RETRIBUTION

THE PROTECTORS #3

SLOANE KENNEDY

CONTENTS

RETRIBUTION

Sloane Kennedy

TRADEMARK ACKNOWLEDGEMENTS

The author acknowledges the trademarked status and trademark owners of the following trademarks mentioned in this work of fiction:

Iron Man
Captain America
Avengers
Spiderman
Cheerios
Ritz Carlton
The Hulk
Hawkeye
X-Men
Harley Davidson

ACKNOWLEDGMENTS

Kylee and Claudia, thank you for being my soul sisters and for everything that position entails! It isn't an easy job, I know. But you guys are the best at it and I'm still wondering what I did to get so lucky to stumble across you two.

Claudia, an extra special thank you for your contribution to this book – you know exactly which one I am talking about. Your beautiful words were absolutely perfect and I'm humbled that you let me borrow them.

SERIES READING ORDER

All of my series cross over with one another so I've provided a couple of recommended reading orders for you. If you want to start with the Protectors books, use the first list. If you want to follow the books according to timing, use the second list. Note that you can skip any of the books (including M/F) as each was written to be a standalone story.

Note that some books may not be readily available on all retail sites

Recommended Reading Order (Use this list if you want to start with "The Protectors" series)
1. Absolution (m/m/m) (The Protectors, #1)
2. Salvation (m/m) (The Protectors, #2)
3. Retribution (m/m) (The Protectors, #3)
4. Gabriel's Rule (m/f) (The Escort Series, #1)
5. Shane's Fall (m/f) (The Escort Series, #2)
6. Logan's Need (m/m) (The Escort Series, #3)
7. Finding Home (m/m/m) (Finding Series, #1)
8. Finding Trust (m/m) (Finding Series, #2)

9. Loving Vin (m/f) (Barretti Security Series, #1)
10. Redeeming Rafe (m/m) (Barretti Security Series, #2)
11. Saving Ren (m/m/m) (Barretti Security Series, #3)
12. Freeing Zane (m/m) (Barretti Security Series, #4)
13. Finding Peace (m/m) (Finding Series, #3)
14. Finding Forgiveness (m/m) (Finding Series, #4)
15. Forsaken (m/m) (The Protectors, #4)
16. Vengeance (m/m/m) (The Protectors, #5)
17. A Protectors Family Christmas (The Protectors, #5.5)
18. Atonement (m/m) (The Protectors, #6)
19. Revelation (m/m) (The Protectors, #7)
20. Redemption (m/m) (The Protectors, #8)
21. Finding Hope (m/m/m) (Finding Series, #5)
22. Defiance (m/m) (The Protectors #9)

Recommended Reading Order (Use this list if you want to follow according to timing)

1. Gabriel's Rule (m/f) (The Escort Series, #1)
2. Shane's Fall (m/f) (The Escort Series, #2)
3. Logan's Need (m/m) (The Escort Series, #3)
4. Finding Home (m/m/m) (Finding Series, #1)
5. Finding Trust (m/m) (Finding Series, #2)
6. Loving Vin (m/f) (Barretti Security Series, #1)
7. Redeeming Rafe (m/m) (Barretti Security Series, #2)
8. Saving Ren (m/m/m) (Barretti Security Series, #3)
9. Freeing Zane (m/m) (Barretti Security Series, #4)
10. Finding Peace (m/m) (Finding Series, #3)
11. Finding Forgiveness (m/m) (Finding Series, #4)
12. Absolution (m/m/m) (The Protectors, #1)
13. Salvation (m/m) (The Protectors, #2)
14. Retribution (m/m) (The Protectors, #3)
15. Forsaken (m/m) (The Protectors, #4)
16. Vengeance (m/m/m) (The Protectors, #5)
17. A Protectors Family Christmas (The Protectors, #5.5)

SERIES CROSSOVER CHART

Protectors/Barrettis/Finding Crossover Chart

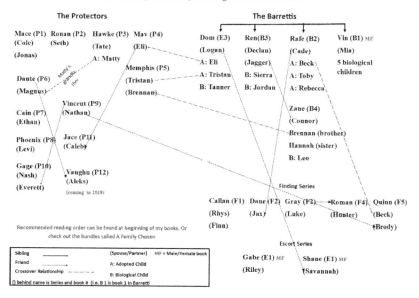

I know I need to keep living
while I wait for you to come home
But I don't know how to tell my heart to stop hurting
since you're the reason it keeps beating on
My days are empty, my eyes full of tears
but the sound of your voice
and the promise of your smile
make it all disappear
You're the other half of my soul
the light that shows me the way
You're my yesterday and my tomorrow
The Angel that keeps me safe

--Claudia Polydoro

RETRIBUTION

noun ret·ri·bu·tion \ˌre-trə-ˈbyü-shən\

Punishment inflicted on someone as vengeance
for a wrong or criminal act.

PROLOGUE

HAWKE

*E*xcitement flooded all my nerve endings as I worked to pick the lock in front of me, but that wasn't a good thing. I needed the familiar numbness back. I needed to not feel anything at all.

Excitement in my line of work accomplished one of two things. It either left you open to making a mistake that could end up getting you killed, or it meant you were so far gone that you'd become as soulless as the men you'd been sent to rid the earth of. In my case, it was still the former, but I often wondered if there would be a point where I'd actually look forward to taking a man's life. Where I thought less about the life or lives I was saving in the long run and more about the satisfaction of finally having some of the power back that I'd lost so long ago...that had been stolen from me when they'd stolen *her*.

But unlike the countless lives I'd taken in the last decade for both the army and for the underground organization I now worked for, this kill *would* be about pleasure. I was going to enjoy watching the man's frantic eyes pleading with me as he desperately promised to give me what I wanted. And I'd let him believe up until the very end that he had a chance of walking away without a bullet in his brain.

He wouldn't. Nor would his partner. They would die the same way she had died. Slowly and painfully. And they would suffer the way she'd suffered. They'd beg the way she'd begged. And I'd finally be able to keep the promise that I'd whispered in her ear as her heartbeat had slowed, the pauses between beeps on the heart monitor she'd been hooked to growing longer and longer.

I'll find them. I'll end them and then we'll be together again.

A sigh of relief went through me when I heard and felt the lock disengage. But as I reached for the knob, I heard the elevator open behind me and I yanked my tools out of the lock and hurried to the stairwell door that was just around the corner from the apartment I'd been about to enter. I didn't hear voices, but I could tell that there were at least two people heading in my general direction. And when I saw two men stop right in front of the door I'd been about to open, I felt a rush of energy surge through me. I'd hoped and prayed I'd find both of my wife's murderers at the same time, but it had been just that...hope. But my hopes were dashed when I realized one of the men wasn't old enough.

"Um, thanks for the ride," I heard the one guy say. His back was to me so all I saw was an average build and a head of thick, brown hair that had a little bit of curl to it. He was wearing a beat up leather jacket and a loose pair of jeans.

"My pleasure," the man with him murmured. He was about the same age as the first guy who I guessed to be in his mid-twenties. But whereas the other guy looked very blue collar, the guy with him was white collar all the way. His suit looked custom made for his tall, muscular body and I had no doubt the thick watch on his wrist cost more than my car.

Even from where I stood, I could tell by the first guy's body language that he was uncomfortable. But if the second guy noticed, he didn't care because he pressed against the first guy until the man had nowhere left to go, since the door was at his back.

"I should get going," the first guy said. "I've got an early morning." Suit guy ignored the clear signals the other guy was sending and leaned down to kiss him. The brown haired guy turned his head away, but that didn't stop suit guy from kissing the man's exposed neck. I couldn't say why the whole thing bothered me, but I didn't dwell on it. Brown haired guy deserved whatever he got because he was clearly the one who lived in the apartment...he was the man I was interested in, but for a whole other reason.

"I could use you again tomorrow night," suit guy said as he took a whiff of the other guy.

"Yeah, sure," brown haired guy said, but he didn't move at all. He clearly wasn't enjoying the other man's attentions, but seemed reluctant to stand up to him.

"Okay, I'll see you tomorrow." Suit guy placed a kiss on the other man's cheek and then pushed back and strode away. I heard the elevator ding but my target didn't move right away. At some point, he'd closed his eyes and leaned his dejected frame against the door. He looked...done.

Rage went through me at the momentary pang of pity and that had me striding out of the stairwell as the guy turned to go into his apartment. I reached the door just as he was closing it. His startled eyes lifted to mine just before I used my booted foot to kick the door open, knocking him on his ass. I pulled my gun from my waistband as I strode into the apartment and slammed the door behind me.

"Please-" the man whispered, but his words dropped off when I pointed my gun at him.

"Where is he?" I snarled.

The man put both his hands up. "Wh...Who?" he stammered.

I leaned down and grabbed him by the hair and yanked his head back until he cried out in pain. "Don't fuck with me," I ground out.

"Please...please," he bit out as tears formed in the corners of his eyes.

I released my hold on him and pressed my gun against his forehead. He let out a choked sob, but I didn't care. I wanted so badly just to pull the trigger. But I couldn't. Because I didn't want to spend another day knowing that even one of the two men who'd raped my wife and left her for dead was still breathing.

"You want to play it that way?" I asked calmly as I finally felt the familiar emptiness creep back into my veins.

I hauled the man up so that he was on his knees and then pressed the gun back against his head. "If the next words out of your mouth aren't his location" – I removed the gun from his head and pressed it against his groin – "this is where the first bullet goes."

The man was crying silent tears, but he didn't say anything. He was shaking uncontrollably, but despite his fear, he remained quiet and I noticed that even though he was crying, his eyes looked blank, like he was somewhere else. I ground my jaw in frustration and began searching for anything I could use as a gag. I didn't have a silencer, but I could come up with creative ways to make the guy talk that didn't require a gun.

Before I could decide what to do next, I heard a knock on the door behind me.

I slammed my hand down over the man's mouth and yanked him to his feet. The move seemed to finally snap him out of his daze. "One word..." I warned quietly as I jammed the gun against his temple.

"Mr. Travers," came a woman's voice on the other side of the door. She began knocking harder. "Mr. Travers, I know you're in there. I saw you pull up out front a few minutes ago!" she shouted in irritation.

The man was frozen in place so I shoved him towards the door. I moved to the other side of the door jamb so that the person on the other side wouldn't see me when he opened it. But I kept my gun pointed at his head.

"Answer it," I ordered.

He shook his head violently.

"Do it!" I snapped.

"No!" he said in a harsh whisper.

The woman continued knocking. "Mr. Travers, we agreed to nine o'clock, no exceptions!"

"Answer it or I'll kill her," I threatened. "Get rid of her or you both die."

The man finally reached for the door and opened it a crack. "Ms. Parks, I'm sorry-"

I nearly pulled the trigger when the door suddenly opened wider, but it wasn't the woman who entered. A little boy no more than five or six years old squeezed through the narrow crack in the door. My instincts kicked in and I grabbed him and dragged him to me, covering his mouth with my hand before he could scream. The man at the door gasped, but the woman he was talking to didn't seem to notice that his attention was no longer on her.

"I'm sorry, Mr. Travers. We had a deal. You want me to watch him longer, you have to pay me for longer!"

I heard footsteps hurry off, but the man staring at me in horror didn't move or even shut the door. "Please don't," he whispered as his eyes fell on the kid who was squirming in my grasp. And that was when I knew I had him.

I kicked the door shut and stepped forward. The man automatically stepped back.

"Where is he?"

"I swear to God, I don't know who you're talking about!"

"Your father!" I shouted.

The man was so caught off guard that he lowered his hands. "My... my father?" he stuttered.

The kid was furiously trying to escape me and it was a struggle to maintain my hold on him without hurting him. I also didn't know what the fuck to do with him – he hadn't been part of my plan. I hadn't even once considered the possibility that the younger of my wife's murderers might be a father. And no way in hell was I hurting a kid...I'd use him to get what I wanted, but I wasn't so far gone in my hatred that I'd actually follow through with my threats.

"I...I haven't seen my father in years," the guy said desperately. His eyes shifted back to the little boy. "It's okay, Matty. Daddy's here. Just be real quiet for a few minutes, okay," he said gently, his voice surprisingly even.

The boy quieted in my hold.

"No loyalty among murderers, huh?" I said.

"Murder?" the man whispered.

My fury was so intense that I released my grip on the boy and he ran to his father. "Get him here now!" I ordered.

"Jesus," the man cried as he grabbed his son and put him behind him. "You're looking for Denny!" he said.

"What?"

"I'm Tate. You're looking for my father and Denny, my brother."

CHAPTER 1

HAWKE

"*Y*ou're lying," I snapped even though in my gut, I knew he wasn't. I couldn't explain how I knew, I just did. And I'd learned long ago to trust my instincts, even when my head was telling me not to. But I kept my gun pointed at the man – Tate – because I also knew he was my only link to the men I was looking for.

"I swear, I'm not," he said with a shake of his head.

"Daddy," the little boy whispered with a tug on his father's shirt.

"It's okay, buddy," Tate murmured as he reached behind himself to put his hand on his son's shoulder. But his eyes never left mine. "Please," he begged.

But I didn't just hear his plea. I heard hers too. How many times had the same word fallen from her frightened lips as she was being brutalized? And it just hadn't been her life she'd been begging for...

"Sir..."

I hadn't realized I'd dropped my eyes to the little boy until Tate's shaky voice got my attention. I knew without question that the kid was the linchpin...even a subtle threat against him would get me what I wanted.

"What's your name?" I asked the terrified little boy.

7

"Sir-" Tate said again, but a hard glance in his direction had him falling silent.

"Matthew," the kid said, his voice soft and uneven. "But Daddy calls me Matty."

Matty had stuck his head around his father's body to answer me, but even before he finished his last statement, Tate was gently pushing the kid back behind him.

"Please sir, I'm begging you..."

I finally lowered the gun and settled my eyes on Tate. "Where are they?"

A slight shudder went through Tate's body. "I...can I put Matty to bed? It's...it's really late."

I studied the younger man for a long moment. I was pretty sure I was right about him being in his mid-twenties and though he wasn't quite as tall as me, he appeared more muscular than I'd first guessed. His brown hair was just a little too long and I found a sudden and very disturbing urge to push back a few of the strands that kept falling over his forehead. I shoved the errant thought away and took in the rest of him. He had a rangy look to him but more than anything, I noticed the strain that made him appear to have lived every single one of his young years and then some. His body said he was in his twenties but his eyes said he was much older...that he'd seen much more than most.

"Give me your phone," I said.

"I...I don't have one."

He must have seen the irritation in my face because his eyes fell to my gun and he said, "I'm telling you the truth. I had one of those disposable ones where you buy the minutes, but I couldn't afford to reload it so they turned it off a couple days ago." Tate swallowed hard when I rubbed my finger over the trigger on the gun. It was a habit on my part more than anything else, but I didn't mind if he thought the move meant something else.

"The phone is in that drawer," he said as he pointed to a small single drawer table by the door. I kept my eyes on him as I checked the drawer and pulled out an older model flip phone. I had to turn it on and sure enough, when I tried to dial, I got a message saying the phone had been deactivated.

"What about a landline?" I asked.

Tate shook his head, but didn't say anything. I wondered how the hell someone managed to go this day and age without any kind of phone, but didn't give voice to my thought. I tossed the cell phone back in the drawer and went back to stand in front of Tate and his son who was peeking around his father's leg to watch me with curiosity.

"Where's his room?" I asked.

"Back there," Tate said, motioning behind him with his head.

I nodded and Tate quickly turned around and picked his son up. He stripped the backpack the kid had been wearing off and dropped it to the floor and then cast me several glances over his shoulder as he went to a small room on one side of the cramped apartment... although apartment was a generous term for the confined space. From what I could tell, the kid's room was the only actual room besides the bathroom. The rest of the space was open and there was a tiny kitchen with a small table jammed against the dingy window. The living room had one couch which was covered with a sheet and on one end was a single pillow and a folded blanket. There was a small, old fashioned TV on a TV dinner tray table in the corner.

As shitty as the apartment was, the kid's room was a whole other story. It was painted bright blue and there were all sorts of posters covering the walls, most of them depicting some kind of superhero. There was a laundry basket full of toys in the corner and the bed had several stuffed animals sitting on top of the Iron Man comforter. Next to the bed was an old milk crate stacked high with books.

"Okay, let's get jammies on," Tate murmured as he searched through the drawers of a faded yellow dresser. I wasn't surprised to see that the pajamas had Captain America all over them. As Tate put Matty down so he was standing on the bed and began to undress him, the little boy kept glancing my way.

"Is he gonna shoot us, Daddy?" Matty asked as he braced his hands on his father's shoulders to steady himself as Tate worked his pants off and replaced them with the pajama bottoms.

9

"No, he's not," Tate said firmly as he got his son's attention. "He... he just got us confused with some other people, okay?"

Undaunted, Matty shifted his attention back to me. "Why does he have a gun?"

I could see Tate didn't have an answer for his son and when he cast a desperate glance over my shoulder, I actually felt a thread of shame go through me. I found myself tucking the gun in the waistband of my pants at my back before I could think too much on it.

"Are you looking for bad guys?" Matty suddenly asked after Tate pulled his shirt off.

"Sort of," I answered before Tate could.

"Are you a policeman?"

Tate's moves in getting his son dressed were quick and efficient and I wondered how much of that was related to practice and how much had to do with wanting to get his son away from me.

"No, buddy, he's not," Tate said. "Come on, climb into bed."

Tate pulled back the covers and Matty took a big leap from where he was standing and landed on one of the pillows. He let out a little giggle and then began positioning all of the stuffed animals underneath the covers on his left side.

"Daddy, I forgot to brush my teeth," Matty said as he tucked a ratty looking stuffed teddy bear next to his body.

"It's okay, we'll skip tonight...but just this once," Tate admonished as he leaned down to kiss his son's forehead. "Sleep tight-"

"No," Matty interrupted. "Story."

"Not tonight, buddy-"

Matty began shaking his head in earnest and I heard Tate let out a rough breath. He gave me a glance and then finally said, "Just one."

Something deep in my belly twisted when I saw the smile that lit up the kid's face as he wrapped his arms around his father's neck. It was quickly replaced with anger and I had no doubt it was written all over my face as Tate glanced at me before going to search for a book. A look of trepidation passed over his features as he kept one hand on the edge of his son's bed as he searched the milk crate for a book – he probably wanted to make sure he was close enough to throw his body over his kid's if I decided to reach for my gun again. Admiration went through me because despite the young man's obvious and well-founded terror, he was holding it together pretty well and I had no doubt it was all for his son.

"Are you an Avenger? Is that how you got hurt?"

Matty's question caught me off guard and I reflexively reached up to run my fingers over the burn scars on my face.

"Matty-" Tate said.

"I bet he's like Captain America, Daddy. He's a secret hero."

"Maybe," Tate managed to get out as he snatched up a book and sat down next to his son on the bed. It took only minutes for Matty's attention to turn from me to the story his father was telling him, and I had no doubt it was because of the way his father made all the different voices for the characters in the book. The kid was out within ten minutes, a slight smile on his small mouth and his teddy bear tucked against his chest. I expected Tate to shift his focus back on me, but to my surprise, he seemed to forget my presence as he leaned down and pressed a kiss to his son's forehead. "Sleep tight, don't let the bed bugs bite."

A mix of longing and rage went through me at the same time and I turned away from the doorway. Sixty minutes...sixty minutes ten years ago was the only reason I was here and not at home with my own kid reading him a bedtime story.

Sixty minutes was all it had taken to wipe out an entire future.

I heard the bed shift and I automatically pulled my gun back out and waited. I didn't really need the weapon, but I always felt better when it was in my hands.

Tate turned off the light as he pulled the door almost all the way shut. I could see a dim blue light coming from the room and I suspected it was a night light of some kind. Tate's whole body drew up tight as he turned his attention on me.

"Kitchen," I said as I waited for him to move past me.

Tate did as I said and I followed him to the kitchen and motioned to one of the two vinyl chairs. The décor of the apartment left no doubt that the dump had either come furnished that way or the man was a thrift store shopper. The only light that was on in the kitchen was the one above the stove so I flipped on the overhead light and went to sit down across from Tate. He had his hands fisted on his thighs but his eyes were darting around the kitchen.

"Don't bother," I muttered as I laid my gun down on the table in front of me and leaned back in the squeaky chair.

"What?" Tate asked cautiously.

"Looking for a weapon," I said. The flash of guilt in Tate's eyes was brief, but then he stiffened. Gone was the man who was terrified for his kid. The man in front of me was...determined. It was the only word I could come up with for the way he pinned me with his gaze. A strange fluttering sparked in my gut.

"Where are they?" I asked, ignoring the unexpected sensation.

"I don't know," he said quietly. His eyes were on my fingers which were resting near the butt of my gun. "I haven't seen them in a couple of years."

"You really want to make that kid in there an orphan?" I threatened as I motioned towards Matty's room.

Tate paled and swallowed hard but as scared as he was, he didn't take his eyes off me. "I'm telling you the truth."

"Then tell me more of it."

"The last time I spoke to my father and Denny was right before I left home with Matty."

"Where's home?"

"Lulling, Texas."

"Never heard of it," I said.

"You wouldn't," Tate quipped. "It's barely even a dot on the map... unless you're looking for Crystal Meth...then it's Mecca."

"Your family deals meth?"

"Don't call them that," Tate ordered softly. "Those men were never my family."

I wasn't sure what to make of that statement, but the hatred in Tate's voice was clear. And it was a good sign for me. "They're dealers?"

Tate nodded.

"They use too?"

"Denny does...at least he did the last time I saw him."

"And your father?"

Tate stiffened but didn't contradict me. "No," was all he said.

"What's his name?"

"Dennis Buckley," Tate responded. "Everyone calls him Buck."

"That lady called you Travers," I said as I thought back to the woman who had been watching Tate's son. Tate remained stubbornly silent. Since my question had been asked out of curiosity rather than necessity, I let it go.

"How did you find me?" Tate asked suddenly.

I studied him for a long moment. "Your DNA was a partial match to the DNA left at a crime scene."

"A murder, you mean," Tate murmured. "How did you get my DNA?"

I ignored the question and studied Tate. He was sitting calmly in the chair, but I could see a slight shudder roll through his frame every now and then and he kept shifting his eyes nervously towards his son's room before moving them back to me as subtly as he could, as if he was somehow hoping I'd forgotten about his son's presence. I felt a shimmer of pity for him at the fear he must be feeling, not for himself but for his kid.

It wasn't until Tate again glanced at Matty's room that I finally noticed what had been bothering me from the moment we'd sat down at the table. Tate's eyes – they didn't match. One was a startling bright blue while the other was a soft, subtle golden brown color. The contrast was intriguing...so intriguing that I caught myself staring at him as warmth settled in my belly.

What the fuck?

"I don't know what else to tell you."

It took me a moment to process Tate's words because as soon as I'd managed to tear my eyes from his, I was dropping them to his mouth. His lips were fuller than I would have expected to see on a man.

"You don't seem surprised to learn your father and brother are

13

wanted for murder," I managed to say as I forced my eyes away from his mouth.

"Sir-"

"It's Hawke," I interrupted, though I wasn't sure why I'd told him that since my name was of no importance in the situation. In fact, it was downright stupid to give the man any clue to my identity.

But Tate's words surprised me. "I don't care," he said. "I don't care who you are or why you're looking for them. I don't care what you're going to do when you find them. Tonight never happened." His eyes held mine as he repeated, "Tonight. Never. Happened."

The guy had balls, I had to give him that. He had absolutely no power, but he was still trying to stare me down. The show of strength should have pissed me off, or in the least, irritated me. But I found myself actually admiring him. Even if his demeanor was begging for trouble, I couldn't help but think that I preferred it to the blank look he'd had when I'd first threatened him before his kid had arrived.

"Daddy?"

Tate jumped to his feet at the sound of his son's voice and he immediately put himself between me and the little boy. "What are you doing up?" Tate asked as he quickly lifted Matty into his arms.

"I forgot Spidey," he mumbled.

I grabbed the gun off the table and followed Tate to the front door where Matty's discarded backpack lay. He rifled through the bag and pulled out what looked to be an eighties era version of a Spiderman doll. Matty smiled sleepily as he clutched the doll to his chest. Tate watched me over his shoulder as he began to head towards Matty's room.

"G'night Captain," Matty called before dropping his head on Tate's shoulder. I watched them disappear into the darkened room and then glanced down at Matty's backpack. I had what I needed.

For now...

CHAPTER 2

TATE

$\mathcal{M}$atty felt like a dead weight against my shoulder as I lowered myself into the chair across from the stern looking older woman. Although she'd been the one to call me up to her tiny, partitioned desk that didn't actually offer any privacy from the people sitting on either side of us, the woman didn't acknowledge me as she continued to punch away on her keyboard. I tried to shift Matty to ease some of the numbness in my arm but when he stirred, I changed my mind and stilled until I felt him settle again. After all, he'd have to be fully awake soon enough.

I let my own eyes drift shut as I felt Matty's warm breath against my neck. I wouldn't have thought my life could get any worse after the night the dark, forbidding stranger had knocked me on my ass and pointed his gun at my head.

I'd been very wrong…again.

That day had been like any of the other endless days that I couldn't seem to escape from. The morning had started off the same with trying to get Matty ready for pre-school. He'd been half-asleep as usual as he'd sat over his bowl of Cheerios and we'd barely caught the 7:35 bus. I'd been fortunate enough to find a small, friendly daycare just a few miles from our apartment that offered pre-school classes to

Pre-K kids and then watched the children for the rest of the day. The place was surprisingly clean and well run and I'd considered myself lucky to have found it since many of the other programs I'd looked at cost considerably more than I made bussing tables at a 24-hour diner in a less than perfect neighborhood.

Work had been as grueling and non-eventful as always and I'd only been twenty minutes late in picking Matty up which was significantly better than my normal hour or sometimes even two-hour delay since the prick I worked for had no issue with making me stay well past my regular hours. And I wasn't in any position to complain since I desperately needed the job. My plan had been to spend the night helping Matty with an art project he'd been working on for school, but the sight of the sleek, red sports car sitting in front of my building had blown that plan to hell. Matty had been upset with me at first when I'd told him that I had to work, but then he'd given me a look that was entirely too understanding for someone so young and I'd been the one fighting back my guilt as I'd handed Matty off to my neighbor, Ms. Parks, to watch for several hours.

My second job wasn't a steady one, but it did pay well so I never said no when Roger Banks called me with an offer to unload the delivery truck that stocked his upscale night club. I'd suspected the man's interest in me went beyond cheap labor, but I hadn't been sure until that day because I doubted any other potential employer would have bothered to drive to my shitty neighborhood to offer me the work when he couldn't get a hold of me via my defunct cell phone.

I'd met Roger through a co-worker at the diner who'd known about my situation, but I'd been too preoccupied with the never-ending demands of my new life to realize the good looking man was flirting with me at first. I should have been interested in him. He was stunningly gorgeous, successful and clearly had enough money to throw around. And he hadn't hesitated to drop hints that I too could benefit from his wealth. But it hadn't been until that same day that he'd shown up that I'd finally figured out what kind of a guy he really was, because as I'd walked hand and hand with Matty towards the red car and watched the man unfold his long, trim body from the obscenely expensive vehicle, Roger hadn't even spared Matty a passing glance. Not once as he'd spoken to me had his eyes shifted to Matty and even after I had introduced the little boy to him, Roger had refused to acknowledge his presence.

I'd spent the rest of the evening avoiding Roger's leering glances as I'd unloaded endless crates of alcohol and it was only the stack of cash Roger had placed in my hand afterwards that'd had me agreeing to his offer of a ride home. He'd followed me up without asking and clearly hadn't cared that I had no interest in his unwelcome advances... advances I'd allowed only because I'd needed the cash more than I'd needed to escape the touch of a man who made me physically ill.

But all of that had been pre-Hawke. Because I'd given up everything the second Hawke had walked out my front door. The moment I'd heard the door click into place, I'd rushed out of Matty's room and flipped the flimsy lock that I'd known wouldn't really keep the man out if he were inclined to return. I'd then grabbed Matty's backpack along with the packed duffle bag I kept stashed in the closet by the front door before going back to Matty's room and throwing some of his clothes into my duffle. I'd jammed the two toys I'd known he couldn't live without into his backpack along with a couple of books and then I'd wrapped a small blanket around Matty's sleeping body and had carried him out of the apartment. He'd woken up briefly, but his unfailing trust in me had had him looking around only for a second before he'd snuggled up against my neck.

After all, it wasn't the first time we'd been in the exact same situation.

I hadn't liked ditching the apartment, especially since I'd just paid the entire month's rent a few days earlier. But I'd had no doubt the dangerous looking Hawke would be back at some point. I'd seen the hatred in his eyes when he'd knocked me to the floor after pushing his way into my apartment. And the way he'd grabbed Matty...no, I wasn't going to risk another encounter with the man. Especially since I knew he probably wouldn't find what he was looking for just because he now had names to go with the men he was hunting.

I'd ended up finding a cheap motel on the other side of town and

Matty and I had spent most of the weekend hiding out there. I'd moved us to another motel two nights later and then another one a few nights after that. I hadn't returned to work at the diner and I hadn't risked taking Matty back to daycare despite his insistence that he had to turn in his art project. The project - which I'd ended up leaving behind in the apartment – was a family self-portrait that had only taken Matty a few minutes to re-create after I'd told him I would hang it on the wall of our motel. Ironically, seeing the two stick figures hand in hand outside a colorful little house next to what I could only assume was a dog, had given me the strength I'd needed when all I'd really wanted to do was let my body fold in on itself in a desperate attempt to escape the reality that was slowly drowning me.

I'd finally started to feel more at ease about a week after Hawke had left, though I still hadn't been brave enough to return to the apartment to try to get the rest of our belongings. I had no doubt that my job at the diner had already been given away and I'd briefly considered going to Roger's club to see if he had any work for me because the little money I had stashed away was dwindling at a rapid rate. I'd even floated the idea of asking Roger for a loan, but then I'd remembered the feel of his clammy lips on my neck and the look in his eyes that said he knew that, in that moment, he owned me. I'd seen that look every day of my life for longer than I could remember and as hard as the last two years had been, knowing that no one had the right to look at me that way again – that Matty would never know that look himself – made every struggle I'd endured worth it.

But all that had changed two days ago when I'd been getting Matty dressed and I'd noticed the bruises. The same bruises I'd seen a few weeks earlier that I'd attributed to him roughhousing with other kids at daycare.

They'd had nothing to do with roughhousing.

And they had changed everything.

Everything.

"Mr. Travers, I'm afraid we're still having some issues with getting the Medicaid paperwork submitted for Matthew. Would you mind confirming this is the correct social security number?" the woman finally said to me as she glanced at me over her glasses and then turned her computer screen my way so I could see the number.

I swallowed hard and said, "That's the correct number."

I'd become a consummate liar in the past several years, but it wasn't something I would ever become comfortable with so I dropped my eyes when I answered her.

She punched the keys on her keyboard and waited several long seconds and then shook her head. "I'm afraid it's not going through. You'll need to contact them yourself to try to resolve this," she said as she shifted her chair and folded her hands on the desk. "Until then, I'm afraid I'll need you to pay up front."

"What?" I asked in surprise. "I…I don't have that kind of money," I whispered.

There was little pity in the woman's eyes as she studied me. I knew what she was seeing. Worn, ripped jeans that were just a little too big for me, a faded green Henley that had stains I still hadn't figured out how to get rid of and a tattered leather jacket that was about ten years out of style.

"We can set you up with a payment plan, but I'll need ten percent of the balance today."

I did the calculations in my head and felt my stomach drop as I realized I didn't even have enough money saved up to cover half the upfront payment she wanted.

I shook my head. "I'm sorry, I…I could do a hundred dollars," I offered desperately, though even that amount would hit me hard. I'd been on such a roller coaster of emotions since my visit to Matty's pediatrician two days earlier, that I hadn't even thought this far ahead.

"I'm afraid that we'll need the full ten percent today before you'll be able to see Dr. Spengler. We do accept credit cards."

I felt bile rising in my throat as I understood what she was telling me. Disbelief coursed through me as I said, "Ma'am, Dr. Spengler said Matty needs to have these tests done today." I looked around the small reception area as if half-expecting to find the older, silver haired doctor the pediatrician had referred us to and that we'd seen for the first time just yesterday. "We…we were here yesterday! He said he needed to do the tests to figure out the best course of treatment!"

I knew my voice was cracking, but I couldn't rein in my terror as the reality settled on me like a heavy, lead blanket.

"I'm sorry, Mr. Travers-"

"Here." The singular, rough word was accompanied by a credit card being tossed down on the desk in front of me. I glanced to my right and felt my heart seize up at the sight of Hawke settling his big frame in the chair next to mine. I automatically tightened my arms around Matty as I began scanning my surroundings for help.

"Captain America," Matty breathed as he shifted in my hold so he could see Hawke.

"I'll be right back with this," the woman across from me said as she snatched up the credit card.

"I'd like to pay the balance on the account with that," Hawke said to the woman as she stood. "Use it for whatever is done today too."

"No," I cut in and both Hawke and the woman shifted their attention to me. "No," I repeated, my head shaking violently. I turned to tell Hawke to get the hell away from us, but then I felt Matty's warm breath against my neck as he let out a tired sigh.

"Daddy, I'm tired," he whispered.

Except he wasn't just tired. He was so much more than that. I glanced helplessly at Hawke and then down at the mop of brown hair beneath my chin. I closed my eyes and forced back the tears that threatened to fall. I managed to nod my head, but I wasn't sure if anything happened until a good minute passed before I heard the woman return.

"I'll let Dr. Spengler know you're here," I heard her say.

Hawke murmured "thank you" and then I felt his hand at my elbow. I forced my eyes open and saw that the woman was on her phone, seemingly uncaring about the events that had just unfolded.

I managed to pull myself to my feet, but I didn't miss Hawke's fingers brushing the back of my arm as he guided me towards a couple of chairs in the far corner of the waiting room. I hated that I noticed it at all. I hated that despite my fear of him, his touch still felt better than Roger's had the night he'd tried to kiss me. I hated that I wanted him to keep touching me.

But more than anything, I hated that I would have given anything in that moment to feel his arms close around me and tell me that everything was going to be okay.

I shoved the ridiculous thought away and pulled free of his hold. He released me without hesitation, but I still felt like a prisoner. Matty had gone quiet against me again and I managed to shift him enough so my arm didn't feel like it was going to fall off my body. As I got him resettled, I glanced at Hawke. I was looking for the gun, but didn't see it anywhere. Which meant nothing since the shirt he was wearing was untucked and I knew the gun could be at his back.

Hawke wasn't a huge guy, but his bearing was. Everything about him screamed danger even as he sat casually in the hard waiting room chair. But I knew I was the only one who saw it because he was so relaxed and at ease that it seemed like he belonged there...with us. I already knew him to be a couple inches taller than me and I guessed he had at least fifty pounds on me. And if his bulging biceps and broad chest were anything to go by, it was all muscle. Tribal tattoos covered his upper arms and disappeared under the navy blue T-shirt he was wearing. His jeans fit snugly across his thick thighs and he was wearing a pair of black steel-toed boots.

I hadn't missed the burn scars on the right side of his face the night he'd broken into my place, but in the light of day, I finally had a chance to study them. The raised, pink flesh covered almost his entire right cheek and jaw and went down his neck which had me thinking the scars might continue lower. The disfigurement should have made him more frightening, but there was something innately beautiful about them. Like they were proof that he'd lived through something that very few people could.

I continued to steal looks his way as I took in the rest of him. Strong, straight nose, wide, firm lips that I knew would be softer than they looked, glittering, unyielding dark blue eyes and closely cropped black hair. The crow's feet around his eyes had me guessing he was older than me by at least ten years which put him in his mid-thirties. I also couldn't ignore the gold band on the ring finger of his left hand.

I was still studying him when he suddenly looked at me and I tore my eyes away from him. I could feel his gaze burning into me as I examined the thin, utilitarian carpet beneath my feet. I was too overwhelmed by everything that was happening so I did what I always did when I needed to escape and began focusing on the things in the waiting room that no one else probably even noticed. The shadows cast by the harsh overhead lights, the angles and planes of the furniture in the room...

"Mr. Travers."

I snapped out of my reverie as soon as the nurse called my name and I quickly jumped up. But I didn't make it even a step before Hawke's fingers closed around my lower arm, his touch sending sparks along my nerve endings at the same time that a cold fear settled in my gut. I forced myself to turn to look at him.

"I'll wait here," he said.

I nearly sighed in relief as I began to plan my next steps. I'd assumed he would insist on accompanying us and I'd have to try to find a discreet moment to signal the hospital staff for help, but all I had to do was make it a couple more minutes until we were free of his line of sight and then I'd tell the nurse to call 911. I managed a nod, but when I took a step forward, he didn't release me and I held my breath.

But with his next words, all my plans died an instant death.

"Whatever you're thinking of doing...don't," he said calmly before glancing briefly at Matty. His steely eyes returned to mine and then his mouth was near my ear, his warm breath skittering across my skin. "Unless you want everyone to know he's not your kid."

CHAPTER 3

HAWKE

ate didn't move after I'd spoken, even after the nurse called him for the third time. I released the hold I had on his arm, ignoring the zaps of energy that were surging through my fingers and up my arm and placed my hand on his lower back to give him a little shove forward. He finally got moving, but I didn't miss the way his breathing had ratcheted even higher than it had been after I'd dropped down in the seat next to him at the check in desk a few minutes earlier. As he walked away from me, I noticed Matty's tired eyes on me where his chin was resting on Tate's shoulder. He gave me a small wave and I had to steel myself not to return it. I wasn't here to make friends with the kid. I was here for one thing and showing the little boy or his father any kind of compassion would make what I had to do all the harder.

But as Matty's eyes stayed on mine as his father neared a doorway leading out of the waiting area, I couldn't stop myself from lifting my hand slightly to acknowledge the child. He smiled just before Tate carried him through the door and I felt my heart constrict painfully as I sat back down in the chair. I could have gone with Tate for whatever tests the kid needed to have, but I'd held back because I didn't want to know what was going on with him. I had no room for pity.

Liar.

My wife's whisper in my ear unnerved me as it always did, but I also felt a pang of warmth go through me. I wasn't a religious guy by any means, but on the rare occasion that I did hear Revay's voice calling me on my bullshit, I welcomed it. Because she had always been the only one brave enough to tell me when I was full of it. And while I wasn't so far gone that I actually believed it was her talking to me, I liked that my subconscious used her voice to remind me when my internal bullshit meter was pinging.

My hope had been to not have to deal with the intriguing Tate Travers or his cute kid again, but I'd suspected even as I'd left his apartment more than a week ago that things wouldn't be so easy. My desperation to confront Buck and Denny Buckley had led me straight from the run down area of San Francisco that Tate lived in to the dusty, remote town of Lulling, Texas. The underground group I worked for employed a young hacker named Daisy Washburne to gather information on potential marks and I'd called her on the way to Lulling to see what she could dig up on Buck and Denny. In short, she'd found nothing...absolutely nothing. Both men had been living off the grid for some time so I had no address, no recent pictures, no nothing to use to find either man. It was beyond frustrating and I'd known the second I rolled into the tiny, insular town, that I wouldn't get anywhere by asking the residents questions – all I would do was give the murderers ample warning that I was on their trail. So I'd reluctantly turned around and headed back to San Francisco and the only lead I had to work with.

On the way, I'd asked Daisy for any information she could give me on Tate, but like his father and brother, he didn't appear to exist because there was no record of him anywhere. Which led me to believe he was still living off the grid for a reason. And after I'd had Daisy check why Tate had submitted his DNA to a private lab for testing, I'd suspected what that reason was.

Several hours passed before the door Tate had disappeared through earlier opened and I stood as Tate walked through it. My first thought was that the stricken look on his face was because of me, but then I noticed that he wasn't even looking at me. His face had gone deathly pale and each step he took looked wobbly and uneven and I instantly stepped forward so I could catch him and Matty if he lost his footing.

"Let me take him," I finally said when Tate teetered back and forth as I reached him. He looked at me as if finally seeing me for the first time and then he shook his head weakly.

"Then at least sit down so you don't fall," I murmured as I motioned to a chair.

"No," he whispered. "I...I need to get him home. The doctor said he needs to rest..."

Tate tried to brush past me, but I put my hands on his arms to stop his forward motion. "Tate," I said as gently as I could. His red rimmed eyes lifted to meet mine and I knew he'd been crying at some point because his eyes hadn't looked that way when he'd walked away from me. My stomach fell as I realized what that meant. "Let me take him," I repeated softly as I held him in place. I had no idea why I hated that it was only the fabric of his shirt I was feeling beneath my fingers and not his skin.

"Here, you can hang on to these," I said as I tugged my car keys from my pocket along with my phone and wallet. I offered him the items and then realized how ridiculous it was to think he'd hand me his child in exchange for them.

Tate shook his head, but after I'd put everything back in my pocket, he studied me for a long time and then said, "Just for a minute."

It was a testament to how tired the man was. I nodded and carefully took Matty from him. I hadn't been sure if Matty was asleep or not, but I had my answer as soon as I pulled him against my chest. His eyes were closed and I could tell from how puffy they were that Tate hadn't been the only one in tears at some point. His warm breath fanned across the skin of my neck and his limp body made carrying him awkward.

"They sedated him," Tate mumbled as he pulled a blanket from Matty's backpack and worked it around the boy's body. Feeling Tate's fingers brush against me as he tucked the blanket in between Matty's body and mine did strange things to my insides…things I hadn't felt in a really long time…things I didn't want to think too much about.

Tate and I began walking towards the exit and I didn't miss the way he stuck right next to me and kept glancing my way. He also kept his hand on one of Matty's shoes as if that would somehow deter me from running off with the kid. Even without the burden of carrying Matty, Tate's pace was still slow and it took us more than ten minutes to finally reach my car in the parking lot next to the hospital. Tate hadn't even realized our destination until I fished around my pocket for the keys and unlocked the sedan.

"No," Tate immediately said as he tried to take Matty from me. I used my body to maneuver Tate back against the car and he instantly ceased his struggles – probably so he wouldn't wake his son up. With Matty's body blocking him on one side and my free arm caging him against the car on his other side, Tate began breathing erratically as he realized I was once again in control. It was exactly the position I wanted to be in, but seeing Tate's fear for his child had me second guessing myself and the reason I'd returned to San Francisco.

Don't.

I closed my eyes as the soft word penetrated my brain. But for once, I ignored the voice and said, "Get in the car, Tate."

The betrayal in Tate's eyes was instant and sharp and bothered me more than I wanted to admit. But I shoved away the urge to gentle my stance and stepped back enough to allow Tate to open the door. He glanced around the empty parking lot and then at me before finally closing his eyes and reaching behind him to grab the door handle. The second he was in the back seat, I handed Matty to him and closed the door. I was glad when Tate didn't try to get back out as I climbed into the front seat. Instead, he worked to get Matty buckled in and then he sat next to him and drew him protectively against his side.

We didn't speak as I pulled the car into traffic and to my complete surprise, Tate fell asleep within ten minutes of leaving the hospital. But his arm never left Matty's small shoulders as he kept him close. I used the time to study Tate with quick glances in the rearview mirror.

Although it had only been a little over a week since I'd last seen him, he looked even worse than he had when I'd confronted him that first night. His face had a gauntness to it that made me wonder if he was steadily losing weight and there were dark smudges under his eyes suggesting he hadn't been sleeping well. Even in sleep, his entire countenance was drawn up tight with tension and I doubted that it was only because of my presence.

Another wave of guilt went through me as I forced my attention back to the road. Tate didn't stir even after I pulled the car to a stop in front of his apartment building. It wasn't until I opened the door and gently shook him awake that he reacted like a startled animal and immediately wrapped his arms tighter around Matty and used his body to cover the still sleeping boy. I swallowed hard as the memory of trying to wrap myself up like that washed over me. I'd been considerably younger, but age wasn't a factor when your self-preservation instincts kicked in. As afraid of me as Tate was, I suspected his reaction in that moment hadn't been about me at all.

"Tate, we're here," I said quietly, but I didn't put my hands back on him.

Tate didn't move for several long seconds and I didn't rush him because I knew he needed to get control of himself; never an easy task when you were scared shitless about where the next blow would hit you. It was several long seconds before Tate finally looked over his shoulder at me and I could see the remnants of sleep still held him because he blinked his eyes rapidly as if trying to bring me into focus. Then he checked to make sure Matty was okay before finally looking around at our surroundings.

"What...what are we doing here?" he asked as he began the process of unbuckling Matty. As he climbed out of the car, Matty in his arms, he said, "We...we don't live here anymore."

"I know," was all I said as I went to the trunk of the car. I kept my eyes on Tate as I pulled both his duffle bag and mine from it. His eyes fell on his bag as I came back around the car.

"You were in our motel room?" he managed to get out.

"That place was a shit hole," I said as I once again put my hand on

Tate's arm to get him moving. "Makes this place look like the fucking Ritz," I added as we walked up the walkway towards the apartment building.

Tate didn't say anything even once we were inside his apartment. He just carried Matty to the little boy's room and then shut the door. I didn't follow him because I knew there was no place for him to go in the windowless room. I used the time to search out the contents of Tate's kitchen and shook my head at the nearly bare cabinets. The fridge had a few items in it, but since I knew Tate had likely left the apartment within minutes of my leaving the week before, I didn't trust that the food was any good. I searched out my phone to find the closest pizza delivery place and ordered some food. I gave Tate a few more minutes and then went to Matty's room to find him. The door wasn't locked so I quietly pushed it open.

The first thing I heard was crying - no, not crying – sobbing. Big, heart wrenching, bone deep sobs...the kind that made it hard to breathe. I didn't see Tate as I pushed the door further open, but I saw that Matty was asleep under the covers. I had to open the door all the way to find Tate. He was sitting on the floor near his son's bed, his back against the wall. His legs were drawn up and he was resting his elbows on his knees as he wept into his hands. I hated that I wanted to go to him, to sit down next to him and pull him against me and tell him it would be okay...whatever *it* was. At that exact moment, Tate looked up at me and even in the dim light I saw it. His naked need for me to do exactly that. But then his eyes shuttered and he leaned his head back against the wall and turned his face away from me.

My chest felt tight as I closed the door and I actually found myself rubbing my fingers over the middle of it as if that would somehow stem the discomfort. I wasn't sure how long I stood there for, but it wasn't until I heard a sharp rap on the front door that I remembered where I was and why I was there. As I went to the door, I kept glancing over my shoulder as if half expecting Tate to come running out of the room seeking help from whoever was at the door. I had already pulled my gun from the back of my pants when I remembered the pizza I'd ordered. After giving the pimply faced delivery guy a generous tip, I took the pizza into the kitchen and put it on the small table. But my appetite was gone and when I didn't hear Matty's door open, I pushed the pizza away and leaned back in the kitchen chair and studied my surroundings.

Everything about this job was going to shit. I was no closer to finding the men who'd killed my wife despite having more information than I ever had before - information that should have been enough to lead me to them and take them out. Yet all I had was a guy who was clearly struggling to be a good father to a kid that wasn't his. And the kid - a fucking cute little kid who was sick...very sick if the look on Tate's face at the hospital had been anything to go by.

And none of it mattered.

Because I was still left with one undisputable fact – Tate Travers was my only hope of getting justice for the woman who'd changed my entire life...who'd *been* my entire life. I steeled myself not to care as I started making plans for how I would get out of Tate what I wanted. Because after all this was over, the young man would still have the kid he'd chosen to raise as his own and I would have nothing.

Nothing except knowing I'd finally kept my promise.

~

*I*t was almost an hour before I heard footsteps heading towards the kitchen. I was still sitting in the same chair, but as Tate entered the kitchen, I looked up and held his gaze as he stood in the wide doorway.

"How did you find us?" he finally asked.

"Tracking device in Matty's backpack," I said. "I put a bug in there too."

"You were listening to us?"

I nodded. I'd tracked Tate to the hospital, but I hadn't planned to go in until I'd heard Tate talking to the woman about his account. The desperation in his voice as he'd talked about his kid needing the tests...

"You knew I'd run," Tate murmured.

"You knew I'd be back," I countered. I nodded to the chair across from me. Tate shifted nervously before finally sitting down.

"You only find Buck when he wants to be found," Tate responded quietly. Although his tears had dried up, his eyes were swollen and red. He looked like hell so I got up and grabbed a few slices of pizza from the box on the stove and tossed them into the microwave. I searched out a cup and filled it with tap water and placed it in front of him. He didn't respond, but he did reach for the cup to take several long drinks. But when I slid the pizza in front of him, he didn't touch it.

"When was the last time you ate?" I asked as I sat back down across from him. Tate merely shook his head. "Eat, Tate," I said. "There will be plenty left for Matty."

Tate's eyes lifted to meet mine but he didn't answer. He looked over his shoulder at the large pizza box sitting on the stove. I hadn't missed the fact that most of the spoiled food in the fridge was geared towards a child's taste. It explained a lot about the man across from me...his lean frame, his lack of funds, Matty's nicely decorated room.

A strange sense of satisfaction went through me when Tate finally took a bite of the pizza, but I tried not to examine too closely why it mattered so much that he'd done as I'd asked. And I definitely tried not to focus on his intriguing, mismatched eyes. Sharp, bright blue and warm, soft hazel...I couldn't help but think they matched the two sides of his personality I'd seen so far. I wondered what they would look like when he smiled, laughed, felt pleasure...

Fuck, what the hell was wrong with me?

I forced myself to remain silent until Tate finished the food and pushed the plate away. He took a couple more drinks of water and then sat stiffly in his chair, his eyes settling on me. His gaze briefly skimmed my entire body and a shot of lust flashed through me.

Jesus Christ, there was no way this was happening to me. There was no fucking way I was attracted to this man...any man. It just wasn't possible. Only my dick was telling me it definitely was possible and I had to lean forward so I could use the table to hide my unexpected reaction to Tate's perusal. It had to be the fucking stress, the anticipation of what was to come.

"What's wrong with Matty?" I asked.

My question had a profound reaction. The pain shooting through Tate was clear and tears instantly pooled in his eyes as he hunched in on himself. He angrily wiped at his face with his shirt sleeve – he had taken his jacket off at some point – and sucked in several deep breaths as he covered his eyes with his hand.

"Leukemia," he whispered so low that I barely heard him.

A chill went through my entire body and I couldn't help but cover my mouth with my hand as I tried to stem the lump of emotion that threatened to close off my throat. I'd expected some kind of serious condition but nothing like that.

"Jesus," I muttered as I sat back in my chair. "Is it...is it treatable?" I heard myself ask, my voice sounding shaky.

Tate nodded. "The doctor said we caught it early. He needs multiple chemo treatments over the next six months. They did a bone marrow test today to see if he'll need a stem cell transplant...that's assuming they would be able to find a match."

"What about you?" I managed to ask.

"They'll test me if he needs one, but usually a full sibling has the best chance of being a match."

"And you're only his half-brother," I said quietly.

Tate lifted his eyes to meet mine. "He's Buck's?" he asked in a rush.

"You didn't know?" I asked. "The DNA test-"

Tate shook his head. "I asked the lab to confirm he was related to me, but I couldn't afford the tests that would have shown if he was my brother or my nephew."

"You didn't know if he was related to you?"

"No," he murmured as he wiped at his face and reached for the glass of water with a trembling hand. "I...I came home one day and he was just there. I asked Denny whose kid he was, but Denny told me to mind my own business. After I took him, I started to wonder if maybe they'd kidnapped him or something...I kept thinking about how worried his parents would be." Tate took a long drink.

"Why did you take him?" I asked.

But Tate just shook his head slightly and dropped his eyes. I got the message.

"Buck and Denny, they...they liked to share women so I knew it was possible that either one of them could be the father."

My gut clenched at Tate's words as an image of Revay's battered body went through my head. The hospital staff had only found one usable DNA sample when they'd done the rape kit, but I had no doubt she'd been brutalized by both men. Tate's statement was confirmation of that fact.

"So you don't know who his mother is?" I managed to ask.

"No, Buck had a lot of girlfriends...so did Denny."

"How old would Denny have been when Matty was born?"

"I'm not a hundred percent sure," Tate admitted. "I don't know Matty's exact age...if he really is five, Denny would have been around twenty-five when Matty was born.

"Was there a specific girl in his life at that time? Or Buck's?" I asked, making sure not to refer to the man as Tate's father.

Another shake of Tate's head. "No," was all he said. His lack of a response told me there was more to it than just that, but I didn't press him. In reality, it didn't matter.

"Look, if I knew more, I'd tell you," Tate said as he finally lifted his eyes. "Just...just leave us alone, please? I can't help you."

I steeled myself to ignore the pleading in his voice as well as the pity I felt for him for Matty's condition. It changed nothing. I held Tate's gaze as I said, "Yeah, you can. And you will."

CHAPTER 4

TATE

*M*y whole body seized up at Hawke's words and I knew I was fucked. I'd been foolish enough to forget for a few minutes that this man was not my friend. My desperation to have someone to share my burdens with had blinded me to who he was and why he was here. And as his hard blue eyes held mine, I felt the knot of tension in my gut build. I willed myself not to escape into my head like I wanted to because I couldn't risk not being completely aware if he went after Matty to get to me.

But focusing was harder than I thought as I kept hearing the doctor's mechanical voice repeating that same word over and over again.

Leukemia.

Cancer. Matty had cancer. My sweet, funny, kind-hearted little boy had cancer.

And he was just that – my little boy. He'd become that the moment I'd stolen him in the dead of night from the doublewide trailer I'd shared with Denny and Buck. I was his father and there was absolutely nothing I could do for him. I'd spent two years trying to protect him from the worst kind of evil, but I couldn't protect him from the disease that coursed through his blood. And I couldn't protect him from the man across from me either. I could try, but Hawke could best me physically and, based on the certainty of his voice a moment ago, he had already bested me mentally by taking away my choices. Despair rushed through me as I realized I was back exactly where I'd been two years earlier...only now I had a new jailer.

"What do you want?" I managed to ask, though my voice sounded like a hoarse croak.

"A couple of days of your time, that's it," Hawke said easily...too easily.

"For what?" I stammered. I hated that the man sat so comfortably in the chair across from me...like we were old buddies just shooting the breeze. I wondered if the son of a bitch liked playing with me because he had to know how scared I was.

"You come with me to Lulling...help me find Buck and Denny-"

"No," I said before the last syllable even left his mouth. "Absolutely not."

I finally saw a reaction in the man – an almost imperceptible hardening of his jaw – and I felt my heart lurch in my chest. "Matty needs to be admitted to the hospital within the next couple of days," I added, hoping that would somehow make this man see that what he was asking was impossible. Even if Matty hadn't been sick, my answer would have been the same, but I didn't tell him that.

"I have some friends who can watch Matty while he's getting treated."

"Friends?" I asked stupidly.

"In Seattle."

I laughed before I could stop myself and stood up. "You're insane," I snapped, my anger replacing my fear.

His irritation was no longer subtle as he got to his feet. I half expected to see him pull out the gun, but he didn't. He just strode towards me and didn't stop until he was just inches away. The kitchen counter was at my back so I had no way to escape him.

"Here's my offer, Tate," he bit out. I hated the way my name sounded on his lips – like a curse. "We leave for Seattle tomorrow. I'll make sure Matty gets the finest care possible and I'll pay for it...all of it, no matter how long it takes. In return, you give me a week in Lulling."

I shook my head emphatically. "I am not leaving my son!"

I expected Hawke to point out that Matty wasn't mine, but he didn't. He just stepped even closer to me, his body almost brushing mine. I could feel the heat from his body drifting over me and I had the overwhelming urge to wrap my arms around him and try to soak some of it up because every part of me felt bitterly cold.

"One of my friends is a doctor-"

"I don't care," I snapped. Since he was taller than me, I was forced to look up at him and the move made me feel small and insignificant. Powerless.

I knew Hawke was done with me when his big hand came up to wrap around my throat. He didn't exert any pressure, he just held me there. It was a warning, a message. But I held my ground and whispered, "I am not leaving my son."

"Very noble," Hawke murmured as he glared at me. "Is that nobility gonna pay for the treatment your kid needs?"

I swallowed hard and didn't miss when Hawke's eyes dropped to where he was holding me. His gaze returned to mine just as quickly and I swore I saw a flash of something in his eyes that seemed out of place. Understanding? Compassion? Respect?

I nearly laughed at the prospect. This man had none of those things.

"Fine, we'll play it your way," Hawke murmured and he released me. But he didn't step away from me. "What do you think will happen to little Matty when the cops show up questioning you about a murder that happened ten years ago? A murder where a partial match to your DNA was discovered?"

Disbelief flooded my nerve endings, then white hot fear as I understood what he was saying. "The...the lab would never give the cops my DNA."

"You really think they gave it to me?" Hawke asked calmly.

And I knew in that instant that he had me. It didn't matter how he'd managed to find my DNA. It didn't matter that he knew I hadn't been involved in whatever murder he was talking about. Even if the cops couldn't use my DNA, that wouldn't stop them from investigating me and that meant Matty would go into foster care. And if he went into the system, I'd never get him back.

I leaned back against the counter for support as my knees threatened to give way. This couldn't be happening. I couldn't have come this far, given up so much, only to have this man take it away from me. To have cancer take it from me. I struggled to draw in air as a dull roaring began in my head. I tried to focus on a spot on one of the cabinets on the other side of the small kitchen, but my vision began to dim.

"Tate."

The soft, gentle murmuring of my name was so different from the angry way it had been said before. I wanted to hear it again. And then I did, but it got better because the warmth I had been craving seeped into a spot just above my elbows.

"Open your eyes, Tate."

I shook my head because I knew what was waiting for me if I did. And then sparks of electricity flared to life on my cheek and I sucked in a soft breath at the sensation. I forced my eyes open and saw Hawke watching me intently, his wide, firm lips slightly parted, his flinty blue eyes focused on me...no, not me, my lips.

I didn't move as I made sense of the flash of heat on my cheek. He was caressing me there, the rough pad of his thumb dragging over my skin. When his finger stilled, I brought my hand up to close around his wrist. But not to stop him, not to push him away. To prevent his escape. To urge him on. To beg him to keep the pain and fear at bay for just another few seconds.

Hawke's eyes drifted from my face to my hand where I was holding him and I saw his eyes shutter and then go dark as he released his hold on me. I cursed my foolishness and quickly dropped my hand.

"We're leaving in the morning," he finally said as he stepped back.

I didn't say anything as he went back to the chair and sat down. It took me a long time to find the strength and the will to move. And when I finally did, I went to Matty's room to start packing his things. Because like so many times in my life, my choice to do anything else had been taken away from me.

~

Since Matty's room didn't have a clock in it, I had no idea what time it was when I finally woke up the next morning. What I did know was that my son's warm little body wasn't lying next to me anymore and I jerked upright and stumbled out of the bed. I ripped the closed door open and scanned the small space and then felt my breath come out in a whoosh when I heard my son's voice. I couldn't hear what he was saying, but it took only seconds to find him. He was sitting with Hawke at the kitchen table and he was talking excitedly about the Spiderman doll in his hands.

"It was Daddy's when he was little," Matty was explaining as he moved the doll's arms and legs into different positions.

I was shaking when I reached the pair and while Hawke looked at me with an unreadable expression, Matty smiled and said, "Hawke says we're going on a trip."

Several things occurred to me as I took in my son and the hard man across from him. One, I probably shouldn't be letting my son call the man by his first name. But I realized just as quickly that I didn't know the man's last name and I wasn't about to ask. I didn't want to know what it was...I didn't want to know any more about him than was absolutely necessary. The other thing I noticed was the half eaten bowl of Cheerios on the table. Since we'd been out of the cereal the day Hawke burst into our lives, I knew what the box and the container of milk next to it meant.

"Where did these come from?" I asked Hawke.

"Hawke and I went shopping while you were sleeping, Daddy," Matty answered, though I kept my eyes on Hawke. He, in turn, held my gaze, unconcerned at the growing anger I knew had to be wafting off of me.

"You took him without my permission?" I said, knowing the question was stupid. This man didn't need my permission to do anything. Whatever he wanted, he took.

Hawke didn't move, didn't smile…didn't do anything but stare at me with his cold, cobalt eyes. "Figured you wouldn't want him eating pizza for breakfast," he finally responded. "And we have a long day of driving ahead of us."

I ignored the challenge in Hawke's tone and went to kneel down next to Matty. He looked tired, but seeing the smile on his face had me feeling marginally better. "Hawke said we're going on a trip," Matty repeated, almost hopefully. I bit back the tears that threatened to fall as I thought about the many days of pain my son would have to endure in the coming months.

"Yeah, we are. Would you like to go meet Hawke's friends?"

Matty nodded. "He said they have a really cool dog. His name is Bullet," Matty said with a laugh.

I smiled and then reached out to press my hand against Matty's forehead. "How are you feeling this morning?" I asked.

"My belly hurts a little," he said. "There's another one, Daddy," he said softly as he pulled his shirt up to show me yet another bruise on his abdomen.

I nodded slowly while I tried to find the strength to speak. "I know, buddy. But the doctors know how to fix it now so you won't get any more."

"Is it gonna hurt like yesterday?" Matty asked, his voice dropping.

"No," I lied as I pulled him into my arms. "But we'll talk about that later, okay? Why don't you go watch some cartoons for a bit and then we'll get ready to go so we can meet Bullet, okay?"

I felt Matty nod against my neck before pulling free of me. To my surprise, he ran over to Hawke and threw his arms around the man before Hawke could even react. Hawke stiffened and tried to hold himself back from the contact, but then I saw the slightest relaxing of his body as he wrapped an arm around Matty's small frame.

"Here, you can play with him for a while," Matty said as he thrust Spiderman into Hawke's hands before leaving the kitchen. I heard the

TV come on a few seconds later. I reached for the dishes on the table and began cleaning up.

"The bruises?" I heard Hawke ask.

My entire body ached from exhaustion and I found myself leaning against the kitchen counter, my stinging eyes focused on the dingy tile backsplash over the sink. "A symptom," I answered. "They were the reason I took Matty to the pediatrician a few days ago. He sent us to a specialist."

"And you got the diagnosis."

I let out a strangled laugh. "I didn't believe him. I knew it was a mistake so when he said I needed to take Matty to the hospital for tests, all I could think was that they were going to look like fools when they told me they'd screwed up in telling me my kid had cancer."

I began washing the few dishes in the sink. "Other kids get cancer. Not mine." I sucked in a breath. "Then the oncologist starts talking about chemotherapy and stem cell transplants and I just lost it."

I heard the chair scrape back and then Hawke was leaning against the counter next to me. I kept my eyes on the dishes in the sink, but at some point I'd stopped cleaning them. "My little boy has cancer," I whispered in disbelief. At some point tears had started to slip from my eyes, but I was powerless to move as the enormity of what was happening hit me all over again.

"You said they got it early," Hawke said, his voice soothing. How could one man be so terrifying one moment and so gentle the next?

"I...I saw the bruises a few weeks ago. I thought he got them from playing too rough," I whispered. I looked at Hawke who was standing much closer to me than I'd realized. "I should have taken him to the doctor that day...what if those three weeks-"

"He's going to be okay, Tate," Hawke said firmly and I closed my eyes when I felt his big hand settle on my back between my shoulder blades. His palm rested there for a moment before drifting up to settle over my right shoulder and he squeezed gently.

The move unlocked something inside of me and I let out a hoarse sob. "I can't lose him!"

I didn't resist as Hawke pulled me to him and when I felt his broad chest pressed against my cheek, I began crying in earnest as I finally got what I'd needed for so long. I wrapped my arms around him and held on for dear life as I let out all the fear and uncertainty that had hounded me in the two years that I'd taken Matty and escaped the life that had been drowning me.

"Daddy?"

I pulled back from Hawke's hold to see Matty standing next to us, his big eyes pooling with tears. Before I could even react, Hawke was picking him up. "He's okay, Matty. He just needs a really big hug, okay?"

Matty nodded as Hawke handed him over to me. Matty wrapped himself around me like a monkey and I let go of another round of sobs when he whispered, "It's okay, Daddy. I'll take care of you," into my ear.

I wasn't sure how long I held him for, but at some point we ended up sitting in one of the kitchen chairs. Matty sat back so he could study my face. "Love you lots," he whispered and I let out a choked laugh.

"Forever and ever," I responded. It was a saying we'd come up with, though I couldn't remember where we'd gotten it from. It had just... been. Like me and Matty. One day we were strangers, the next we were family. It had just happened.

"I'm okay now," I said to him as I used a dish towel that had magically appeared on the table in front of me to wipe away my tears. "Why don't you go finish watching your cartoon?"

Matty nodded. He looked over his shoulder at Hawke who had returned to the chair across from us. I spared the man a glance and was surprised to see what I was sure I hadn't last night...compassion.

"I think Daddy needs Spidey," Matty said in all seriousness to Hawke. "He's sad."

Hawke nodded and pushed the doll across the table so Matty could reach it. He grabbed it and handed it to me. I was too emotional to speak so I gave him a nod and then pulled him back against me for another hug. His hold on me was unfailing and unhurried and I wondered again how I'd been lucky enough to have this kid in my life.

"Go on," I finally said. Matty hopped off my lap and left the kitchen. I felt completely drained as I put the doll on the table and tried to wipe away the last remnants of my breakdown from my face. I forced myself to look up at Hawke. "You said your friend is a doctor?"

Hawke nodded. "He's already in the process of finding the best oncologists at Seattle Children's Hospital. Matty will get the best care possible. They'll want to see the results of the tests Matty had done yesterday."

I managed a nod. "I'll call them from the car," I said. As much as I hated being forced into this situation, I couldn't help but feel relieved that Matty would be getting what he needed despite my lack of funds. Dr. Spengler had explained that Matty would have to be in the hospital for weeks at a time since the chemo would destroy his immune system. He'd get about a week or so between each phase of chemo where he could leave the hospital, but it would be at least six months before the first round of treatment was completed. The cost for his care would be staggering and since I had no documents proving Matty's identity, I wouldn't have been able to rely on any government programs for assistance. And after the prior day's fiasco with the woman insisting I pay for part of the services up front, I couldn't even be sure Matty would get any kind of care since I couldn't afford to pay for it.

"I'll find a way to pay you back," I managed to say as I leaned back in the chair.

"You don't-"

I put up my hand to stop Hawke's words. "I'll keep my end of the deal, but I'm not a charity case. The money is a loan," I said firmly.

Hawke didn't respond in any kind of way and I wasn't sure what that meant. He was once again distant and unreadable. I forced myself to hold his gaze as I said, "If we find Buck and Denny, I need you to make sure-"

"I won't let them near you, Tate."

A shiver ran down my spine at his declaration. How many times

41

had I wished there'd been someone to say those exact words to me? How many times had I curled in on myself as blow after blow had fallen across my battered body and dreamed that someone like the man across from me would step in and stop it?

Too many times.

Too many to believe his words.

But I had to hope that whatever connection he'd managed to forge with my son would carry over to what I was about to ask of him.

"I need you to make sure that Buck and Denny never get to Matty," I said firmly. "No matter what happens to me, Matty comes first. I don't care what you have to do...Buck never lays a hand on him." I swallowed hard as even the thought of Matty being exposed to Buck's brutal "lessons" made me want to throw up. "Promise me," I whispered unashamedly.

Hawke studied me for so long that I had to fight the urge to squirm in my seat. I hated that my mind feared the power he had over me, but I hated even more that my body craved it and him in a way I'd never known before.

"No one touches Matty," Hawke finally said. "Or you," he added. And then he leaned forward and pinned me with his hard eyes. "Ever."

I forced back the dual need to believe him and to tell him not to make me a promise he couldn't keep and merely nodded my head. "I'll go pack," I said.

"Eat something first," Hawke murmured. He got up before I could respond and then he was setting the Cheerios and carton of milk in front of me. I wasn't actually hungry, but there was something about the way he watched me that had me reaching for the bowl and spoon he slid in front of me. I had no idea what he was thinking, but for the first time since he'd forced his way into my life, I actually didn't feel afraid of him.

And I had no idea why.

CHAPTER 5

HAWKE

*I*t took us more than an hour to finally get on the road since I'd vastly underestimated the amount of stuff one kid needed. While Tate just had a small bag, he'd packed as many of Matty's books, toys and stuffed animals into my car as he could, leaving only just enough space for Matty in the back seat.

Which meant Tate was sitting in the passenger seat next to me. And the fact that his close proximity bothered me was a problem. A big one.

I hadn't meant to touch Tate when he'd broken down about Matty's condition. But as his voice had cracked and then finally broken, I'd found myself desperate to take away his pain and I'd pulled him against me. His arms had wrapped around me like a drowning man, but instead of trying to extricate myself from his hold like I should have, I'd held him tighter. His tears had seeped through my shirt and my own eyes hadn't been immune. And then Matty had appeared and everything had gotten more fucked up.

Because the harder I tried to maintain my distance from Tate and Matty Travers, the more they sucked me into their lives. And the guilt of what I was doing was eating me alive. My threat to turn Tate's DNA over to the cops had been an empty one, but I'd made sure he wouldn't know that. I'd gotten what I wanted, but I couldn't get the image of Tate's look of betrayal out of my head. Which was ridiculous because I owed him nothing. I didn't give a shit what he thought of me.

I didn't bother to wait for Revay's voice to whisper in my ear that I was a liar because I already knew I was. Just like I was lying to myself about what Tate's body pressed up against mine had done to me.

I'd wanted him. I still wanted him.

A man.

A fucking man.

My entire life had only ever been about women...well, one woman. Sure, I'd noticed other women in the years I'd been with Revay, but not one of them had stirred even an ounce of the same desire in me that my wife had. Even in the years since I'd lost her, there'd been no one that had made me burn with need.

Until now.

I'd been around plenty of gay men and women in my life. Hell, the man I considered the closest thing I had to a best friend was openly gay and I'd spent the last couple of weeks protecting the man he'd been in love with for several years. It wasn't something that was foreign to me, but feeling my body react to Tate's hard body definitely was. I hadn't even once looked at a man in the same way I did a woman. There was no way what I was feeling was real... it was some kind of fucked up fluke. It had to be. Because not only could I not be attracted to a man after a lifetime of wanting only women, I could not be attracted to the son of one of my wife's murderers.

And if that wasn't bad enough, I'd had to contend with Matty when he'd shuffled into the kitchen this morning in his superhero pajamas. I would have expected him to be afraid of me after what I'd done to him and his father that first night, but instead, he'd studied me for a moment, his Spiderman doll hanging loosely in his hand, and then he'd climbed up into the chair across from and just stared at me. He'd then announced that he didn't think I was Captain America because my name was Hawke. That meant I must be more like

Hawkeye and he'd begun asking me why I carried a gun instead of a bow and arrows.

I'd managed to use his hunger as a distraction and had taken him down to a small grocery store a block from Tate's apartment. And while he'd gotten off the topic of me being a superhero in hiding, he hadn't stopped rambling from the moment we'd left the apartment. Worse, he'd grabbed my hand as we'd walked and simply looked up at me and said, "Daddy says." I'd taken that to mean Tate had a rule that Matty needed to hold a grown-up's hand, but I hadn't had a chance to ask him that because he'd started in on explaining who he thought would win if Spiderman and Captain America got into a fight.

It wasn't until we'd gotten back to the apartment and I'd slid a bowl of Cheerios in front of Matty, that I'd managed to get a few snippets of information out of him. Like that his father did dishes in a restaurant, slept on the couch and they moved around a lot. The latter hadn't been described that way of course – Matty had made it sound like a game where winning was about being quiet and quick. It was a telling statement of what Tate's life was like.

And that should have made me feel better about what I was doing. It didn't.

Because even if Tate and Matty got what they needed out of the deal, I'd still taken Tate's choice away. I'd terrorized him, threatened him and used his kid to get what I wanted. And then I'd reveled in the way his body had lined up perfectly with mine as I'd held him. I hadn't cared that all the places where I'd been touching him were hard instead of soft. Or that he hadn't smelled like flowers and that his muscles had rippled beneath my fingers. Or that his hold on me had been desperately tight instead of soft and comforting.

I could easily end this when I got them to Seattle. I could keep my end of the deal because the money for Matty's care meant nothing to me. I could entrust them to Ronan's care and be done with this whole thing.

But I wouldn't be done because I'd have to live with knowing I'd failed Revay in every way. And I couldn't do that. I wouldn't.

I felt the hairs on the back of my neck standing up and I glanced over to see Tate watching me. I cursed the fact that my dick twitched at the momentary flash of need I saw in his eyes. "What?" I bit out a little too harshly.

"Nothing," Tate murmured as he shook his head and turned his attention back out the window. We'd been on the road for a couple hours, stopping only once to buy a booster seat for Matty along with some snacks that I never would have even thought to buy for a little kid.

"What?" I repeated, forcing the irritation from my voice because, strangely enough, I wanted him to talk to me.

Tate turned back to me and then glanced at the back seat. I looked up in the rearview mirror and saw that Matty was asleep, his head resting on his shoulder and Spiderman clutched to his chest.

"Who was it?"

"Who?" I asked.

Tate hesitated and then finally said, "Who did Buck and Denny kill?"

I felt pain shoot through my chest. Since I needed a moment to recover, I managed to get out, "You don't seem surprised they did it."

Tate dropped his eyes to his hands. "I stopped being surprised by the things they did a long time ago." Tate began twisting his fingers around each other. "Who was it?"

I blew out the breath I hadn't realized I'd been holding. "My wife."

I was surprised when Tate didn't look at me. He barely even acknowledged that he'd heard me. The only change in his tense frame was that his fingers had stopped moving. "When?" he finally asked.

"September, 2005."

"What was her name?"

More pain bloomed in my chest. I rarely said her name out loud and I always felt a searing pain on the few occasions that I did. "Revay," I managed to whisper.

Tate fell silent. Most people always apologized to me when they learned I'd lost my wife, but Tate said nothing. It was strangely comforting. Like he knew that telling me he was sorry would solve nothing, would do nothing to even make a dent in the agony that consumed me.

"Did they ever say anything about her? About that time?" I forced myself to ask.

Tate didn't need to ask who I was talking about. "I don't remember. I learned a long time ago not to ask questions."

"How old were you then?"

"Thirteen."

"What about your mom? Was she around?"

Tate was quiet for a moment before saying, "No, she wasn't."

"So your parents were divorced?"

Tate shrugged. "No idea."

I figured the conversation was over when Tate turned his head to look out the window. But to my surprise, he started talking again.

"I don't remember her, but I used to dream about this woman when I was little. It was always the same dream. She had this really bright, long red hair and she was wearing some kind of uniform…a nurse maybe. It was just her and me and Denny sitting around this small table, holding hands, and she was saying grace. That's it…that's all I ever see." Tate glanced down at his hands again. "That was how I picked Tate."

"What do you mean?" I asked.

"When I left home, I knew I needed a new name. She used to always call me Tate in the dream."

I wanted to ask him what his real name was, but I held back because I could see by the way he'd started twisting his hands again, that he was already tense. He cast a look over his shoulder at Matty who was still asleep. Then I felt his eyes on me and I could tell he wanted to say something.

"What?" I asked, keeping my voice low and gentle.

"I wish I'd been stronger back then," he said quietly. "Maybe she'd still be alive if I'd said something…anything."

I tensed at that because I knew who the *she* he was referring to was, but when I shot Tate a glance, he was once again looking out the window. I fought the urge to reach my hand over to grab one of his so he would stop clenching them together. But my body refused to listen to my brain and before I knew it, my palm was settling over his warm skin. He stilled instantly and I heard the slightest intake of breath. Electricity fired through my blood when I once again felt his eyes on me.

I'd intended to tell him that it wasn't his fault, but I got lost in the sensation that was coursing through my body and what it meant. My brain could deny it all it wanted, but the fact that my dick was even now swelling with need was proof that it wasn't some fluke.

I wanted Tate.

Badly.

And I had no idea what that meant.

CHAPTER 6

TATE

I wasn't able to take a deep breath until Hawke removed his hand from mine. The contact had been brief, seconds only, but my whole body felt like it was on fire. Desire wasn't an entirely new feeling for me, but I'd never felt it to this extreme.

Growing up in a small, rural town in Eastern Texas hadn't exactly provided a lot of options for a teenage kid with a homophobic father and brother to explore his sexuality, but I'd lucked out when I'd discovered that a classmate I'd been tutoring in English Lit, Reggie Kimball, was hiding the same secret I was. Reggie had been two years older than me and had already fooled around with a couple other guys when he'd cornered me in the gym's locker room at school one day and kissed me.

He'd never allowed me to call him my boyfriend, even when it was just us, but I'd let him take my virginity just the same. The sex hadn't been at all what I'd expected, but I'd never protested when he'd asked if he could fuck me. Because even though I'd never found pleasure in the act, I'd lived for what came after…those few minutes when Reggie would be lying on top of me, his length buried deep inside of me, his breath against my neck, his heavy body covering mine like a blanket. In those moments I became someone else – we both did. And I was safe...and free. There was no doublewide trailer to go home to, no bruises to try and hide, no fear that one day the heavy fists wouldn't stop. But it would only last as long as it took for Reggie to recover, pull free of me and slap me on my ass and tell me I was the best fuck he'd ever had.

A couple months after Reggie had left for college, I'd visited a gay club in nearby San Antonio on a night Buck and Denny were out of town. I'd been picked up within minutes of walking through the door, but instead of going to a motel like I'd hoped, the guy had fucked me in a darkened area at the back of the club. As he'd come, I'd heard other grunts all around me and I'd realized other men had been watching us. Humiliation and fear had coursed through me and I'd run as soon as the man had slipped free of me. I never went back.

It wasn't until I was almost twenty-one that Reggie suddenly returned to town after having dropped out of college. He'd been just as arrogant and callous as ever and I'd still been just as desperate for the connection with someone who needed me, even if it was in a fucked up way. He took, I took...it had just worked for us and some-where along the way, he'd become the closest thing to a friend that I'd had.

But not once had I ever felt with Reggie what I felt when Hawke touched me. Even now, minutes later, I could still feel my breath sawing in and out of me as my body drew up tight with excitement. I knew that Hawke had only meant the gesture to be about comfort, but my body didn't seem to care. I shifted in my seat to try to ease the discomfort in my jeans as my dick continued to swell.

I wanted to laugh out loud at the irony of the situation. For the first time in my life, I was feeling true desire and it was for a straight man who was just using me to get what he wanted. He'd terrorized, threatened and ultimately blackmailed me, but my body chose this moment, this man to come alive for.

I willed my cock to settle down as I turned my attention back on the scenery flying by. My thoughts drifted to Hawke's wife and pity rushed through me for the faceless woman. Because I knew in my heart what Buck and Denny would have done to her before they'd taken her life. I'd been honest with Hawke when I'd said I didn't remember any discussion of his wife between Buck and Denny, but I knew from years of watching my father and brother use and abuse women, that they would have taken pleasure in hurting the woman. I also knew that they were very good at not getting caught. Which would explain why Hawke's wife was gone. And it also explained why he'd threatened me...it was something I wouldn't have understood before Matty came into my life – that unconditional love you had for someone else, that they had for you. I would do anything to protect Matty and if I lost him, I knew I wouldn't survive it. The man next to me knew that pain, had lived it for ten years now. I couldn't fault him for wanting what he did. And the fact that I had to pay for it right alongside Buck and Denny...maybe it was justice coming full circle. For not having had the courage to find someone who would make sure Buck and Denny were stopped.

"Daddy, I gotta pee."

Matty's voice startled me from my thoughts and I turned to see that he was rubbing at his eyes.

"Okay, buddy, we'll stop in a second."

I glanced at Hawke. His entire countenance had grown hard and cold and I could feel the tension wafting off him in waves. He gave me the slightest nod, but didn't speak and he never once glanced at Matty in the rearview mirror. It was like we were no longer there.

We stopped at a fast food restaurant, but to my surprise, Hawke didn't come in with us. We were still technically his prisoners, but I suspected he knew I needed his help just as badly as he needed mine, more so even, and that I wouldn't be asking anyone to alert the authorities. Once we were done in the bathroom, I took Matty's hand and led him up to the counter and scanned the menu. Ignoring my own growling stomach, I ordered Matty some chicken nuggets and fries and herded him back to the car as he tried to search through the bag for the toy the advertisement for the meal had promised. Once he was buckled in, I got back into the passenger seat and waited, but Hawke didn't put the car in gear. His eyes finally lifted to check the rearview mirror and then he glanced at me. His jaw tightened and then he turned the car off and got out without a single word and stalked off towards the restaurant.

"How you feeling, buddy?" I asked as I turned so I could watch my son devour his meal.

"Look, Daddy," he said as he proudly held up the small plastic airplane. "Can we go see this movie?"

"Maybe," I hedged as my stomach churned. I knew I needed to explain to Matty why he'd be spending much of the next six months in the hospital, but I had no idea how to do it. I could feel the tears threatening all over again so I turned around and stared at the cars flying along the Interstate. By now, I should have been used to the feeling of not knowing what was going to happen…it had become a way of life for us. But all I wanted was for my kid was to have a normal life. Play dates, birthday parties, a house with a yard, a dog… and I couldn't give him any of that.

Hawke pushed out through the restaurant door, a bag in one hand and a cup in another. He practically ripped open the driver's side door. He shoved the bag at me and put the cup in the cup holder before jamming the key into the ignition and starting the car. I held the bag on my lap, trying to ignore my cramping stomach as the smell of the food hit me. Once the car was moving, I tried to hand the bag to Hawke but he pushed it back at me and muttered, "Eat."

I looked at him in surprise. "But-"

"Just shut up and eat, Tate," Hawke snapped.

"Oooh, he said a bad word," Matty called from the back seat.

"Eat your lunch, okay, Matty?" I managed to say, though I couldn't take my eyes off the man next to me who had yet to look at me. When he finally did, I felt my throat close up at the flash of softness I saw as he quietly repeated his order for me to eat. The hardness returned almost instantly, but I didn't focus on that. Instead, I opened the bag and did exactly as he said.

I ate.

∽

*H*awke's emotional distance continued to grow throughout the drive north. We had to stop several more times for Matty to go to the bathroom and while Hawke never complained, I couldn't get a read on him. He didn't interact with me or Matty, but at a gas station, he bought Matty some ice cream and when Matty saw a children's play area in a park across the street from the next gas station we stopped at, Hawke pulled the car up to it after we'd gassed up and Matty and I had played for almost a half an hour before getting back in the car to continue on our journey.

We'd stopped for dinner an hour earlier at a truck stop that had a restaurant attached to it, but when I'd only ordered a small soda, Hawke had ended up ordering me a burger, fries and even a piece of pie. I'd tried to offer him money to pay for both Matty's and my meals, but he'd shot me such a dark look that the protest had died in my throat.

Matty had spent most of the meal coloring the children's paper placemat in front of him and I knew even he'd sensed Hawke's withdrawal. We'd gotten back on the road after that and Matty had fallen asleep a few minutes later.

Darkness had started to fall when I glanced at the clock in the dashboard and saw that it was eight o' clock.

"Hawke," I said softly.

Because it was dark in the car, I couldn't be sure that the man next to me actually flinched when I said his name, but he did turn to glance at me. "What?"

I ignored the irritation in his voice. "Are we stopping for the night soon?"

"We're driving through," came his terse reply.

"Don't we have like six hours to go?" I asked.

"Five."

"Matty's tired. He needs a bath and he needs to sleep in a bed. Can we just stop at a hotel? I…I'll pay for it," I offered even though I knew a hotel room would eat up much of the little cash I had left.

Hawke didn't respond in any way. Anger surged through me, but I quelled it and said, "Please."

The only reaction I got was Hawke drumming a couple of his fingers on the steering wheel. The red glow from the lights on the dashboard let me see a little of his face and I could tell he wasn't happy. But I didn't give a shit. My son came first. Before I could repeat my request, Hawke turned on the blinker and steered the car off the Interstate at the next exit. There was only one small motel just off the freeway and I could only hope it was reasonably clean because the outside appearance was not encouraging. Hawke was already out of the car a second after he slammed it into park and he was back a moment later with the room key...a single room key.

I kept my mouth shut as he drove us around to the other side of the motel and parked in front of our room. There were only a couple of other cars in the lot. As I pulled Matty from the backseat, Hawke got our stuff from the trunk and then opened the door. I breathed a sigh of relief when he flicked on the lights. It wasn't a pretty room, but it looked clean. I carried Matty to one of the two beds and sat down.

"Matty, do you feel like taking a bath tonight?" I asked softly against his head. I felt him nod against my chest and I couldn't help but smile. My kid loved his baths.

Hawke dropped mine and Matty's bag on the bed next to me. I looked up to see him staring at Matty. I was surprised to see that the mask of indifference had disappeared and in its place was an intense look of longing. His eyes shifted to me and I sucked in a breath at the impact it had on me. God, what I would have given to have him lean down to brush his lips over mine. I didn't know if Hawke saw something in my gaze because his eyes went dark with some unnamed emotion and then he shuttered them and suddenly turned and left the room. No explanation, no saying when he would be back. I shook my head as I held Matty tighter. I needed to get a fucking grip. If Hawke had any idea of the direction my thoughts kept wandering in, he'd kick my ass for sure.

I took Matty into the bathroom and got his bath started. He woke up enough to play with his new toy and his Spiderman doll in the tub, but as soon as I got him out and started drying him off, he started to drift again and by the time I put him in one of the beds, he was completely out. Hawke still hadn't returned so I used the time to change into a pair of sweats and a T-shirt and then went to the bathroom to brush my teeth. After rinsing, I used a hand towel to dry my mouth and turned to leave the bathroom when I saw Hawke watching me from the doorway. I managed to stifle a gasp at his sudden presence because I hadn't heard the door open.

"I'm done in here," I managed to choke out as I willed my speeding heart to slow down. I put the towel down on the counter. Hawke hadn't moved at all and I felt excitement flood my system as his eyes stayed on me. I couldn't pinpoint what he was thinking, but I knew what I was thinking...or rather, what my body was.

Since Hawke's big body was blocking most of the doorway and he didn't seem to be in any rush to move, I was forced to try to get past him without touching him. It would have worked if he hadn't stepped forward just a little bit as I was walking past. The move had me pressed back against the doorframe and I froze in place as Hawke's body brushed mine. The contact lasted only seconds, but it felt like forever as his chest skimmed mine. Even through my T-shirt, my skin burned and lit up with sensation and I sucked in a harsh breath as he held the position for a brief moment. I looked up to see that Hawke's eyes were on me - on my mouth to be exact - and I licked my lips in anticipation. His whole body drew up tight and we both held there. The air sizzled around us and heat flooded my entire system as my cock filled in eagerness. And I knew if I didn't move, he'd notice it because his crotch was almost brushing mine. If he just moved forward a little bit...

The whole thing ended when Hawke stepped past me into the bathroom and began to shut the door. I moved out of the way and felt my knees nearly give out as the door clicked into place. I stumbled to the bed I was sharing with Matty and dropped down on it and tried to catch my breath. I knew the encounter hadn't lasted more than a few seconds and that I'd read way more into it than it had been, but it was just more proof that being in Hawke's presence was dangerous in so many ways. Anxiety crept over me as the feeling of being trapped took over. Two years ago I'd risked everything to escape the life that had been forced upon me. And now it was happening all over again. Hawke, cancer...I couldn't escape those things. Despair sank into my bones as I crawled into bed next to Matty and rested my head on the pillow next to his. But just as quickly as the hopelessness had come over me, the second Matty rolled and pressed himself up against my chest, it receded and I wrapped my arms around my son. Whatever came tomorrow and the next day and the day after that...I'd handle it. I had to. Because it wasn't about me anymore. It hadn't been about me for a really long time.

~

By the time the car rolled past the heavy iron gate that blocked the driveway at the end of a secluded dead end, my anxiety was sky high. Matty hadn't stopped talking for more than a minute or two ever since Hawke had driven the car onto the ferry that took us from the mainland to Whidbey Island and Hawke had been cool and distant since we'd left the motel this morning. Luckily, Matty hadn't noticed his surly attitude, but my frustration had grown more and more every time he answered Matty's curious questions with blunt, one or two word responses.

"Is Bullet nice?" I heard Matty ask from the back seat.

"Uh-huh," was all Hawke said back to him.

It wasn't until the car was parked in front of the huge Tudor style mansion and Hawke and I had both gotten out, that I finally got a chance to lay into the man like I wanted. As I moved past Hawke to get Matty out of the car, I bit out, "We didn't ask to be here. He's just a kid and he doesn't deserve you treating him like shit."

Hawke grabbed my arm before I could reach for the door handle. His hold wasn't gentle, but he wasn't hurting me either. Just like the night before, he looked at me like he wanted to say something, but instead, his eyes dropped to where his fingers were pressed against my bare skin. I was no longer surprised by the current of electricity that passed through me or the way heat began spreading out from the place where his skin touched mine. But what surprised me was rather than releasing me, Hawke drew me closer to him. And instead of just gripping my arm, his fingers began rubbing back and forth over my heated skin. I held my breath as he continued to draw me forward until we were almost touching. Everything around us ceased to exist as his eyes held mine and I saw the unspoken apology there...at least, that's what I thought it was. I saw something else too, but I couldn't be sure about it either because it seemed too farfetched to be possible.

Longing.

For what, I didn't know. But he had yet to let me go and I had yet to move away.

It wasn't until a cold, wet nose pressed against my hand that the spell was broken. I looked down to see a large German Shepherd sniffing me and then glanced up to see a man standing at the entrance to the house. His eyes weren't on me, though. They were on Hawke who hesitated for a moment before releasing me and stepping back. The dog circled him excitedly several times, but Hawke ignored him and went around the front of the car. I forced my attention back to getting Matty. His initial excitement about the dog seemed to have faded once he got a look at the huge animal because he clung to me as I lifted him out of the car. His legs were wrapped around my waist and his stranglehold on my neck sent a clear message that he wasn't ready to be put down yet so I carried him around the car.

The dog followed us, but I was glad when he didn't jump up to try to reach Matty.

"Is he nice, Daddy?" Matty whispered against my ear.

"I think he is, buddy," I said.

"His name is Bullet."

I expected the voice to belong to the intimidating man who'd been watching us just moments before, but it actually came from a young man making his way down the entry way stairs towards us. I saw Hawke and the other man deep in conversation and had to force myself to focus on the younger man. I guessed him to be close to my own age, maybe a little younger. He had thick blond hair and a kind face and he immediately held out his hand to me.

"I'm Seth Nichols."

"Tate," I answered and I shook his hand.

"And who's this?" he asked as his eyes fell on Matty.

Matty's head was pressed against my shoulder and he turned it so he could see Seth better. "Matthew but my Daddy calls me Matty."

Seth smiled. "Is it okay if I call you Matty?"

Matty nodded against me. "Is Bullet nice?" he asked timidly.

"Very," Seth responded. "He knows some tricks. You want to see them?"

Another nod from Matty. As Seth showed Matty the dog's tricks, I lifted my eyes to watch Hawke as he talked to the other man. His eyes shifted to me and whatever conversation he was having ceased. He held my gaze for a moment and then strode into the house. The other man came down the stairs towards us and I resisted the urge to step back.

He was bigger than Hawke by a couple of inches. His hair was coal black and his gray eyes were studying me. Just like Hawke, I couldn't get a read on him and I automatically tightened my arms around Matty in response. But as soon as the man's eyes moved from me to Seth, his entire countenance changed dramatically. Even before Seth put out his hand, I knew what they were to each other.

"Tate, this is my boyfriend, Ronan. Ronan, this is Tate," Seth said as he motioned to me. "And this is Matty," he said with a big smile as he put his hand briefly on one of Matty's legs.

Ronan nodded at me as he pulled Seth against his side. "Hi, Matty."

I barely noticed Ronan and Seth talking to Matty because I was lost in the way the two men held onto each other. My childhood hadn't exactly given me a lot of opportunities to see how two people in love behaved with one another, but seeing two men being so openly affectionate was overwhelming and a rush of envy went through me. I'd hidden my sexuality for so long that I'd just assumed it was something other gay men automatically did as well when they were in the presence of other people. But the two men in front of me weren't hiding anything…not from me, not from my son, not from each other.

"Daddy, can we?"

I realized I'd missed Matty's question entirely when I noticed him and both men watching me expectantly.

"Can we what?"

"Can we take Bullet for a walk?" Matty asked. His voice had started to lose some of its shyness.

"There's a nice beach down by the water," Seth explained.

"You sure you're not too tired?" I asked.

Matty shook his head.

"Okay," I said.

"Can Hawke come?"

Ronan answered before I could come up with an excuse because I had no doubt the man had no interest in spending any more time with us if he could avoid it.

"Hawke was pretty tired so he went inside to take a nap," Ronan said. "You sure you don't want to take one?"

The man's question had the desired effect because it took Matty's focus off of Hawke.

"Noooooo," Matty said with a laugh.

But as I followed Ronan and Seth around the side of the house towards the backyard, I realized that even though Matty wasn't thinking about Hawke anymore, I couldn't say the same thing.

CHAPTER 7

HAWKE

*D*espite the sweat that was dripping down my forehead and into my eyes, I saw Ronan the second he walked into the large gym that was located in the lower level of the house. I'd been waiting for him to come find me because I knew he wasn't going to wait very long to get the information he wanted. But I didn't let up on the punches I was laying into the heavy weight bag that hung from the ceiling in the corner of the gym. And when Ronan came over to hold the bag steady so I could take out even more of my frustration on it, he didn't say a word. I lost track of how much time had passed as I pounded on the canvas bag and even when my arms began to burn, I continued. Because it was the only thing that was keeping me from hunting down Tate and dragging him to me so I could finally see if his lips were as soft as they looked. If his taste was sweet or heady or a mixture of both.

I would have had my answer out in the driveway if we hadn't been interrupted. I knew that without a shadow of a doubt. I could pretend as much as I wanted, but it wouldn't change the fact that I was attracted to another man. Or that I felt the same spark of electricity with Tate that I'd only ever felt with my wife. And that in itself was unacceptable to me. Because Revay had no equal…there would never be anyone as good and kind and gentle as she'd been. There'd never be anyone who knew me inside and out like she had, who knew what I needed before I did. And I had absolutely no desire to know someone in the way I'd known her. She had been and still was my other half. No person, man or woman, would ever change that. My body might have some fucked up thoughts about Tate Travers, but my mind was clear. Tate was a means to an end, nothing else.

Liar.

I let out a loud curse and slammed my fist into the bag one last time before I finally gave in to my body's demand to stop. It took what little energy I had left to stumble to a nearby weight bench and sink down on it. As I used my teeth to loosen one of the boxing gloves on my hands, Ronan moved past me. He was back a moment later with a towel and a bottle of water. I swiped at my drenched hair and face with the towel and then took several pulls on the water. I didn't look at the other man as I began unwrapping my hands.

"Where are they?" I asked.

"Backyard," was all Ronan said.

"Did you get the appointment with the oncologist?"

"It's tomorrow morning. They can get him admitted the day after if they get all the test results in time."

I nodded. "Tate called them from the car. He had them email the release to your email address. He'll sign it today."

We both fell silent, but I knew it wasn't over. My hunch was confirmed when Ronan said, "So that's it? I don't hear from you for two weeks and when you do finally call, it's to ask me to find a place that will treat a kid with leukemia. What the fuck is going on, Hawke?"

I took my time working the first wrap off, but my intent wasn't to annoy Ronan, though I'm sure it did. No, I did it because I was trying to gather my courage to admit to this man, to my friend, what I'd done. Shame wasn't something I felt often, but from the moment I'd held my gun on Tate and his son even after I knew that Tate wasn't one of the men I'd been looking for, it was all I felt. But even now as it coursed through me, the need for vengeance was still stronger.

"His father and brother killed Revay," I finally spit out.

"Tate's?"

I nodded, unwilling to share the fact that they were also Matty's father and brother. In my mind, Matty was Tate's son and always would be despite what the DNA said.

"Fuck," I heard Ronan mutter and I looked up to see him turning away from me so he could begin pacing. It was something he'd done in front of me before, but I knew he'd let very few other people see him like this.

The Ronan I knew was very different from the persona Ronan shared with others and that had always been strangely comforting to me. I'd met Ronan ten years earlier when Revay and I had been wheeled into the ER at Brooke Army Medical Center the night she had been attacked. Although I'd been badly burned, I'd still been conscious and the ER had been in such a state of chaos that no one had noticed when I'd climbed off the gurney I'd been rolled in on and searched out the room Revay had been taken to. A young doctor had been frantically working on her with only a single nurse to help him. He'd spared me only a glance as he'd worked on my wife and he hadn't tried to make me leave which I wouldn't have done anyway. I was never sure if he'd let me stay because he'd known it was what I'd needed or because he'd known I wouldn't have left.

Either way, his eyes had connected with mine for the briefest of moments and then his only focus had been Revay. I hadn't been able to make sense of any of the words he and another doctor on the other side of the large room had kept yelling to each other, but I had understood exactly what it meant when my wife's heart monitor had begun screaming and the line on it had gone flat. Everything afterwards had been a blur as the doctor had begun slicing into her body with a scalpel. For all the gruesome things I'd seen and done during my career in the army, I hadn't been able to bear to watch my wife's blood pour from her body as the heart monitor reminded me she was already gone, so I'd dropped to the floor and covered my head with my hands and sobbed like a child as I'd tried to come to terms with the fact that my best friend had left me. I'd had no idea how long I'd sat there for, but I'd steeled myself for the words that would confirm my worst fear when I'd felt a hand come to rest gently on my shoulder.

I hadn't heard the words...I hadn't heard anything the doctor had said to me. What I had heard was the steady, rhythmic beeping of my wife's heart monitor and I'd scrambled to my feet to take her burned, bloody hand in mine as she was being moved to another floor. I'd had three days with her after that. Three days to tell her everything I'd thought I'd have a lifetime to say. And despite the agony my own burns had been causing me, I'd only felt true pain when she'd told me she loved me for the last time, just before a tube had been inserted into her throat to help her breathe. Three days and then she was gone.

I hadn't seen Ronan after that night in the ER, but our paths had crossed again four years later when I'd learned of an attack on Ronan and his lover, Trace, who'd happened to be Seth's older brother. Ronan and Trace had been ambushed by several soldiers from Trace's unit while they'd been stationed at Bagram Air Base in Afghanistan. Both men had been brutally beaten and then each had been sodomized with a metal pipe. Ronan had survived the attack. Trace hadn't. My heart had gone out to the surgeon and his dead partner, but it wasn't until I'd overheard some soldiers bragging about the attack a month later that I'd seen an opportunity to pay Ronan back for what he'd done for me. I hadn't even felt a speck of guilt when I'd abducted the man who'd been the ringleader of the attack, and I'd had no issue with helping Ronan seek out his own form of justice when the army refused to acknowledge the brutal crime or punish any of the men involved. After that, I'd watched as Ronan took out every last man who'd tortured him and stolen his future away, and a few months later when Ronan had built an underground organization that could do the same thing for other victims, but on a larger scale, I hadn't hesitated to sign on.

"Does he know where they are?" Ronan asked.

I shook my head. "They were living in Lulling, Texas, but Tate left two years ago and hasn't been back. I think he's been running from them...he and the kid."

"Any idea why?"

"I think they were abusing him…Tate. Not sure about Matty – it sounds like Tate got him out of there in time," I responded. "I went to Lulling last week, but didn't find anything. Daisy can't find a trace of either of them so I don't even really know who I'm looking for. I didn't want to blow my advantage by asking around."

I reached for the water and took several long drags on it before I began working on the wrap on my other hand. I steeled myself for what was to come because it wouldn't take Ronan long to figure out the right questions to ask.

"How'd you end up with them again?"

"I put a tracker and bug in the kid's backpack."

"Jesus, Hawke," Ronan muttered. "Was he at least able to give you anything else?"

I shook my head.

Ronan finally stopped pacing. "I can give you some guys…maybe they can help you-"

"No," I interrupted. "I've got a handle on it."

I didn't miss the look of disappointment on Ronan's face, but I didn't have time to dwell on what it meant because his next question was the one I'd been waiting for.

"What can I do to help?"

I removed the wrap from my hand and dropped it on the bench and then folded my hands together. "I need you and Seth to watch Matty for a while. A few days, maybe a week."

"You mean watch Matty and Tate," Ronan said carefully.

"Just Matty."

"Why?"

I sucked in a breath. "Because Tate is coming with me to Lulling."

Ronan was quiet for so long that I looked up at him. "What the fuck did you do?" Ronan finally asked angrily.

"Tate agreed to come to Lulling with me to help me find his father and brother-"

"Bullshit!" Ronan yelled. "No father agrees to leave his kid while he's undergoing chemotherapy! What did you do?"

"What the hell difference does it make?" I asked, unwilling to tell Ronan the truth about the extent of my blackmail.

"Tell me or I'll ask him!"

My own temper flared to life and I shot to my feet. "I told him if he didn't come with me, I'd turn his DNA over to the cops."

Ronan shook his head in disbelief and took several steps away from me. I hated the way he was looking at me...like he didn't know who I was. He was quiet for an unnaturally long time before he spoke again.

"Is this what she would have wanted, Hawke?" Ronan asked quietly. "Justice at the cost of an innocent man and his child?"

I snapped at the mention of Matty. "What she would have wanted, Ronan?" I shouted. "She would have wanted to raise our son!"

Ronan stilled, but before he could say anything I barreled on. "What about what I want? Huh? A few days, Ronan. A few days away from his kid! A kid he gets to come back to, a kid he gets to watch grow up! What about my kid? My little boy?"

"Revay was pregnant?" Ronan asked gently.

I didn't bother to answer because a cold, familiar feeling settled over me. I fought the urge to run my fingers over the burns that made my skin tingle uncomfortably.

I barely recognized my own voice when I said, "My kid's rotting in a grave with his mother. Tate's kid is safe and happy and God willing, will be healthy someday. I don't get a someday, Ronan. All I have left to look forward to in this fucking thing I call a life is watching those men die. Tate is my only chance to finally end this!"

I snatched the towel off the bench and didn't bother looking at Ronan again because I didn't want to see what I knew would be in his eyes now instead of disappointment.

Pity.

CHAPTER 8

TATE

"*Y*ou heard?"

I looked up at Ronan as he came to a stop in front of me. When I'd heard Hawke striding towards me from the gym, I'd taken a few steps back into a darkened hallway. But as I'd heard Ronan's footsteps approaching, I'd stepped out of my hiding spot.

I nodded.

"How much?"

"All of it," I admitted. "I didn't mean to eavesdrop," I added. "I wanted to get the release signed."

"Sure," Ronan responded, but he didn't move away from me and at the moment, I didn't care. Because all I could focus on were Hawke's final words.

"Where's Matty?"

"Still in the backyard," I murmured. "He and Seth are throwing a ball for Bullet."

I hadn't been surprised that Matty would warm up to Seth as quickly as he had because there was something so innately kind about the young man, that it would have been impossible for anyone, man or child, not to gravitate towards him. When I'd asked Matty if he wanted to stay outside with Seth or come inside with me while I got the release form ready to send, he'd barely paid me any attention as he'd waved me off.

"Tate, I'm sorry, Hawke shouldn't have threatened you."

I wasn't sure if I managed to respond in any kind of way because I was still reeling from what Hawke had said. Not only had Buck and Denny murdered Hawke's wife, they'd stolen the life of his unborn son too. I felt my stomach rolling and I briefly wondered if I would have to ask Ronan where the nearest bathroom was.

"I know Hawke, Tate. It was an empty threat. He never would have gone through with it. But if it makes you feel better, I can make the DNA test and results go away," Ronan said.

I had no idea how the man could manage something like that and I realized it didn't really matter. Like with Hawke, I was completely out of my element. "No, he and I...we have a deal. I need to keep up my end."

"What kind of deal?" Ronan asked.

But instead of answering Ronan, I shook my head and kept my mouth shut, though I had no idea why. I didn't owe Hawke anything.

"He offered you something, didn't he?"

"I should get back to Matty," I whispered, but Ronan gently grabbed my arm before I could get away from him.

"You and Matty are safe now, Tate. Money, protection, support... you have all those things here."

I looked up at him at that. "Why? You don't know me."

Ronan released my arm. "Seth and I both know you. We were you."

I didn't know what to make of the cryptic statement and truth be told, I was still too caught up in everything that had happened in the last few days - hell, within the last few hours - to actually want to try and understand it. "I should get that release form done," I said quietly.

"Sure, my laptop's in the kitchen." I followed Ronan out of the hallway, but my thoughts were still on Hawke and I wondered what the hell I was supposed to do next.

~

*M*y limbs felt heavy and sluggish as the barista handed me my coffee. The small coffee stand near the entrance of the hospital had been a blessing in disguise because I couldn't stomach the sludge they served in the cafeteria. I was on my second visit of the day, my first being when I'd left the hospital to go back to the hotel to shower and change and try to grab a few hours of sleep.

It had only been ten days since Matty had been admitted, but it felt like a lifetime. The day after arriving at Seth and Ronan's house, I'd taken Matty to the children's hospital in Seattle. I'd expected to make the journey by myself and had been trying to get up the nerve to ask Ronan and Seth if they had a car I could borrow, when Seth had knocked on the bedroom door of the room Matty and I were sharing and had asked if he and Ronan could come with me. I'd barely managed to hold it together at that point because I hadn't been at all prepared to try to deal with understanding all the information the doctors would be throwing at me to explain the treatment plan for the next six months.

Ronan had driven us to the hospital and he'd kept Matty entertained on the ferry to the mainland while I'd had a chance to talk to Seth. I hadn't seen Hawke since the day before when he'd stormed out of the gym. On the one hand, I'd been relieved because I wasn't sure when Hawke was going to insist that I keep up my end of the deal. On the other hand, I'd missed the distant, brooding man, though I had no idea why.

The visit with Matty's new oncologist had gone well and Ronan had stayed with me to ask the questions I hadn't thought of while Seth kept Matty busy by playing with him in the waiting area. The doctor hadn't tried to gloss over the seriousness of Matty's illness, but he'd been very optimistic that Matty would respond to treatment, especially since we'd caught the disease so early. After the appointment, Ronan and Seth had suggested we go down to the waterfront for lunch. Matty had had a chance to play the various arcade games that were housed in the same building as the restaurant and then we'd explored the aquarium. The fun had continued once we'd returned to the house on Whidbey Island and by the time we'd sat down to a dinner of hamburgers and hot dogs on the patio, Matty had barely been able to keep his eyes open. I'd put him to bed shortly after that and had used the quiet time to explain to Matty that he was sick and would need to spend some time in the hospital. I wasn't sure how much Matty had really understood, but it hadn't mattered because just before he'd drifted off to sleep, he'd murmured something about superheroes always getting better even when they got hurt.

I'd gone back downstairs after that to talk with Ronan and Seth about them watching out for Matty after I had to leave with Hawke to go to Lulling. They'd both been sitting at the kitchen table, hands joined as they'd poured over some papers that they'd spread out in front of them. I'd watched them in silence for a moment as they'd talked and laughed amongst themselves and I'd envied the easy conversation and the loving touches between them. And none of those things had stopped when they'd spied me. Instead, they'd waved me over and as I'd sat down, they'd started going over the plans they'd made on how to split up the time spent staying with Matty in the hospital so he'd never be by himself. I'd lost it at that point and had started sobbing uncontrollably as I'd realized I wouldn't have to face this by myself. Seth had held me as I'd cried and when I'd finally managed to get control of myself, there'd been no judgment or recrimination. We'd simply picked up where we'd left off and made our plans.

The following morning, we'd taken two cars to the hospital. Ronan and I had gone directly to the hospital to get Matty admitted while Seth had taken Bullet to the nearby hotel we'd be using as our home base for the foreseeable future since their house was too far away to travel back and forth to. I'd been nervous about the admission process in terms of the financial aspect, but the woman at the desk had merely slid a piece of paper in front of me and pointed to the billing section and asked if the information was correct. I'd felt Ronan's eyes on me as I'd read the name on the page, but he hadn't said anything.

Michael Hawkins.

Michael.

At first the name didn't seem to fit the harsh man, but the more I'd said it to myself over and over in my mind, I'd found that I liked the way it sounded in my head and as soon as I'd been by myself, I'd actually spoken it out loud just to see what it felt like. I hadn't asked Ronan where Hawke was staying though he clearly hadn't been staying at the house or I would have seen him. I'd kept hoping he would show up at some point, though I had no idea what I would have said to him if he had.

Matty had been a trooper for all the various poking and prodding he'd had to endure, but he'd had his first meltdown when he'd woken up after receiving anesthesia so that doctors could put in a central line. The central line had been inserted under his collarbone and was threaded under the skin until it came out of his upper chest. It was meant to make the administration of the chemotherapy drugs easier, but Matty had cried when he'd realized that the strange looking device would be staying in his body for the foreseeable future. He'd been inconsolable until the moment Ronan had leaned down and whispered something into his ear. I'd only heard the words "super-hero juice" but whatever he'd said had been enough for Matty to settle down and I'd held him in my arms until he'd finally fallen asleep. It was at that moment that I'd known I'd be able to leave my son in the care of the two men who were fast becoming friends.

Matty's first chemo treatment had been done the following night while he'd been asleep and Ronan had stayed with me the entire night while Seth went back to the hotel to get some rest. Matty had reacted better than expected to the medication, though he was nauseous the next morning and hadn't eaten anything. By lunch time, he'd been sitting up in bed and had taken a few tentative bites of the mac and cheese the nurse had brought him. He'd spent the rest of the afternoon napping, watching cartoons and coloring and when Seth had arrived to relieve us, Ronan and I had gone to the hotel to get some sleep.

As planned, we'd each taken shifts and while I'd spent every hour that I wasn't sleeping by Matty's side, Ronan and Seth alternated so that the only time I was ever alone with Matty was when he was asleep. I usually managed to snag a few hours of sleep myself at those times, but after only ten days, the physical and emotional stress were taking their toll on me.

Hence the many coffee runs.

But as tough as the days had been, we'd gotten some really good news the previous day when the doctor had spoken to us about the bone marrow biopsy they'd done. The fact that the disease hadn't progressed enough that Matty would need a stem cell transplant had helped ease some of the constant fear and anxiety that plagued me day in and day out.

I took a few sips of the coffee as I made my way to the elevator. The bitter liquid helped clear my muddled thoughts and I threw out the coffee before I entered the ICS ward. The unit was home to nearly a dozen immunocompromised kids and it was both humbling and encouraging to see the children of all ages and their families who were going through the same things Matty and I were. I hadn't had a chance to talk to any of the other parents yet, but Matty had already made friends with a little girl named Susie who was a year younger than him and was halfway through her course of treatment. He'd spent some time playing with her in the toy room and I'd nearly cried when I'd gotten to see my little boy being the kid he was meant to be. In those few minutes, he hadn't been sick and I hadn't had to deal with the prospect of losing him.

"Daddy!"

I smiled as Matty welcomed me before I'd even gotten the door to his room completely open.

"Hey, buddy," I said as I hurried to the bed and carefully wrapped my arms around him. I gave Seth a smile over Matty's shoulder.

"Seth and I are playing Tic Tac Toe," Matty said excitedly as he pointed to a piece of paper with dozens of Tic Tac Toe squares on them.

"He's beating me," Seth announced grumpily.

Matty chuckled. "You can win next time," he promised.

"Deal," Seth said with a laugh. "Hey, didn't you want to show your dad something?" Seth asked.

"Oh yeah," Matty said and then he was searching the bed for something. He finally pulled out a doll I didn't recognize. "Look what Hawke brought me!"

My heart lurched at the mention of Hawke and I felt a sliver of disappointment go through me that I'd missed his visit. "Wow, cool," I said.

"It's Hawkeye," Matty explained.

"That was so nice of him," I said. "Did you say thank you?"

Matty nodded, but then his face fell. "He said he had to go away for a while."

"Hawke said that?"

"Uh-huh. He said he might not be able to come back."

I glanced up at Seth who gave me a slight nod. "He left this for you," Seth said as he reached for a folded over piece of paper sitting on a small table next to Matty's bed.

My fingers shook as I saw my name scrawled across the front of the note. Inside were just a few words, but they shook me to my core.

Take care of your son, Tate. --H

My knees felt weak and I had to search out a chair. I shook my head in disbelief and I looked up at Seth. "Did you read this?"

Seth shook his head and I handed him the note. He read it and then folded it closed.

"When did he leave that?" I asked

"About an hour after you left."

I leaned back in the chair and watched Matty play with his doll. Hawke was letting me go. I couldn't believe it.

"Why would he do this?" I asked. I had no doubt that Seth knew exactly what Hawke's plans for me had been since I was sure Ronan would have told him.

I wasn't sure if Seth was going to answer me or not, but before he even had the chance, there was a knock on the door. Mira, the second shift nurse entered.

"Hi Matty," she said.

"Hi," Matty returned and then he was holding up the doll. "Look what I got."

"Hawkeye," Mira said knowingly. "He's my favorite."

"How come?" Matty asked as Mira came farther into the room.

"Because he doesn't have any actual super powers, but he's just as brave as all the other Avengers." Mira bypassed Matty's bed and came up to me.

"The billing office asked that I give this to you," she said as she handed me a piece of paper.

"What is it?" I asked.

"Your receipt."

Mira turned her attention to Matty before I could question her further. I studied the piece of paper and felt my heart constrict painfully in my chest when I saw Hawke's name again in the payer section. I shifted my eyes to the bottom of the page and sucked in a breath when I saw the balance. It was a negative number. A really big number.

"What is it?" Seth asked.

I glanced up to see that Mira had left at some point and Matty and Seth were once again playing Tic Tac Toe.

"He prepaid the bill," I managed to say. "For Matty's treatment."

Seth's eyes held mine for a brief moment and I swore I saw a hint of a smile drift over his lips before Matty demanded his attention again. I sat back in the chair and let my eyes fall back on the receipt.

What the hell did this mean?

CHAPTER 9

HAWKE

I held the rifle against my shoulder as I watched the headlights bounce along the dirt road that led up to the house. I'd grabbed it long before the car even made the turn from the secluded highway that bordered the property, because it was rare to see any kind of vehicle making the journey across the pass this time of night. And since my only neighbor owned a huge cattle ranch, I knew the man was already in bed since he was up before the sun even rose. It was likely just some poor soul who'd taken a wrong turn somewhere and gotten lost and was seeking directions, but I was hoping the rifle would make it clear that I wasn't in the mood for chit-chat.

Because I had work to do.

The drive from Seattle to Rocky Point, Wyoming had taken nearly twelve hours, but instead of getting the rest my body was demanding when I'd finally spied the lone light on the slight rise as I'd crested the last pass, I'd immediately started putting my plans into motion. Not having Tate as part of the equation anymore would make finding Buck and Denny much more difficult, but what I couldn't get with a few subtle questions, I could take with brute force. Someone in Lulling would tell me where the bastards were one way or another.

From the moment I'd admitted to Ronan that I'd lost not only my wife, but my son as well, I'd been a man possessed. Only I hadn't had anyone or anything to take my rage out on, so I'd drowned myself in alcohol in the small, secluded motel I was staying at. Ronan had called me several times and left messages asking me to go to Matty's first appointment with the oncologist or to join them for dinner, but I hadn't called him back. I hadn't wanted to see Matty and I definitely hadn't wanted to see Tate. And not only because my growing need for the other man was slowly driving me crazy. No, I hadn't wanted to see either of them because that fucking voice had gotten louder and louder in my head.

My wife's voice.

My beautiful, gentle wife who'd given up everything to be with me. My wife who'd been carrying the child we'd been trying for years for.

And she'd kept saying the same three words over and over to me until the doubt grew like a cancer inside of me.

This isn't you.

I'd done my best to ignore the words, but I'd heard them in every heartbeat, in every breath. I'd figured that if I set a timetable, the relentless torment would stop, so I'd sobered up long enough to get in my car and drive to Seattle in the dead of night so I could confront Tate and tell him when we were leaving. To my surprise, I hadn't had any trouble finding out what room Matty was in because someone had put my name down as an authorized visitor. A little bit of sweet talk with one of the nurses had gotten me around the fact that at just past midnight, it was too late for visitors and I'd been led to Matty's private room. She'd explained to me that the chemotherapy drugs were being administered to Matty while he was asleep and had warned me not to wake him up. She'd also told me that Matty's father was spending the nights with him.

I'd pushed open the door after steeling myself to face Tate, but all the pity for the man and his son that I'd forced away during my drive to the city had come roaring back when I'd seen Matty curled up on his side, his Spiderman doll and teddy bear clutched against his chest. There'd been only a small light on above Matty's bed, but it'd been enough to see where the line from the IV bag entered his body through two cannulas that were sticking out of his skin beneath a huge bandage. I'd managed to quietly close the door behind me as my eyes had drifted to Tate who'd been asleep in a large chair next to Matty's bed. His hand had been extended onto Matty's bed, his fingers resting on one of the little boy's arms.

I'd willed myself to wake Tate up and tell him we were leaving in a couple days, but instead of moving towards him, I'd gone to the other side of the room and dropped down into an identical chair to the one Tate had been sitting in and I'd watched them both sleep. I'd stayed until light began filtering through the window and as I'd gotten up to leave, I'd walked right up to Tate. But instead of shaking him awake, I'd merely stood there watching him sleep, his features relaxed. Right before I'd left, I'd run my fingers through his thick hair, marveling at its softness as it had curled around my fingers.

I'd spent the next day at Seth and Ronan's house shredding my body in their gym in the hopes that the brutal workout would distract me from what I needed to do. And hours later when I'd made the trip to the city again, I'd been determined to follow through with my plan. Only that night ended up like the first one. And so went every night after that. At some point, Revay's voice had quieted in my mind and when it was finally silent, I'd known it was time to finish what I'd started. So twenty-four hours ago when I'd walked out of Matty's room, I'd let my fingers rest in Tate's hair like I had all the other nights, but then I'd gone a step further and leaned down to brush my lips over his temple. He'd stirred just enough so that his lips were achingly close to mine and I'd finally given in to my need to taste him and had brushed my mouth over the corner of his. The result had been electric and it had taken everything in me to step away from him.

I'd driven back to Whidbey Island just as the sun had been rising over the mountains behind me and for the first time in the ten years since I'd lost Revay, I'd felt a few moments of peace. I'd gone back to the motel and slept for a couple of hours before gathering my things. My plan had been to return to the hospital only long enough to take care of the hospital bill, but when I'd spied a toy store on the way to the ferry dock, I hadn't been able to curb the need to leave a little piece of myself behind with the little boy who'd reminded me what true strength was all about.

Matty's smile as I'd entered his hospital room had turned me inside out and when he'd put out his arms expectantly, I'd hugged him and fought the sting of tears I'd felt burning the backs of my eyes. I'd only glanced at Seth once because the young man's knowing eyes had had me wanting to retreat in on myself. I'd had no doubt that he'd known what my plan for Tate was and I hadn't wanted to risk the same look of censure in his eyes that I'd seen in Ronan's that first day.

I'd listened as Matty had proudly explained how brave he'd been for all the tests and procedures that had been done on him and that he'd made a new friend named Susie, but my heart had nearly broken when he'd asked if I would spend the night like his daddy did. The doll I'd bought him had helped appease him when I'd explained that I had to leave for a while and I hadn't lingered after that. Partly because I hated hurting the little boy who'd clearly grown fonder of me than he probably should have, considering the shitty way I'd treated him. But mostly because I hadn't wanted to run into his father. My obsession with Tate was spiraling out of control and I'd been terrified that even being around him for the few seconds it would take to say my goodbyes would have had me wanting something more than I should.

So for the first time in my life, I'd run. I'd taken the coward's way out and I'd left a note...a fucking note. And I hadn't even had the balls to actually tell Tate I was sorry for what I'd done. I'd gotten in my car and started driving and as the miles had flown by, I'd forced all thoughts of Tate from my mind and I'd done what I did best. I planned.

But a stranger showing up in the dead of night wasn't part of my plan. I had no reason to think it was anyone but a harmless tourist who'd gotten lost while looking for nearby Yellowstone National Park, but my years of tracking hardened, evil men had skewed my reality and I was always on the alert for any possibility. Hell, truth be told, my faith in humanity had been fucked up from the moment I ran into my burning house and found my wife lying on the floor of our bedroom, her body covered in blood as flames had licked at her skin.

The car rattled to a stop about ten feet from me, but the glare from the security light above the garage made it impossible to see the driver's face. But the second the door tentatively opened and brown hair appeared, I knew who it was and my stomach dropped out. My mouth went dry as Tate's eyes connected with mine and I felt heat wash through my entire body before setting up camp in my gut.

Neither of us spoke after he closed the car door and for the life of me, I couldn't break the connection we had just from staring at each other. I still didn't understand how I could suddenly be attracted to a man, but what I was struggling with even more was my level of attraction. The idea of touching another man, tasting him, should have made me at least wary. But the only messages my brain was sending me was how good Tate would feel in my arms, beneath me, surrounding me.

Tate's eyes finally shifted to the rifle I had in my hand and I automatically pointed it towards the ground. I'd terrorized this man enough, even if my threats had been empty ones.

"What are you doing here?" I managed to ask as I forced my gaze from Tate and focused on putting the rifle back in the bag of weapons I'd been putting in my truck. I tried to keep my breathing even as I heard Tate approach me. When he didn't answer me, I made myself turn to face him and saw that he was less than a foot from me...it would be so easy to draw him forward into my arms. I wondered if he would come willingly. I suspected he was gay based on the encounter he'd had with the man the night I'd broken into his apartment, but I could have read that situation wrong. After all, Tate hadn't seemed to be enjoying the man's attentions. And his physical reactions to me when I'd pulled him against me at Seth and Ronan's house, as well as in the hotel room the night we'd driven up to Seattle from California, could have just been fear on his part.

"Why?" was all Tate asked, his eyes searching mine out. A shiver went through his body and I wondered if it was because of the cool night air or something else. He was wearing the same jeans he typically wore and I was glad to see they actually looked like they fit him better now. And while he still looked tired and a little too pale, he didn't have the same gauntness he'd had when we'd first met.

I ignored his question simply because I didn't want to answer it... because none of the answers I had were easy ones.

"How did you find me?"

I employed an online postal services company to receive my mail since I didn't spend enough time at the house in Rocky Point to pick up my mail on a regular basis, so I'd used my virtual post office box address for the hospital paperwork.

"Ronan gave me your address."

Irritation went through me because I'd never told Ronan about this place and I certainly hadn't given him the address. Which meant he'd used alternative means to locate me.

I pushed past Tate, ignoring the rush of sensation that went through me when our bodies briefly connected. I strode into the garage and began searching through the cabinet where I stored my weapons.

"So you're going after them by yourself?" I heard Tate say behind me.

"Go home, Tate," I said without looking at him. "Go be with your son," I added as I carried a couple of clips over to my work table and began adding bullets to the first one.

"What about our deal?"

I put down the clip I'd been loading and turned to face him. "You and I both know it was never a deal," I finally said. I ended up grabbing the clip again so I could keep loading it because I didn't trust myself enough to have my hands free when Tate was once again within reaching distance.

Tate appeared agitated as he glanced around the empty, well-lit garage. "They won't talk to you," he eventually said. "They're all afraid of Buck."

"Then I'll make sure they're more afraid of me."

I turned back around to the work table and reached for the second clip. But then Tate was whirling me around, and to my surprise, he actually shoved me back against the work table, his hands fisted in my shirt. "Please don't do this," he whispered.

They were the last words I expected to hear.

Tate's hands relaxed enough to release my shirt, but instead of pulling them away, he opened them so they were flat on my chest and I barely kept it together as the heat burned through the thin fabric of my shirt. He stared at his hands for a moment and then lifted his eyes to meet mine. I saw the flash of heat go through them and I wondered if he saw the same thing in my gaze. I nearly groaned when his tongue flicked out to moisten his lips and then he was pulling his hands away from my chest, the tips pressing into me for the briefest of moments before he stepped back. At least I had my answer about whether his physical reactions to me had been about fear or something else.

Anger and frustration consumed me as I grabbed the clips and the box of bullets and strode back to my truck. Tate hadn't moved when I returned to the garage and began closing up the nearly empty gun cabinet.

"I know you came to the hospital every night."

I stilled, but didn't turn to face him. I tried to lock the cabinet, but my fingers wouldn't cooperate.

"One of the nurses mentioned it when I told her Ronan and Seth would be staying with Matty because I had to leave for a few days."

"What the hell do you want, Tate?" I ground out as I jammed the lock closed and turned to face him. "I fucked up," I snapped. "I know that! I'm trying to do the right thing here!"

"Just tell me why," Tate said softly.

I bit out a curse and strode past him, grabbing his upper arm as I went. I pulled him out of the garage and hit the button on my way out. I nearly dragged him to his car, but he didn't fight me. I reached for the door handle on the driver's side, but he got between me and the door and wrapped his hand around my wrist to stop me from opening it. I let out a harsh breath as he moved forward just enough so that our bodies were touching. I felt Tate's free hand settle on my waist and I closed my eyes as a wave of need crashed over me.

"Tell me," Tate whispered, his mouth dangerously close to my ear.

I could have told him a lot of things; things that were all some version of the truth. But as I felt his body heat seep into me and his soft lips press against the skin just below my ear, I couldn't do anything but tell him the truth I'd been denying from the moment I'd realized he wasn't one of the men I was hunting.

"I didn't want to hurt you anymore."

Tate let out a long breath, like he'd been holding it, and the sensation skittered over my flesh where his mouth was still touching me. At some point I'd wrapped my arm around his waist...to hold him there, to be able to pull him closer, I wasn't really sure why. All I knew was that his body fit mine perfectly and instead of feeling strange or unnatural, it just felt...right.

"I'm coming with you," he finally said.

I sighed and forced myself to push back from him. I missed the contact immediately, but I made myself take a few more steps back, widening the distance between us. "Go home, Tate. Take care of Matty," I said firmly. "When things settle down, Ronan can help you start over. Don't worry about the money-"

"I'm not doing this for the money," Tate interrupted. I waited for him to say more, but he didn't. I shook my head and went to my truck to close the door.

"Matty wanted you to have this," I heard Tate say from behind me. I turned around and felt my heart lurch at the sight of the Spiderman doll he was holding out to me. I took it and studied the faded patches of paint. "He said he could help you fight the bad guys."

A chuckle escaped my lips and I lifted my eyes to study Tate who was standing tensely in front of me, his arms hanging loosely by his sides, the hands fisted. "I'll follow you to Lulling," was all he said and I knew by his determined expression that he meant it.

A mix of emotions went through me as we stared at each other. There was no denying that Tate could give me the information I needed to help make my search easier. But even the idea of spending the next several days in such close proximity to him was playing havoc with my senses. "What about Matty?" I finally asked.

"Tonight was his last round of chemo for this phase. He has to stay in the hospital for the next three weeks so that his immune system can recover, then he can go home for a week before we start the whole process over again. Ronan and Seth are amazing with him and when I told Matty that you needed my help, he gave me Spiderman to give to you." Tate let out a little laugh. "I guess since I'm not a superhero, he figured you could use all the help you could get."

I knew Tate's last statement was meant to lighten the mood, but I couldn't bring myself to laugh or even smile. Instead, I closed the distance between us and put my hand at the back of his neck to hold him still. He sucked in a breath as I dropped my mouth near his, but I bypassed his lips and moved my mouth to his ear. "You're a hero every fucking day, Tate," I said softly. "Don't ever forget that."

And with that, I released him and moved past him. "Come on in," I said as I started for the darkened house. "We leave in a few hours."

CHAPTER 10

TATE

The skin along the back of my neck was still tingling where Hawke had held on to me and it took me a moment to gather myself together enough to follow Hawke into the house. I was still reeling from both his words and his touch, but the part that had me struggling to move forward was the way he'd looked at me...if I hadn't known better, I would have thought he had been feeling the same pull of desire that I was.

From the moment I'd read Hawke's note, then re-read it, I'd obsessed over what to do next. He'd given me exactly what I'd wanted – freedom. But he'd given me much more than that. And it wasn't just the money for Matty's care. No, he'd given me something nearly as valuable. He'd given me people to lean on.

I hadn't really put much of my faith into Ronan and Seth sticking around as Matty's treatment continued, especially since Matty's young age meant he only had so much patience before he had one of his meltdowns. But in the ten days since Matty had been admitted, neither man had waivered in their commitment to supporting both of us and I'd finally realized they weren't doing it out of some obligation towards Hawke. They were doing it simply because they were both good men and because they genuinely cared about Matty...and me. It was a hard adjustment for me, having friends, and I was sure I'd shown my initial mistrust early on when I'd staunchly refused to stay away from the hospital for more than an hour or two. But neither Ronan nor Seth had ever seemed offended by my overprotectiveness.

I'd also had a chance to talk to both men in turn and while they'd never probed me about my past, they'd been open about their own struggles to find each other. I'd felt an immediate kinship with Seth because of our close proximity in age, but it was Ronan's past that I'd understood more. His own childhood had been bleak and he'd admitted that he really hadn't understood what it had meant to be a part of a family until he'd met and started dating Seth's older brother, Trace. He'd lost that for a while after Trace's death, but he hadn't needed to say the words for me to know that he'd definitely found it again with Seth. And I'd finally understood what Ronan had meant when he'd said that he and Seth knew me, that they'd once been me. It had given me hope that maybe I could one day have what they'd had. I'd also felt a sliver of hope take root deep inside me that when all this was over, when Matty was better, he and I might have found our own little version of a family.

But none of it would have happened if Hawke hadn't stormed his way into our lives. He'd bullied, threatened and terrorized me, but he'd never actually hurt me and I did believe what Ronan had said about Hawke not going through with his threats to give my DNA to the police. I couldn't say why I'd believed that, but somewhere along the way I had. Maybe it was the little things he'd done for me and for Matty. Making sure I ate, buying Matty ice cream and letting him play at the park after spending hours in the car.

And then the damn note.

I'd known within minutes of reading it over and over again that I couldn't leave things that way. Even if by some miracle I could have found a way to pay him back for what he'd done, it wasn't money that he needed from me. He'd given me my son and possibly even a new unofficial family…things I couldn't give back to him. But I could help him find peace. I could help him ease some of the torment of losing his wife and child.

The decision to leave Matty hadn't been easy, not because I didn't trust Ronan or Seth because I absolutely did – no, the decision had been one of the hardest in my life because for the past two years everything in my life had been about what was best for Matty. And if my little boy hadn't been as strong and as brave as he was, I wouldn't have been able to walk out of that room, his beloved Spiderman doll clutched between my fingers. But any doubts I'd had about my choice had fled the moment the night nurse had told me about Hawke's nighttime visits. I'd wanted to ask her more, like what had he done when he visited, how long had he stayed, had he really been there each night? But I hadn't had enough time since I'd had a flight to catch.

Ronan had taken care of all the travel arrangements for me and had even bought me a cell phone so that I would be able to stay in constant contact with them. My brain was overwhelmed by the sheer number of dollars that I was accruing in unofficial debt, but I'd tried not to focus on that as I'd driven the rental car over the numerous mountain passes that were still covered with snow despite it being spring. The GPS on the phone had gotten me to Hawke's house which I was supremely grateful for, since it was so dark when I'd arrived that I never would have found it based on written directions alone. I hadn't been able to make much out about the property other than there seemed to be no immediate neighbors based on the lack of any other kind of light besides the single lamppost next to what I'd finally realized was the garage as I'd gotten closer. The garage with an older model blue pick-up truck in front of it.

And Hawke.

As I made my way up the path towards the house, lights inside started turning on. It was too dark to make out the outside of the house other than it appeared to be an older farmhouse with two stories. There was a porch running the length of the front of the house and I couldn't help but notice the faded rocking chairs sitting off to one side.

Two chairs.

I let myself in through the screen door and tried to get my bearings since Hawke had disappeared. The first thing I noticed about the house was the smell...not bad exactly, just stale. Like it had been a while since it had been opened up long enough to let fresh air in. The second thing I noticed was a very fine layer of dust on the furnishings just inside the door.

"Here," Hawke said as he came around the corner and held out a bottle of water.

"Thanks," I said.

"I don't have much to eat, but I can take something out of the freezer-"

"No," I responded quickly. "I ate at the airport."

Hawke nodded and I felt a shiver crawl up my spine as his eyes swept my entire body. If I'd known for a fact that he was gay, my insides would have been doing a happy dance at his obvious interest. I knew it was possible he was bisexual, but I didn't want to risk pissing him off if I was wrong and did or said something that set him off.

"Let me show you around," he finally said. He didn't speak as he gave me the tour of the lower floor so I focused my attention on the small details I managed to pick up as we strode through the house at an almost unnaturally fast clip.

The furniture, what little of it there was, looked brand new, though the décor, like the wallpaper and fixtures, looked like they were from the seventies. The bigger pieces of furniture were still wrapped in plastic except for one chair. There also weren't any pictures save a small one, right above the fireplace in the middle of the mantel. I couldn't make out much from the picture other than to tell the guy was Hawke and he had his arms wrapped around a pretty blonde woman, presumably his wife.

The kitchen was devoid of any kind of appliances on the counter expect for a small coffee machine and the mismatched larger appliances also looked like they were decades old. There was no table in the small nook that likely would have served as an eating area.

"The bedroom's upstairs if you want to crash for a while."

Hawke's voice caught me off guard because he'd been so quiet the rest of the time. "Um, yeah, I'd love to get a couple hours sleep."

"Is your bag in your car?"

I nodded and before I knew it, he was handing me his bottle of water. We were back by the front door and as I waited for him to return, I glanced back at the picture on the mantle in the living room. There was a TV in the room but the single armchair that wasn't wrapped in plastic wasn't pointed at the TV. It was facing the fireplace and the picture above it.

I ripped my eyes from the curious arrangement when I heard the screen door open. Hawke barely looked at me as he carried my bag past me and up the stairs. I followed him to the second floor, but he didn't give me a tour. There were several closed doors that we passed until we reached the room at the end of the hallway. "It's the only one with a big mattress," Hawke murmured as he led me inside the sparsely furnished room.

There was a bed but no headboard and the bedding included a simple comforter and two pillows. A dresser and nightstand were the only other pieces of furniture in the room.

"Is this your room?" I asked.

"Yeah," Hawke said as he went to put my bag on the bed. "I wasn't expecting company," he said as he tried to straighten the comforter.

"It's fine," I said quickly, though the idea of sleeping in the man's bed sent a ridiculous thrill through me. "But I can't just take your bed," I added.

"I don't need it tonight," Hawke responded and then he was brushing past me, grabbing his water as he went.

"Where will you sleep?"

"I'll be in the living room," was all he said.

"Hawke," I called before he completely left the room.

He stilled but didn't respond. It was like he didn't even want to look at me. I definitely hadn't been right about him looking at me the same way I looked at him.

"You won't leave, right?" I asked.

He didn't answer me right away, but when he did, he finally turned my way. "No, I won't leave. Get some sleep, Tate. We have a long drive ahead of us."

Hawke closed the door and I took a deep breath and looked

around the empty room. I went to grab my bag so I could search out my toothbrush, but when I saw the pillows lying at the head of the bed, I let my fingers trail over one of them before picking it up and putting it to my nose. It smelled like Hawke.

Fucking perfect.

∽

"*T*ate, wake up."

I'd never exactly been a morning guy, but having a heavy hand shaking me awake brought back a slew of memories, and I jerked away from Hawke and threw up my arm to protect my head before I could stop myself. Humiliation flooded through me as I realized what I'd done and I slowly lowered my arm to see that Hawke was watching me with an unreadable expression.

"Sorry," I murmured.

"Ronan's on the phone," Hawke said as he held up his cell phone.

"Is it Matty?" I nearly shouted as I scrambled upright and grabbed for the phone.

Hawke gently put his hand on my shoulder to hold me back and quickly said, "Matty's fine, Tate. He's completely fine."

I blew out a breath and pressed my hand to my thudding chest. "Thank God," I whispered.

"Ronan just wanted to make sure you made it okay last night. He said you didn't text him and you didn't answer your phone."

"Shit," I said as I grabbed the phone off the nightstand. "I forgot to charge it last night. It's dead," I said as I held the phone up to show him.

"I have a charger in the car," Hawke said. "Here, talk to Ronan."

I took the phone from him and reassured Ronan I was fine and apologized for forgetting to let him know I'd made it. Hawke watched me for a moment before leaving the room and a glance to my left showed it was still dark outside. I listened as Ronan gave me a rundown on Matty's final night of chemo. I pulled the phone away from my ear long enough to check the time and saw that it was only four in the morning so I knew Matty would still be asleep.

"How you holding up?" I heard Ronan ask.

"I'm good," I said.

"And Hawke?"

I wanted to laugh at that. The man was so unreadable that I had no fucking clue how he was doing. "He didn't ditch me, so I guess that's a good sign," I finally said.

Ronan chuckled. "I wish I could say he'll warm up, but Hawke is... well, Hawke is Hawke."

I smiled at that. "Thanks, Ronan. For everything."

Ronan didn't respond right away and for a second I thought he'd hung up on me without saying goodbye. "It's a good feeling, isn't it?" he finally said.

"What is?"

"Knowing you don't have to do it alone anymore."

I swallowed hard at that and managed to say "yeah" before my throat closed up with emotion. I'd suspected I'd found something in Seth and Ronan that I'd been needing for a long time, but to hear Ronan confirm it was nearly too much.

"I'm going to send some pictures to Hawke's phone in a few minutes since yours is dead, okay?"

"Yeah, okay."

"And I'll have Matty call you as soon as he wakes up."

"Okay," I whispered as I dashed at a stray tear that fell. "Thanks."

"We'll talk soon, Tate. Take care and trust in Hawke...there's no one better to have at your back."

I managed to say goodbye and then climbed out of bed so that I wouldn't keep Hawke waiting. It took me just a few minutes to get cleaned up in the bathroom and then I was hurrying down the stairs. I stopped in the living room to see if Hawke was in there, but it was empty. I was about to turn away when I noticed the mantle...the picture was gone.

"You ready?"

I turned to see Hawke standing near the front door. I nodded and handed him his phone but it beeped just as I was giving it to him. I saw that it was a picture from Ronan. "Can I?" I asked Hawke.

He nodded and unlocked the phone for me and gave it back so I could scroll through. I laughed as I realized what I was seeing. In the first picture, a dozen pieces of paper lined the wall of Matty's hospital room. They all had multiple Tic Tac Toe games on them and on each page was a big "M" in the right hand corner and Matty was standing proudly next to them, a huge smile on his lips as he pointed to the pages. The next picture was of Seth standing in front of only one piece of paper with an "S" written on it. His over exaggerated pout was laughable as he pointed to his meager winnings. The very last picture was of Matty standing side by side with Seth, but this time Matty was wearing a paper crown that he'd clearly colored himself.

I laughed and didn't resist when Hawke took the phone from me and scrolled through the pictures himself. A brief smile ghosted his lips, but when his gaze shifted to mine, his eyes went dark again and then he was turning away from me.

"We should get going," he said.

I followed him out of the house and put my bag in the back of the pickup truck. He'd moved my rental car at some point so it was parked next to the garage. He said nothing as he climbed into the truck next to me and in fact, it was almost an hour before he said a word…and that was only to ask what fast food place I wanted to stop at for breakfast.

The drive to Lulling was well over twenty hours and by hour fourteen I was sure Hawke was a robot because he was showing no signs of fatigue and he'd ignored both my offers to take over driving for a while. We'd stopped only when we'd needed gas or food and I'd long ago given up on trying to draw him into conversation. I'd talked to Matty a few times throughout the day which helped pass some of the time because I always felt better afterwards, but as we drew closer and closer to Lulling, I could feel the tension overtaking my body.

We'd just crossed over the border into New Mexico when Hawke finally exited the Interstate and stopped at a small restaurant that was attached to a gas station. We ate in silence and then gassed up the car,

He'd changed into a pair of athletic pants and a black T-shirt and his hair was still wet.

I shook my head, desperate to find the right thing to say. "I'm sorry, I saw the picture in your house and I was curious-"

"She's not a part of this!" Hawke shouted. "Do you understand me?"

I didn't. Not at all. His anger was over the top and I stood up so I could try to ease my way to the bathroom. If I just got out of his sight for a while...

"I didn't mean to upset you-"

Before I could even finish, Hawke was closing the distance between us, the picture forgotten as he tossed it on top of his bag. I froze as he grabbed me by the upper arms, his hold bordering on painful. I expected him to yell at me or hit me, but all he did was hold me like that, his body seething with rage.

But his next words nearly stole my breath.

"I don't want you," he said in a gutted whisper.

I couldn't even register what he meant until he gave me just the slightest shake and again said, "I don't want you." But even I heard the doubt in his voice and I realized the fury in his gaze wasn't about me at all, or at least not about what I'd done.

I was at a complete loss to even comprehend what was happening. I'd been so sure that I'd only imagined that Hawke was feeling the same pull of desire that I was, but now as I watched him drawing in ragged breaths, his tormented eyes holding mine, I knew I'd been wrong. But whatever he was feeling wasn't something he wanted to be feeling. At some point, his hold had loosened enough so that he could rub his thumbs back and forth over my skin and the effect was intoxicating. I could feel my own body tightening up with excitement and my adrenaline spiked as my need to escape him disintegrated. But I couldn't ignore the naked pain in his gaze. As much as I wanted him, I knew he needed to make the next move and I would accept it, whatever it was.

"I know," I said gently. "It's okay, Hawke."

I could see his body warring with his mind and I didn't know which one had won the battle until his hands tightened on me. A sudden rush of air escaped his lungs, but instead of drawing me closer, he released me long enough to reach for the button on my jeans. My need grew to exponential proportions as he jerked the button free, dragged the zipper down and shoved my pants and underwear down in one quick move, his rough palms dragging over my skin. A split second later he spun me around and shoved me down on the bed. I got no reprieve as his hands closed over my hips and he yanked my ass up. His fingers bit into my skin as he split me open and a tremor of fear and excitement went through me when I felt moisture dribble onto my hole.

I closed my eyes as more of what I now realized was spit coated my opening. I had seconds to stop this because I knew what was coming. But I remained silent as I felt Hawke's cock push between my cheeks. More spit hit my ass a second before the broad head of Hawke's dick suddenly shoved inside of me without warning or finesse. Pain tore through me as my body tried to accept the intrusion, but there was no time to adjust as Hawke pulled back just a little before slamming his hips forward again. Tears stung my eyes as another wave of pain went through me, but I bit into my lip to stop myself from making any kind of sound.

To my surprise, Hawke suddenly stopped all together and when I looked over my shoulder at him, I saw him looking at where we were joined and I saw shame flash across his face. But I also saw something else. Need...raw and unbridled. He lifted his eyes to mine and when our gazes met, he opened his mouth like he wanted to say something. But he didn't speak, he just stood there, his fingers digging into my hips, his cock pulsing in my ass. And he shook his head just slightly. Whatever internal struggle he was going through hurt me more than the physical pain that was still thrumming throughout my entire body and that was why I gave him a brief, but very clear nod. He didn't move for several long seconds, but I didn't miss the relief on his face. And then he drew back and slammed into me again, driving more of his cock inside of me.

Despite the fact that Hawke was hurting me, I wanted him...no, needed him. I should have been physically repulsed by what was happening to me, but in truth I craved it – knowing Hawke needed me so badly. And it wasn't just his rock hard cock buried deep inside me that told me that. It was in every frantic move as he pumped into me, in the way his fingers dug into my skin to keep me from moving. And it was in the way he folded his body over mine as soon as he'd bottomed out inside me. His skin burned mine with the intense heat his body was giving off and I could feel his breath sawing in and out of him because his lips were pressed against the back of my neck.

The pain began to recede somewhat as Hawke drove into me over and over, but it was when he wrapped his arm around my chest and closed his hand over the front of my shoulder that I felt my own body finally responding. His hold on me meant there was no space between us and I could both feel and hear every grunt and groan as he pummeled me with brutal thrusts. I knew everything was happening too fast and that I would have no way of catching up to Hawke, so I closed one of my hands over the arm he had wrapped around my chest and took in every sound, every feeling as he fucked me. And when he came just seconds later, I reveled in the way he shouted my name in my ear. Liquid heat burned my stinging channel as Hawke continued to thrust into me as he rode out his orgasm and when his weight forced me down on the bed, I groaned as his body pinned mine and I sank down flat on the bed. His body covered mine like a blanket and despite the need still rolling through my own body, I could have stayed like that for hours. But even as Hawke's dick continued to pulse inside of me, he was pulling back and I stifled a moan as his thick length finally pulled free of my aching body.

Hawke dropped to his back beside me, but I didn't turn to look at him. Because the pleasure I'd felt just moments ago had started to wane as I realized what I'd allowed to happen. I'd let him use me...and I'd taken pleasure in it. He'd admitted that he didn't want me, but I'd been too desperate for a connection with him to care. I forced myself to get up and kept my eyes averted as I pulled up my jeans. I could feel Hawke's semen dripping from my ass so I didn't bother trying to search out my duffle bag as I stiffly walked to the bathroom. Every part of my body hurt as it started to come down from the high and I felt lightheaded as soon as I entered the bathroom so I leaned against the counter so I could get my bearings. After a couple of minutes, I managed to straighten and studied myself in the mirror. My skin was flushed with color, but there was no other evidence of what had just happened. I could feel it everywhere else though. I forced myself to back up and pull my shirt off. I started pushing my jeans down, but stopped when I saw the bruises on my hips. I ran my fingers over them in wonder.

It took me a moment to realize I was no longer alone and when I turned to look at the door, I saw Hawke watching me. I hadn't thought to lock the door and I hadn't heard it swing open either. He said nothing and neither did I – we just stood there watching each other. I tried to get a read on what he was thinking, but his eyes were shuttered. When he finally started moving, it wasn't to leave. Instead, he came into the bathroom and I automatically took a few steps back until the backs of my legs hit the edge of the bathtub. I saw a flash of something in his eyes, but he kept coming at me. He'd pulled his pants back up at some point and he was still wearing his T-shirt. I waited for him to speak – for him to say he was sorry or that it was a mistake. But he said nothing and I couldn't stop myself from flinching when he reached for me. Except he wasn't reaching for me, he was reaching past me to turn the shower on. When he straightened, his body was so close, it was nearly brushing mine.

I expected him to leave at that point, but he remained where he was, and when he reached his hand up to my face, I managed not to move this time. His thumb skimmed my lower lip and came to a stop on the spot where'd I'd been biting myself to keep from making a sound. He massaged the tender flesh for a moment before trailing his fingers across my cheek and then down my neck. My skin came alive with sensation wherever he touched me and despite my aching body, my dick began to react to the contact. I could only stand there in stunned silence as Hawke gently began exploring me with his hand. My chest, my nipples, my abdomen – he left no part of me untouched. And when his hand reached the bruises, I dropped my eyes to watch his fingers gently skim over the discolored skin. At that point, I didn't need to hear the apology because I felt it everywhere.

Hawke ceased his exploration of the bruises and used both his hands to carefully push my pants and underwear down and I sucked in a breath when he dropped to his knees to help me work them off completely. He ignored my half hard cock as his hands trailed up my legs and then up my sides before moving to my back. He stood back up as his hands came to rest on my ass and I stiffened when he pushed his fingers into my crease. But he didn't press a finger inside of me. Instead, he swiped it through the moisture still surrounding my hole. He pulled his hand back and studied the sticky, white fluid covering his finger and part of me wanted to lean down and take a taste. But then Hawke's eyes lifted to meet mine and I couldn't move, could barely breathe. Because the emotion that hadn't been there before was flooding his gaze now.

Regret, longing, need. It was all there in spades.

And in that moment, I knew I would give him anything he wanted. Because I knew what he was feeling. How many times had I been there myself? So desperate for another's touch? To feel something besides pain?

Hawke settled his hand on my hip and then he was drawing me forward. I went willingly and when he dropped his mouth to mine, I lifted to meet him. The kiss was achingly tender and sweet and it hit me hard. Harder than a passionate kiss ever could have. Emotion flooded my system all at once and it took everything in me not to cry as Hawke cupped the back of my head to keep me from escaping. But I had no intention of going anywhere and I wasn't about to let him go either so I wrapped my arms around his neck. And when he finally probed the seam of my lips with his tongue, I opened instantly. Even though the kiss was deeper, it was still painfully gentle and the moment Hawke released my mouth so we could catch our breath, I buried my face against his neck so I wouldn't make a fool of myself. Hawke's arms closed around me and he held me like that even as the bathroom began to fill with steam from the hot water that was still raining down just behind me.

It could have been minutes or hours before Hawke gently pushed me back enough so that he could reach for the hem of his own shirt. I'd wondered if the burn marks on his face extended down the rest of his body, but I only barely noticed that they did when he pulled the shirt over his head. He was as perfectly built as I'd suspected, but my eyes immediately went to the tattoo scrawled across the left side of his chest. Words – dozens of them – covered the muscles just above his left nipple and continued all the way down to his waist. I didn't get a chance to study them, though, because Hawke bent to push his pants off and then he was drawing me back into his arms, his mouth closing over mine. I felt the burn scars as I put my hands on his sides, but I didn't focus on them as Hawke kissed me because his mouth was doing things to me that I wouldn't have thought possible. True, I'd only ever been kissed by Reggie, but I wouldn't have ever guessed a person could say so much with something as simple as a kiss. But nothing about Hawke was simple and I knew in my gut that no other kiss would ever feel like Hawke's.

Hawke kept the kiss short and I had a terrible fear that he would leave me when he drew back a little bit so I closed my hand around his bicep. "Don't go," I whispered desperately.

Hawke didn't respond to my plea with words, but when he kissed me again, I knew he wasn't leaving me. He turned me and urged me into the shower and then he was climbing in behind me. The hot water felt like heaven against my skin, but did nothing to minimize my growing desire. I was facing the wall as Hawke got into the shower, but when I tried to turn to face him, his hand settled on my upper back. I barely felt the cold of the tiles pressed against my chest as Hawke's body lined up with mine, his half hard cock nudging my ass. At that point, I didn't care how much it would likely hurt if he fucked me again – I just wanted to keep feeling his skin against mine. Lips skimmed the back of my neck as hands trailed along my sides and came to rest on the fronts of my thighs. They stayed there for a moment before sliding up my groin, brushing over my swollen cock and then palming my chest.

I let out a protest when they disappeared altogether and Hawke put some space between us. I felt the hot water hit my back and for a second I was afraid Hawke had left me, but a glance over my shoulder had me realizing he was reaching for the small container of body wash on one of the shelves in the shower. And then Hawke's hands were back on me, his soapy hands washing me. I groaned at the feel of his fingers gently massaging me and when his hand slipped between my ass cheeks to clean me, I felt nothing but pleasure. The gentle torment continued when he turned me around and washed my front. He touched every part of me except my aching cock and I couldn't help but wonder if the idea of touching my dick repulsed him. I let my eyes drift down his body and was glad to see that his dick was half-hard. I was tempted to reach for it so I could feel how the thick flesh felt, but I didn't want to do anything to stop Hawke's ministrations so I remained where I was and let my eyes drift closed.

"Tate," I eventually heard Hawke whisper against my ear just before a soapy hand closed around my dick. I cried out at the contact and Hawke stole into my mouth. His grip on my cock was firm and he began dragging up and down it with agonizingly slow pulls. As Hawke's tongue sensually played with mine, his hand followed suit and he drove me higher and higher until I was helplessly thrusting against his hand. I settled my hands on his shoulders to keep myself upright. Hawke's free hand was braced against the wall next to me and I could hear his own breathing increasing as he began stroking me in earnest. He dragged his lips from mine and rested his face against mine as we both looked down to where his hand was frantically jerking me off. I could feel the orgasm building in intensity and a shiver of fear went through me as it grew and grew, but didn't crest. I needed to come so badly, but I couldn't.

"Hawke," I cried in frustration.

"It's okay, Tate," Hawke said against my mouth. "I've got you."

I felt Hawke shift his hand just slightly and I gasped when I felt his dick sliding against mine. I looked down to see him fisting us both at the same time. The contact felt so good that I couldn't stop myself from reaching down to close my hand over Hawke's where he held us both. The feel of his strong fingers did me in and I cried out in relief as my orgasm crashed over me. It was violent and uncontrollable and if Hawke hadn't wrapped his free arm around my waist at that exact moment, I wouldn't have been able to stay upright. I felt Hawke moan against my neck as he followed me over and despite the hot water raining down over us, I still felt our combined releases sliding down my dick. I released the hold I had on Hawke's hand and wrapped both my arms around him as I rode out my orgasm. His body shook beneath my touch as aftershocks rocked through him and despite my still sore ass, I wished he'd been inside of me when he'd come. Because as close as we were in that moment, it wasn't enough.

It would never be enough.

~

I stayed in the shower for several minutes after Hawke cleaned us both off and then kissed me gently before climbing out and grabbing a towel to dry himself off. After collecting his clothes from the floor, he'd left the bathroom without a word or a look back and I'd started to feel so cold inside again that I'd known no amount of hot water would warm me up.

I took my time getting dried off and since I hadn't brought any other clothes into the bathroom with me, I was forced to put my jeans back on. I left the underwear off though, since they were still damp from the semen they'd collected as I'd pulled them up earlier.

I half expected the room to be empty when I exited the bathroom, but to my surprise, a dressed Hawke was sitting on the edge of his bed, his hands clenched in his lap. His bag and the picture had been moved off the bed at some point. He looked up at me briefly, but I saw none of the pleasure I'd seen in his eyes just a few minutes ago when he'd come in my arms. My intent had been to grab my sweats and go back to the bathroom to change, but one look at Hawke had me moving to my bed and I ignored the pain in my ass as I settled my weight onto the mattress and waited for Hawke to say whatever it was that he clearly needed to say.

"I'm sorry," he whispered with a shake of his head. "I didn't mean to hurt you."

As much as I would have liked to tell him he hadn't, he would have known I was lying. There was just no way to deny the rough fucking had been painful, so I told him the truth.

"I don't regret it."

His eyes shifted to mine and he finally nodded. "I didn't use a condom," he said softly. "I got tested in the military a long time ago and I was negative," he managed to get out, but then he dropped his eyes once again. "I haven't been with anyone since Revay. She was the only one I've ever been with."

The admission had me struggling to find words.

"Even after she was gone, she was the only one I ever really wanted," Hawke continued, his words so quiet I could barely hear them.

"You don't owe me any explanations," I finally said, still stunned at what he was telling me. "I tested negative a couple of years ago and haven't been with anyone since then."

Hawke nodded and stood up. He turned to climb into his bed and I couldn't get past how different he seemed. Gone was the confidence, the hardness. Instead, he seemed...broken. I waited until he was under the covers before I stood up and turned off the light on his side of the nightstand. Just as I turned to collect my clothes so I could change, I heard him speak again.

"She's my wife, Tate."

Present tense, not past.

A knot formed in my throat at the need in his voice. "I understand, Hawke," I whispered, hoping my words would ease him in some way. And in that moment, I lost a little bit of my heart to the beautiful brooding man who'd loved his wife so much that even ten years after he'd lost her, he refused to let her go.

CHAPTER 11

HAWKE

"Can you pull over at the next rest stop?"

The sound of Tate's quiet, wary voice jerked me from my daze and I glanced at him, but immediately regretted it because another round of shame flooded my entire system followed by a hearty bout of desire as I remembered the feel of his tight body surrounding me in unfathomable heat.

"Yeah," I murmured and forced my eyes back to the road.

We'd only been on the road for a couple of hours, but it was more words than we'd spoken to each other from the moment we'd both woken up when the alarm clock on my phone had gone off. Of course, I hadn't actually been asleep. In fact, I hadn't been able to find even a few minutes of solace in the darkness of sleep last night after Tate had turned the lights off.

I'd fucked another guy.

I'd betrayed my wife.

I'd hurt Tate.

Under other circumstances, I probably could have dealt with the first one, but I was too caught up in the second and third to even contemplate what the whole thing meant in terms of my sexuality.

Something inside of me had snapped when I'd seen Tate holding

Revay's picture. I'd spent the entire day fighting my growing need for Tate as he'd sat quietly next to me in the car and in that moment, it had all come back in a rush along with a heavy dose of guilt and I'd turned my combined sexual frustration and emotional anguish on Tate. And instead of shoving me away, he'd let me in.

I'd already jerked off in the shower to visions of Tate bent over in front of me, but my already half-hard dick had swelled to painful proportions when I'd seen the permission in Tate's gaze and I'd known that nothing would stop me from taking what he'd been offering. I'd had no control after that.

Absolutely none.

Not even enough to try to find something to use as makeshift lube. My mind had been screaming at me that using spit to ease my entry into Tate's body wouldn't work, but I hadn't cared. My need had been too great and once Tate's body had engulfed my aching flesh, I'd been a goner and it had been sheer force of will that had given me the strength to stop when the shame of what I'd done had hit me. And then Tate had looked at me and he'd known what I was going through. One nod granting me permission and I'd unleased everything I had on him and had rutted into him like an animal.

And he hadn't uttered even a single protest.

Revay and I had tried anal sex once early on in our relationship, but it wasn't something she'd enjoyed and I'd known it had been uncomfortable for her even with generous amounts of lube. So I had no doubt how much pain my actions had inflicted on Tate. And even if I hadn't known, I wouldn't have been able to miss the stiffness in Tate's gait this morning as he'd gotten ready to go. The only good thing, if there could be such a thing, was that I'd been so consumed with lust that I'd come within less than a minute and a dozen strokes.

Without a condom.

And it had been the most explosive orgasm I could ever remember having.

So not only had I betrayed my wife, the sex had exceeded what I'd had with the woman who'd been my entire world.

I hadn't been able to stay away from Tate when he'd gotten off the bed to go to the bathroom. All I'd wanted to do was curl into a ball and drown myself in memories of Revay, but my guilt had been a living thing and I'd forced myself to get up and follow him to make sure he was okay. He hadn't noticed when I'd opened the door and I'd stood there in stunned silence as I'd watched Tate run his fingers over the bruises on his hips where I'd gripped him to keep him from moving away from me. And then he'd looked at me and I'd felt the invisible pull between us that I'd been feeling from the day I'd met him. Everything had floated away in that moment and it had been just me and him, both hurting, both needing something we could only find in each other. So I'd made love to him. Afterwards, I'd wanted to deny that that was what we'd done, but I couldn't make any other words fit.

It hadn't been as simple as making out or getting each other off, and it hadn't been anything like what I'd done to him on the bed because that had been pure, raw fucking. No, it had been more than that. It had been about exploring his body, understanding every line, plane and curve. Feeling every texture, tasting the unique flavors of his mouth, his skin. Hearing every sound he made, the way he begged, the desperation, the way my name sounded when it fell from his lips.

My plan had been to have that moment only be about Tate's needs, but when he'd struggled to find his own orgasm, I'd needed more. I'd needed to share it with him, so I'd taken us both in hand and for the third time in less than an hour, I'd come again.

It had been fucking perfect.

Until it wasn't.

Because the memories had rolled over me like a tidal wave. My beautiful wife, my son, the future I should have had. All of it stolen away by the father and brother of the man who'd just shattered my entire world with three little words.

It's okay, Hawke.

Three little words that had given me permission to let go of the past for a few minutes, to feel things I'd never expected to feel again...

"Hawke, it's this exit."

"Huh?" I managed to say as Tate ripped me from my thoughts for the second time.

"The rest stop," Tate said quickly.

I managed to jerk the truck to the right before I completely passed the exit and I saw Tate grab onto the armrest as the truck swerved sharply. "Sorry," I muttered as I maneuvered the pickup to a stop in front of the nearly deserted building that housed the bathrooms.

Tate got out of the car before I even put it in park, but instead of heading towards the building, he started walking in the opposite direction. Concerned, I got out and followed him. He stopped by some picnic benches under a large tree and climbed up on one so that he was sitting on the tabletop. I stopped in front of him, but didn't speak because I could see from the agitation on his face that there was something he needed to say. I steeled myself for the angry words I knew were coming.

"I promised myself I wouldn't do this," Tate murmured as he rubbed his hands together and tapped his foot on the bench. "But I'm fucking scared to death, Hawke."

His words caught me off guard, but he continued before I could say anything.

"I know you're messed up about what happened last night, but, please, I need you to be with me one hundred percent before we get to Lulling," Tate whispered. "Because more than anything right now, I need to know that I'm going home to my son when this is all over."

God, I was a complete shit.

I mulled over the best words to say as I sat down next to Tate. He was right of course. The events of the night before *were* a huge distraction for me, but not enough that I wouldn't have been aware of any danger we were in and I had no doubt that the second we rolled into Lulling, I'd be on full alert. But Tate wouldn't have known any of that. He'd risked so much to help me and I couldn't even get myself together long enough to reassure him that I would keep him safe.

Although I'd told myself the night before as I lay sleepless in my bed that I wouldn't touch Tate again, I did just that and put my hand on the back of his neck. I waited until he finally looked at me before speaking. "I'm with you, Tate. One hundred percent. You are going home to Matty."

Tate let out a small breath and nodded and I resisted the urge to pull him into my arms. I hadn't really considered what he was going through as he was forced to face a past that clearly had been hard for him. The few things he'd said about Buck and Denny along with the signs I'd seen that he'd been physically abused were likely just the tip of the iceberg. Not to mention the fact that he'd taken Matty with him when he'd run...I hadn't wanted to know more of Tate's story when I'd blackmailed him into helping me, because I wouldn't have been able to even voice the threat.

But now?

Now I wanted to know. I wanted to understand everything that made this man tick. I wanted to know how someone who'd been raised by a monster like Buck had turned out to be so sweet and giving and so fucking strong.

"Will you tell me about the night you left?" I asked as I forced myself to release my hold on Tate's neck.

"I didn't leave, I ran," Tate said with a slight laugh that held no humor whatsoever. He looked around the quiet rest stop. There were no other cars and the only sound besides the wind blowing through the leaves above us was the din of the Interstate traffic.

"I'd been saving up for almost a year," Tate said. "I knew I'd need at least a few thousand in the bank to pay for a bus ticket and to get an apartment in the city – I'd figured someplace like Dallas would be a good place to start over."

Tate had started rocking his upper body back and forth slightly as he spoke. "I worked at a dry cleaning store so I planned to leave on the day I got paid. I cashed my paycheck on the way home – it was only a few hundred dollars but it felt like a million since it was buying me my freedom."

"How old were you?" I interrupted.

"Twenty-two," Tate said. "I'd made plans to leave that night. Denny usually passed out after spending most of the night getting high and Buck spent most Friday nights with whatever woman he was fucking at the time. My plan was to go home, lay low until things were quiet and then grab my shit and go."

"It didn't happen that way."

Tate laughed and shook his head. "Not even close. Buck wasn't home when I got there, but Denny was. Only he wasn't alone."

"Matty," I guessed.

Tate nodded. "I walked into the trailer and the first thing I see is Denny shooting up. And there sitting on the floor in front of the TV is this little kid. I asked Denny who he was, but all he said was that it was none of my business."

Tate's agonized eyes shifted to me. "I told myself he wasn't my problem, that I needed to stick to my plan." He dropped his eyes to his hands again. "I left him there, Hawke," he whispered brokenly. "Denny was passed out and the kid was asleep on the floor and I just left. I was so fucking selfish-"

"Hey," I said, grabbing one of Tate's clenched hands in mine. "You went back," I said firmly as I linked our fingers together. "You went back. That's all that matters."

Tate nodded and used his free hand to swipe away the tears that had formed in his eyes. "I made it to the end of the driveway before I turned around. I was freaking out that Buck would come home early so I didn't even wake him up. I just grabbed him and took him. He... he had this huge bruise on the side of his face and I knew I'd made the right choice."

"What happened after that?"

"He didn't wake up until we were on the bus. I asked him what his name was, who his mom was, that kind of thing. But he wouldn't speak to me...not a word. I finally got him to tell me he was three by asking him to hold up his fingers to show me how old he was. Once we got to Dallas, I got us a motel room. He wouldn't eat or drink anything and he started crying and wouldn't stop. I didn't know what to do so I just started talking to him. I told him I was scared too. And then I started talking about all the superheroes I used to read about when I was a kid and he finally quieted."

"And you gave him your Spiderman doll," I ventured.

"It was stupid to take the doll when I left, but I'd had it for so long-"

"It's not stupid, Tate. We hang on to the good things in our life for as long as we can."

Tate squeezed my hand and gave me a wobbly smile. I couldn't stop myself from reaching out to wipe away a lingering tear that slipped down his face. He stilled at the contact and I was powerless to tear my gaze from his. Tate was the one to finally break the connection and I felt a tug of pain when he carefully pulled his hand free of mine.

"Matty finally started talking to me a few days after I took him. He told me his name was Matthew, but he didn't know his last name or his mom's name. I kept hoping he'd remember them eventually, but if I even asked him about the day he showed up at my house, he'd shut down. I thought about going to the police, but I was afraid they'd arrest me for kidnapping," Tate explained.

I nodded in understanding because my guess was that was exactly what would have happened. "What happened after that?"

"I managed to find a job with a guy who landscaped yards. It wasn't an actual company or anything, just his personal business, so he let me bring Matty with me on jobs in the beginning until I found him daycare and he paid me under the table. I started looking for an apartment, but since I needed money for the security deposit and first month's rent, I needed to get to my savings account. They didn't have any of my bank's branches in the Dallas area so I opened a new account and submitted a request to transfer the money. It...it never occurred to me..." Tate said quietly before his voice dropped off completely.

"What?"

"Matty and I were on our way back to our motel and I saw them."

"Buck and Denny?" I asked solemnly.

Tate nodded. "They were standing outside our room and the door was open. They were talking to a maid. I picked up Matty and ran. I'd made a habit of carrying a change of clothes for Matty and myself back and forth to work and Matty never went anywhere without his doll and his teddy bear so that was all we had."

"You think someone at your bank in Lulling told Buck where you were?"

"I don't have proof, but I think it was my ex, Reggie. He was a teller at that bank."

"Did you get the money at least?"

Tate shook his head. "I was too afraid that they'd be able to track me, even if I just checked to see if the money had been transferred. I had enough on me to get me and Matty to El Paso, but we only stayed there for a few weeks...long enough for me to earn enough money doing odd jobs. Then we moved again. Albuquerque, Denver, Salt Lake City...once we reached San Francisco, I knew I had to take a chance and settle down long enough for Matty to have some normalcy in his life."

Tate looked at me, his eyes shrouded with uncertainty. "I didn't know what the fuck I was doing, Hawke. What if the running, the hiding, are all Matty remembers?"

I wanted to reach for Tate again...badly. But I kept my hands clasped together in front of me as I pinned him with my gaze. "Matty's an incredible kid, Tate. He's happy, sweet, funny, kind-hearted...that doesn't just happen. He's like that because of you – because of every-thing you did for him. The only thing he's going to remember from all this is how amazing his Dad is."

A small smile graced Tate's mouth and I desperately wanted to lean in and kiss him. I had no doubt that he would have let me. I suspected Tate knew my train of thought because he sucked in a breath and stared at my mouth. I nearly groaned when he parted his lips and his tongue darted out to moisten them. God, how I'd loved kissing him last night.

"We should get going," Tate murmured and then he was dragging his eyes away. He climbed off the picnic table and cast a glance over his shoulder at me. I climbed to my feet, but as he began walking towards the car, I reached out to grab his arm.

"You mind driving for a bit?" I asked as I fished the car keys out of my pocket and held them out.

He studied me for a long moment and then nodded. I gave him the keys and followed him back to the truck. My eyes grew heavy as Tate got us back on the road and even though I tried to focus on the scenery flying by, I couldn't stop myself from turning my head to watch Tate. He glanced at me and shot me a sweet smile and my last thought before my eyes drifted shut was how right it felt to have him looking at me like that.

CHAPTER 12

TATE

I needed to get a grip. That was all there was to it.

Easier said than done as I cast another glance at Hawke as his eyes closed and his features relaxed enough that the never-ending look of pain that always seemed to be etched into every line of his face finally disappeared. I forced my attention back to the road even though all I really wanted to do was reach over and touch Hawke. It didn't matter where...I just wanted to feel him.

Which was exactly why I needed to get a grip. Because while my heart was doing crazy ass flips in my chest at the memory of Hawke's hand on my neck and his fingers wrapped around mine, I needed to remember that last night was a mistake. Hawke hadn't wanted me, not really. Even if by some chance he was bisexual, it didn't mean he wanted to be with me...at least not in the way I needed. I was a means to an end for Hawke, nothing more, and last night had only been about him needing release. If we were lucky enough to find Buck and Denny and Hawke did what he needed to do, I doubted it would really change anything for him. I'd seen the proof for myself.

That single chair in his house facing the picture.

I couldn't compete with that. I wasn't even sure I wanted to. Loving someone that much...

I shook my head and focused on the road in front of me. I wasn't ready for this. I never would be. Even the lure of not having to worry about Buck and Denny finding me and Matty someday wasn't enough to ease my fear.

"Hey."

I turned to see Hawke watching me, his eyes heavy with exhaustion. "It's going to be okay," he said softly and I held my breath when he reached out to gently pull my right hand free of the steering wheel that I'd been gripping so hard the skin over my knuckles had gone white.

I nodded and held my breath as he linked our fingers together. He stared at our joined hands where they were resting on the armrest and I waited for him to pull away. But he didn't. He merely closed his eyes again and when I went to shift my hand into a more comfortable position, he tightened his grip on me, refusing to let me go.

I couldn't help but smile.

Yeah, I was fucked. Totally and completely.

～

*H*awke woke up the second I slowed the truck down several hours later to stop for gas. I missed the warmth of his hand when he released me and straightened in his seat.

"It's ten more miles to Lulling," I said. "Can you take over?" I asked.

He nodded. "You okay?"

No.

"Yeah."

Hawke tilted his head at me knowingly and I chuckled. "Okay, no," I admitted. "But I will be," I said as I met his probing gaze. He nodded and got out of the truck. I got out and went to the passenger side and searched out my phone so I could call Ronan. I'd already talked to Matty twice today, but I needed to hear his voice one more time.

"Hey Tate, how's it going?" Ronan asked as soon as he answered.

"Good," I said, though I knew I hadn't managed to keep the shakiness out of my voice because Ronan was quiet for a long moment before he responded.

"Everything okay?"

"Um, yeah," I said. "We're just about to drive into Lulling and I...I..."

When I couldn't finish the sentence, Ronan said, "Hold on, okay?"

I nodded even though I knew it was stupid since Ronan couldn't see me. I sucked in several deep breaths to try to keep my tears at bay.

"Daddy?"

A knot of emotion got stuck in my throat at the sound of Matty's voice, but before I could answer him, my phone switched to video and I saw Matty's smiling face. "Hi Daddy!" Matty said with a huge grin.

"Hi, buddy," I managed to grate out.

"Daddy, look," Matty said and then he was turning the camera's view and I laughed at the sight that greeted me. Both Seth and Ronan were sitting in full costume next to Matty's hospital bed. Seth was dressed as Spiderman and Ronan was covered from head to toe in a green muscle suit. He was holding a Hulk mask in his hand. I started laughing and when Hawke got into the truck a second later, I handed the phone to him. He smiled and I heard the phone click as he pushed a couple of buttons.

"You better not have just taken a picture!" I heard Ronan call out as the image on the phone changed back to Matty. Hawke shifted in his seat so Matty could see both of us.

"It's costume day," Matty announced and then the image wobbled for a moment and I could tell either Ronan or Seth was now holding the phone so we could see all of Matty. I'd expected to see him dressed as Iron Man or Captain America, but he wasn't.

He was Hawkeye.

I shifted my gaze to Hawke whose eyes had warmed over with emotion. "You look great, Matty," Hawke said, though his voice was hoarse. He shot me a quick glance and I felt my heart clench at what I saw. Not pain, not anguish...happiness. Genuine happiness.

"Did you catch the bad guys yet?" Matty asked and Hawke ripped his gaze from me and focused on Matty.

But he seemed to be struggling to speak so I said, "Not yet, buddy, but soon."

"And then you'll come home?"

I swallowed hard. "Yeah, then I'm coming home."

"Hawke too?"

Fuck, now I was the one who couldn't speak.

"We'll see," Hawke hedged, his voice still not quite right. Luckily, we were saved from the additional questions I knew would be forthcoming when Matty looked off screen as Seth said something to him.

"Daddy, we gotta go…the parade's starting! Love you!" Matty said in a rush and then he was climbing off the bed. The video switched to Ronan and despite his ridiculous get up, his face was somber.

"You guys be careful."

"We will," Hawke said firmly. Ronan stared at the screen for just a moment before nodding.

"Call us tonight."

And with that, the call ended and Hawke handed me the phone. He straightened in his seat and started the truck. But instead of putting the car in gear, he just sat there. He didn't look at me when he said, "Thank you, Tate." Then he put the car into drive and that was it.

We didn't speak again until we passed the sign welcoming us to Lulling.

CHAPTER 13

HAWKE

The anticipation I should have felt as we rolled into Lulling was surprisingly non-existent and I knew why. Because of the man sitting next to me. Because of the feelings he'd started to stir in me.

And with those feelings came a bone-deep fear that I hadn't felt in ten years. Not since those final moments as I'd carried Revay through the smoke and flames of what was left of our house and I'd known I wouldn't be able to make it to the front door. But back then there'd been half a dozen firemen who had been able to pull us out of the wall of flames. The only thing that stood between Tate and whether or not he would get to go home to his son was me. It was a burden I wasn't sure I could carry...or that I even wanted to.

"Turn in here," I heard Tate say, though he sounded far away. I glanced at Tate who was sitting stiffly in the passenger seat. At some point he'd grabbed the arm rest on the door and I could see his blood-less fingertips digging into the smooth material. His left hand was fisted and rubbing up and down his thigh. I was tempted to reach for him, but decided against it. I needed to be on full alert. I kept my eyes on the road as I reached behind my back to pull out my gun and I ignored Tate's sharply indrawn breath as I settled it in my lap.

The driveway Tate had pointed to wasn't really a driveway at all. With the overgrown trees and brush, it barely counted as a road. Tree limbs and branches dragged over the truck as I tried to avoid some of the bigger ruts in the muddy road. The sound of wood scraping over metal was eerie and I could see Tate's breath ratcheting up as the overgrown vegetation blocked out much of the sunlight as we made our way farther down the path. The dense greenery wasn't a good sign that we'd find what we were looking for and that fact was confirmed a moment later when we finally entered a clearing and saw a doublewide mobile home that had vines and bushes growing all around it. Junk and trash littered the entire front yard and there was a rusted out older model sedan sitting off to the side on blocks, its engine gone.

I stopped the truck near the door and turned to face Tate. "Stay behind me. You see anything or anyone, you get down and stay there till I tell you it's okay, got it?"

Tate swallowed hard and nodded. We both got out and met around the front of the truck. Even though the place had clearly been deserted some time ago, I kept my eyes open and my gun in my hand as I placed Tate behind me and headed towards the front door.

It was easy to get into the trailer since it wasn't locked. Several windows of the trailer had been broken at some point so the smell inside wasn't as rancid as it probably could have been, but it also meant that various wildlife had managed to find their way into the structure and the second we stepped inside, I saw several rats scurry for cover. The inside didn't look much better than the outside and whenever Buck and Denny had left, it didn't appear they'd taken much with them because there were several pieces of furniture in the living room along with an older model TV.

As disappointed as I was to find the place completely deserted, I also felt a pang of relief because it meant I could focus the majority of my attention on Tate who'd gone deathly pale as soon as we'd stepped into the place. He moved past me and examined the living room. He didn't say anything as he walked towards the back of the trailer. The kitchen and the two bedrooms we passed were in the same state of shambles, but Tate didn't stop until we reached the very last bedroom at the back of the trailer. He had to wrestle with the door to get it all the way open because there was so much debris on the floor. But while the other rooms had just looked like someone had been in a rush to leave, the last room looked like a tornado had hit it.

Or someone in a rage.

"Your room?" I asked as I looked at the shredded mattress, scattered clothes and broken knickknacks.

Tate only nodded. There were a couple of posters on the wall, but they were torn, their pieces dangling precariously.

"I loved this room," he finally whispered as he moved to the foldable plastic table in the corner that had clearly been turned into a desk. "Doesn't really make sense, does it?" he said as he fingered what looked like the pieces of a torn photograph. He glanced over his shoulder at me. "I hated this place, them, but this room...it was the only place I ever felt safe even when I wasn't." Tate shook his head in confusion.

"It makes perfect sense to me," I admitted.

Tate looked at me almost hopefully.

"It was your escape," I said. "They may have still been able to hurt your body in this room, but they couldn't reach you here," I said as I pointed to my head.

Tate glanced around the room and then nodded. He returned his gaze to me. "Did you have a place like that?"

I shook my head "No, not a place...a person."

"Your wife?" Tate asked softly.

For once, the mention of Revay didn't send a searing pain throughout my entire body. "Yes, but she wasn't my wife then."

"Tell me," Tate whispered and even though he wasn't anywhere near me, his voice felt like a caress.

I should have told him no or made an excuse about not having time, but I couldn't force the words out. To my surprise, I wanted to tell him.

"I met her in the third grade. I'd moved to town a few months earlier but hadn't gone to school right away so that day had been my first. The desk next to hers was the only one open. A lot of the other kids were laughing at me because my clothes didn't really fit me and I...I hadn't showered in a while so I guess I smelled kind of bad."

The humiliation of that day as I'd walked between the row of desks came back to me and I could almost still hear the snickers all around me. I'd managed to hold my head up high and had kept my eyes trained on the empty desk the teacher had pointed to, but when the kids had started making oinking sounds beneath their breath, I'd wanted to curl up in a ball and die.

I didn't realize I'd sat down on the edge of Tate's old bed until I felt his fingers threading through my hair. At some point he'd moved between my spread legs and one glance at his face and I knew I'd voiced my humiliation about what the kids had done to me out loud.

He didn't say anything, he just kept caressing me and that made it easier for me to continue.

"I didn't even notice Revay at first because I was trying so hard not to cry. Then the teacher tells us to get our books out so we can each read a section. I hadn't gotten my books yet so I thought the teacher would just skip me. But when she said my name, everybody turned around to look at me and I could see some of the kids making silent oink oink sounds. I wanted to fucking die right then and there," I whispered and I actually had to blink back the tears that threatened to fall.

"What happened?" Tate asked as he continued to gently soothe me with his touch.

"The room was totally quiet, all eyes on me, the teacher waiting... and then there's this loud screeching sound and I look over and there's Revay, standing up just a little and sliding her entire desk over. She was a tiny thing even back then and I could only watch in fascination as she pushed it across the aisle until it hit my desk. Then she opened her book, plopped it down in between our desks and pointed to the paragraph we were on."

Tate chuckled and I looked up at him.

"That was it," I murmured. "I knew she was going to change everything for me. And she did."

"She was amazing," Tate said with a smile. Not a question, not speculation...he said it like he knew it for a fact.

"She was," I said with a nod of my head.

"Thank you," Tate whispered and then he leaned down to brush his lips over mine. The kiss was achingly sweet and way too quick. He dropped his hand from my hair and began to step back, and I saw the tension in his gaze as if he'd just then realized what he'd done.

"For what?" I asked, grabbing him by the wrist before he could completely pull away from me.

"For sharing her with me," he said, clearly startled that I'd stopped him from moving away.

Some unnamed emotion inside of me burst and I felt warmth spread out to all my limbs. But it wasn't the same rush of heat I felt whenever I touched Tate or he touched me...it was different. It was deeper, stronger.

In that moment my need wasn't about lust and I refused to release Tate when he took another step back. Instead, I drew him forward but I closed my legs so that he had no choice but to awkwardly straddle me. His eyes filled with confusion until I tugged him down until he was sitting astride me. And then his eyes cleared and he met my lips as soon as I lifted them. As I let my tongue steal into his mouth for a taste, I wrapped my arms around his waist and I was rewarded with his arms closing around my neck.

I loved kissing Tate. There was just no way around it. I didn't care that I could feel just the slightest hint of stubble where his skin scraped over mine or that he was hard in all the places I'd only ever experienced softness as I let my hands roam along his back. I loved that his need ran just as deep as mine and he held nothing back from me as his tongue dueled with mine before slipping into my mouth. I loved that his grip on me was hungry and desperate and there was nothing tentative as he held my face in his hands so he could take over the kiss. And nothing about the erection I could feel pressing against my abdomen turned me off. If we'd been in any other place, I would have already been settling Tate's body beneath mine on the bed.

I ended the kiss before the desire became too much to contain and my guess was that Tate understood because he didn't resist the move. Instead, he let out a rush of breath and pressed his face against my neck as he drew our bodies closer together. I held him for several minutes as we waited for our racing hearts to settle and I forced my arms to release him when he finally crawled off of me. His face was flushed with color as he looked around the room and then back at me. I saw a hint of a smile as he said, "I think I love this room even more now."

I laughed and stood up. Tate moved to his closet which was also in a disarray and I watched him pick up an older looking camera from off the floor. He examined it and then flipped something on the camera and it began making whirling noises. He opened the back and popped the film canister out of it a moment later and looked at it.

"What's on the film?" I asked.

"I don't remember," Tate said quietly. "I forgot about this one."

"This one?"

Tate looked up at me. "Uh, yeah, I sold the few cameras I had before I left."

"You were a photographer?"

Tate chuckled and shook his head. "I took pictures. Big difference."

"But that was what you wanted to be."

A wan smile drifted across Tate's mouth. "A lifetime ago, yeah, I guess." He tossed the camera on the floor.

"You don't want to take it?"

"The lens is cracked," Tate said. "It would cost more than it's worth to get it fixed. I guess they didn't think to check it for film," he added as he pocketed the roll of unprocessed film.

"Did you take these?" I asked as I moved to his desk and looked through a few of the scattered photos.

"Yes."

I switched my attention to the torn up picture Tate had been playing around with. It looked familiar and I realized why when I glanced over my shoulder at one of the torn posters which I now saw was a blown up copy of the photo. "This was one of your favorites," I observed as I looked at the smaller photo again. It had been ripped into four pieces, but Tate had pushed the pieces into place enough so I could see what the picture had been of. It was a black and white photograph of two black birds, smaller than crows, in the process of taking flight, one slightly higher than the other. Heavy clouds hung in the sky above them...a coming storm they were flying right into.

"It's beautiful," I said as I glanced at Tate who was standing next to me, his shrouded gaze on the picture.

"I still remember that day. It was the summer I turned fifteen. Buck had just beaten the shit out of me for something – I don't even know what – and I snuck out after I heard him drive off in his truck. There was this old barn about a mile away that I liked to take pictures of...I kept waiting for the light to be just right. It was a perfect night. I could smell the rain in the air and the thunder was so loud you could feel it under your feet. I felt so free...and then I saw these birds and I just started snapping away until they were gone. And I knew that would be me someday."

Tate let out a harsh laugh. "Seven years," he whispered. "Seven years of pinning all my hopes and dreams on that picture; of thinking I'd someday be strong enough to face the storm instead of run from it." He shook his head and turned away. I watched him give the room one final look before he left. I reached down to pick up the two largest pieces of the picture and held the torn edges together. I saw the things Tate saw.

But I saw something else too and that had me reaching down to collect the smaller pieces and putting them all carefully into my pocket before I followed Tate from the room.

CHAPTER 14

TATE

I could already feel Hawke's devastating kiss fading to the back of my mind as I moved around the dilapidated trailer. I would have liked to have kept the taste and feel of him with me as the memories started to come back to me one by one, but the past was just too strong. Because everywhere I looked, I saw and heard everything that had had me dreaming of the day I could escape the endless nightmare.

"You okay?" I heard Hawke ask from behind me where I stood at the entrance to Buck's bedroom.

"He never closed his door when he was with his women," I murmured. "I made the mistake of watching him and Denny with one of them once when I was younger. Buck ordered me to join them."

"What did you do?"

I could feel the bile rising in my throat. "I said no and tried to leave, but Buck came after me. He kept asking me if I wouldn't fuck her because I was a faggot. I knew what he'd do to me if I admitted I was gay so I told him I was scared."

"How old were you?"

"Thirteen."

I closed my eyes when Hawke's big hand settled on the back of my neck.

"What happened?"

"By the time Buck dragged me back in here, Denny had the woman on her knees on the floor. She looked high, but when Buck told her to suck me, she reached for my pants. I started crying when she put her mouth on me. Buck started fucking her from behind and Denny was giving her instructions on how to suck me. When I couldn't get it up, he shoved me aside and asked the woman if she wouldn't rather suck a real man."

I turned away from Buck's room and faced Hawke. "Buck started calling me Cryin Chris after that. Denny's favorite was Sissy Chrissy. Chris…that's my real name…Christopher."

Humiliation was coursing through me as I tried to move past Hawke, but he used his body to crowd me back against the door frame. "Tate," he whispered and then he kissed me softly.

"Tate," he repeated along with another kiss.

Every time he said my name, he deepened the kiss that followed. I'd thought the kiss in my room was just another chance occurrence because Hawke had been in a vulnerable state, but as his tongue met mine, I couldn't help but hope it meant he was feeling even a little bit of what I was feeling. When he finally released me, my knees felt like jelly.

"We should look around to see if we can find some evidence of where they went," Hawke said, his voice husky with desire.

I nodded and locked my knees. I followed him to the kitchen and began looking through the drawers while Hawke searched through the debris on the floor. Unfortunately, the work didn't help me tune out the memories of all the times I'd been tormented and tortured by both Buck and Denny.

I had no memory of a time when Buck had been kind to me, but that wasn't the case with Denny. I'd often wondered if the few times I remembered Denny protecting me when we were kids were really memories or just fanciful dreams like the one I'd had about the red-haired woman who'd called me Tate.

Denny had been older than me by eight years, so by the time I was Matty's age, Denny had been a teenager and we'd had little in common. But I had distinct images of him sitting on the floor with me playing with my little green army men or reading to me from one of his many comic books. And there was even one recurring image where Denny had shoved Buck away from me after Buck had grabbed me by the arm and twisted it until the bone had snapped. I'd collapsed on the floor, screaming in agony as my big brother had taken the rest of the beating that had been meant for me.

I couldn't pinpoint a specific event that had led to the change between me and Denny. At some point, he'd just grown more and more distant and one day when Buck went after me for accidentally spilling some of his beer as I'd been bringing it to him, Denny had stood off to the side and watched for a minute or two before disappearing into his room. I'd spent the next several days making excuses in my head for Denny's defection, but I hadn't been able to deny the truth any longer when everything had changed less than a week later.

I'd been exploring the woods behind our trailer when I'd come across two stray puppies and I'd carried them back to the house where Denny had helped me get them cleaned up and fed. We'd spent hours playing with the puppies and he'd named his Comet while I'd named mine Ranger after one of my favorite cartoons. But when Buck had come home, I'd seen something in his eyes as we'd shown him the puppies and asked if we could keep them. He'd looked almost...giddy.

I hadn't understood what he'd meant at first when he'd started talking about only being able to afford one of the puppies and that we'd have to choose which one to keep. But Denny had gotten it because his face had fallen and he'd looked back and forth between his puppy and mine. I'd still been confused when Buck had grabbed both puppies and taken them outside. We'd followed him and I'd asked Denny what was going on as I'd watched Buck put the puppies down on the driveway and then grab a shovel from the back of his truck. Buck had looked at Denny before holding out the shovel. By the time I'd finally figured out what was happening, Denny had straightened next to me, strode over to Buck and grabbed the shovel. My scream of denial had come too late and wouldn't have mattered. Ranger had yelped once and after that, all I'd heard was the sickening sound of the shovel striking flesh over and over again. I'd fallen to my knees and thrown up and when I'd finally had nothing left to expel, Buck had walked past me, a triumphant smirk on his face. Denny had followed, his puppy in his arms. He hadn't even spared me a glance as he'd left me there on the ground.

Everything had changed after that. Buck had still been my judge and jury, but Denny had become the executioner. And he'd been every bit as ruthless as Buck. I'd stood no chance and I'd spent the next fifteen years of my life in hell on earth.

"There's nothing here," I heard Hawke mutter in frustration as he tossed a stack of papers he'd been holding in his hand to the ground.

"I know of a couple more places we can look," I said.

Hawke cast me a glance and nodded, but he didn't look reassured. And in truth, I suspected our luck wouldn't improve. And while I'd dreaded the prospect of having to confront Buck and Denny, the idea of Hawke not being able to find the closure he so desperately needed actually bothered me more.

I ended up being right.

After we left the trailer, I directed Hawke to several different locations including the two places Buck had used as meth labs. The first had clearly been abandoned some time ago and the second had been obliterated by what I suspected had been an explosion. We'd checked out a couple of bars Buck had often frequented and while one had gone out of business, the other had been open. But instead of going inside, Hawke and I had sat in his truck across the street and watched people come and go for nearly two hours before he'd started the car up. And not once had he spoken even a single word to me.

As Hawke drove us to a motel on the outskirts of town, I tried one last time to draw him out by saying, "There are a few places we can ask around tomorrow."

Hawke didn't respond in any way and I could see his anger simmering just under the surface. Once we reached the motel, I followed him inside to check in because it was the same motel where

Reggie and I had hooked up at on a couple of occasions and I was hopeful the owner would know something about Buck and Denny's whereabouts. But I didn't recognize the woman behind the check in desk and when I asked if she was new, she said she and her husband had just bought the place a couple months earlier. When I asked about the Buckleys, she had no idea who I was talking about.

Once we were in the room, Hawke began getting a few things out of his bag. I was unpacking my own things when he handed me his credit card.

"Order something for dinner if you're hungry. I'm going to take a shower. Don't answer the door. I'll be out before the food gets here."

I flinched at his cool, dismissive tone, but I took the credit card and set it down on the nightstand. I listened as the shower came on and I couldn't help but think of how eerily reminiscent it was of the night before just before Hawke had fucked me. I used the time to call Matty, but as happy as I was to hear his excited rundown of the costume parade, I couldn't escape the dread I felt that Hawke was pulling away from me again. I'd been so sure after he'd kissed me for the second time in the trailer that maybe something had changed for him, but now I wasn't so sure.

After hanging up with Matty, I called the front desk and asked for the number of a restaurant that would deliver. I ordered a pizza along with a couple of sodas and then searched out the remote control for the television. When Hawke came out, I turned the TV down and said, "I ordered a pizza. It should be here in about twenty minutes."

"Fine," was all Hawke said, not even sparing me a glance.

I grabbed my bag and went to the bathroom where I took my time showering and by the time I returned to the main room, the pizza was sitting untouched on the table by the door and Hawke was slouched on the far side of his bed, his back to me. I could tell he was holding something in his hand and I had my suspicions as to what it was. They were confirmed a second later when he cast a glance over his shoulder at me and I saw the picture frame. He leaned down, presumably to put the picture in his bag, and I turned away and busied myself with putting my own bag away.

"You should eat something."

I couldn't help but laugh at the order.

"What?" Hawke asked testily.

"Nothing," I murmured.

"You've got something to say, just say it."

My own anger was growing but I forced it back and said as evenly as I could, "It doesn't matter."

"Fucking Christ," Hawke snapped, but he didn't say anything else and that in itself sent me over the edge. I spun around to find that Hawke was in the same exact position and the fact that he wasn't even looking at me pissed me off even further.

"You know what Hawke, fuck you!"

That got his attention and he looked over his shoulder at me, but I found that I didn't give a shit at the cold look in his eyes. "Do you have any idea how hard it was for me to come here?" I ground out. "I left behind my son! I came back to a place that has a starring role in my worst nightmares! I'm risking coming face to face with the two men who took nothing but pleasure in tormenting me for nearly my entire life! And I did it all for you!"

Hawke stood up and came around the bed, his big frame stiff with unspent anger. "You did it because you felt indebted-"

"I did it for you!" I yelled. "You want to treat me like some cheap fuck, fine! You want to take your frustration out on me, then fucking do it! But don't do what you did to me in that trailer." I hated that my voice broke at the last part, but I held my ground as Hawke closed the distance between us. I felt raw and exposed and I suddenly wished I'd just kept my mouth shut.

"What did I do in the trailer?" Hawke asked, his voice softer now. But when he reached for me, I yanked my arm out of his reach and stepped back. He just kept coming at me though, and I had nowhere to go once the backs of my legs hit the bed.

"Don't," I managed to get out as Hawke's body crowded mine.

"Don't what?" Hawke whispered, his voice strained.

"Don't pretend like you care," I finally said and I was helpless to prevent the pleading that crept into my voice.

Hawke studied me for a long time before he leaned down and put his mouth next to my ear. I was trembling with need long before he even spoke.

"One thing you should know about me...I don't pretend," Hawke said, his lips skimming the sensitive skin just behind my ear. He wasn't touching me anywhere else, but he may as well have been because my whole body was drawn up tight with excitement. "And Tate?"

When he didn't continue, I drew back enough so I could look him in the eye.

"I care," he said softly, his blue eyes piercing straight through me. "I fucking care."

His mouth was on mine an instant after the last word left his lips and I couldn't stifle my cry of pleasure as our tongues met. Fingers threaded through my hair to hold me still and then my head was tilted back, exposing my neck. I used my hands to find purchase on Hawke's waist as his lips teased my skin. But he stopped kissing me a moment later and instead drew me against his chest.

"Sorry for today," he murmured. "I really thought we were going to find something. I just need this to be over."

I should have kept my mouth shut, but my need for answers was too great.

"And when it is over? What happens then?"

CHAPTER 15

HAWKE

J was taken aback by Tate's question and I knew it was my silence that had him dropping his arms from where they'd been wrapped around me. But instead of stepping away from me, he whispered, "No, don't answer that" and then his hand snaked around the back of my neck to pull me down for a kiss. I automatically opened for him and it took just one swipe of his tongue over mine to push his words to the back of my mind. I wrapped my arms around him and pulled him flush against my body. He moaned into my mouth when our erections brushed together and when I slid my hand down to cup his ass, Tate whispered, "I need you" against my mouth.

My plan was to lower him to the bed so I could explore every inch of him, but when I felt his palm sliding over my pants until it found my bulging cock, I stilled and closed my eyes. Tate continued to kiss me as he began rolling his hand over my aching dick, but I had trouble concentrating on the deep, drugging kisses. And when I felt his hand actually disappear inside my pants, I tore my mouth from his so I could watch the outline of his hand as his fingers pressed into my heated flesh.

"Oh fuck," I whispered as Tate's entire hand closed around my cock. I really wanted to see his hand on me, but before I could even reach for my pants to push them down, Tate pulled his hand free and began lowering them himself. My body was humming with excitement and I couldn't resist lowering my head to seek out Tate's mouth again. But I only managed to steal a few kisses before I felt the cool air of the motel room wash over my length. Instead of fisting me again, Tate used his thumb to trace the ridge beneath the head of my dick and then he flicked it over the slit on my crown. A shudder went through my entire body, but I was helpless to do anything as I watched Tate explore me. Pre-cum began welling up at the tip and Tate swiped at it with his finger. I expected him to use it as lube, but when he lifted his finger to his mouth, I was sure I stopped breathing. His eyes went glassy with desire as he licked the fluid from his finger and I couldn't stop myself from yanking his mouth to mine.

My control was completely shattered as I tasted myself, but as much as I would have liked to grab Tate and push him down on the bed, he made it clear he was in charge when he began stroking me with heavy drags. His rough hand was so different than anything I'd ever felt before and the sheer size and strength of that had me seeing stars as he exerted the perfect amount of pressure. Tate's free hand slipped beneath my shirt to skim over my abdomen and then he was pushing the hem upwards.

"Off," he demanded. The rough order had more pre-cum leaking from my body and I quickly did as he said and yanked the shirt off and tossed it aside. Shivers of need began to roll through me as Tate stroked me, but when his mouth closed over one of my nipples and sucked, I nearly came on the spot.

"Shit, I'm not going to last," I muttered as Tate laved his tongue over my nipple before teasing it with his teeth.

"Yes, you will," Tate said against my chest as he ran his tongue around the entire nipple before searching out the other one. "Because Hawke," – I looked down at him when he paused – "I'm just getting started."

I let out another foul curse when he bit down on my nipple again. As much as I was enjoying his power over me, I needed to see more of him so I grabbed the hem of his shirt and pulled it up. He released his hold on my dick and pulled back from my chest long enough to let me remove the shirt, but he resumed his sensual torture the instant the garment was free. I wrapped one hand around the back of his head, more to feel him than to control him, and I let the other hand drift past the waistband at his back and brush over his tight ass. Tate moaned against my skin when I trailed my finger along his crack, but I lost the contact when he suddenly dropped to his knees in front of me. I knew exactly what was coming next, but instead of putting his mouth on me, Tate looked up, the unasked question clear in his eyes.

The fact that it was a man who was about to take me into his mouth wasn't lost on me, but I couldn't find it in me to care because it wasn't just any man who was about to be this first for me. It was this man. This sweet, beautiful, strong man who, after all I'd done to him, was brave enough to get on his knees before me...to bring me pleasure without asking for any in return. Just nodding would have gotten me what I so badly wanted, but I needed Tate to understand what he was doing to me so I whispered, "Please."

Tate stilled for a moment, his beautiful blue and golden brown eyes going bright with surprise and then filling with pleasure. He nuzzled my groin and then flicked his tongue against my pulsing dick. It felt like I'd been zapped with a thousand volts of electricity, but before I could even beg him for more, his entire mouth closed over my crown. I let out a rugged groan as he swirled his tongue around me and I reached out with my hands to grab his head. I was tempted to thrust into the wet heat, but I forced myself to remain still so I could just experience every second of pleasure Tate was dragging from my body. As he sucked more of me into his mouth, Tate's fingers began pushing my pants farther down my body. I was prepared to step out of them, but Tate surprised me again when his hands closed over my ass. He stilled when I tensed briefly at the unexpected contact, but when he went to remove his hands, I quickly said, "No, don't...leave them there."

The sight of Tate looking up at me as he sucked my dick was the most erotic thing I'd ever seen in my entire life, but the feel of his rough palms kneading the globes of my ass came in a very close second. Between Tate's mouth and his fingers, I was quickly losing control of my impending orgasm, so I only let him have a few more seconds of me before I reached down and pulled him to his feet. I sealed my mouth over his, loving the taste of my own musky flavor. I pushed him down on the bed, but didn't follow him. Instead, I stood over him and stepped out of my pants before reaching for his. Once they were gone, I stepped back just enough so I could take in my fill of him. Everything about him intrigued me and despite the exploration I'd done of his body the night before in the shower, I knew it wasn't enough. And as I lowered myself so that I could settle my body on top of his, I realized it would never be enough.

I took my time kissing Tate and I smiled when he shifted his legs enough so I could settle between them. Our cocks were nestled against one another, but I kept my attention on Tate's mouth as I nipped, sucked and licked every part of its sweetness. Tate's breath was sawing in and out of him as he took pleasure in everything that I did to him and I didn't miss when he wrapped his legs around my lower body. I wondered if he was afraid I was going to leave him at some point or if he was just desperate to touch as much of me as he could. Because that was exactly what I wanted.

The night before I'd used mostly my hands to learn about Tate's body, but tasting him was so much better. I tortured his nipples the same way he'd tortured mine and I bit back my own need to rub my dick against his when he began bucking up against me with his hips. His eyes were closed and his head was thrown back as sweat began glistening all over his flesh. His full lips were parted as he tried to draw in enough air and I couldn't resist covering his mouth with mine. I loved that as lost in his own pleasure as he was, he kissed me back with everything he had. His fingers were wrapped around my upper arms, the pads pressing into my own heated skin. I continued to brace my own upper body weight with one arm so that I could snake my other hand beneath Tate's body to palm his ass.

"Yes," he hissed when I lifted him up so that he was pressed even more closely against my groin. My plan had been to continue to explore Tate's body, but I could feel my own body getting closer and closer to release, so I began rolling my hips over Tate which slid our dicks together deliciously.

"Oh God," Tate moaned and his eyes opened and he looked down at where we were as closely connected as we could be without being intimately joined. He flipped his eyes up to mine and then grabbed my neck and yanked me down for a kiss. "I need you inside of me," he breathed against my mouth. I kissed him hard and slowed down my undulating hips enough to get his attention.

"No," I said. "Your body needs time to heal."

Tate shook his head violently, but I kissed him again before he could protest verbally.

"This feels so fucking amazing, Tate," I managed to get out as I began rocking against him once more. "Don't you feel it?"

Tate nodded, his lips skimming mine with the move. "Promise me," he grated as he bucked against me to increase the friction. "Promise me this isn't the last time we're together like this."

I knew it was a promise I shouldn't make, especially since I had no idea what tomorrow or the next day would bring. But the idea of not feeling Tate's body wrapped around mine again wasn't fathomable to me so I nodded. "I promise," I said against his lips. "I'm going to make you feel so good the next time I get inside that tight hole of yours," I vowed.

Tate groaned at my words. I began humping against him with less finesse as I said, "I'm going to fuck you just like this, Tate. Facing you. Just so I can watch those beautiful eyes of yours go wide when I slip inside of you."

Tate sucked in a harsh breath and his hold on my arm became almost painful.

"You'll try to hold on to me tight, won't you, baby? You'll try to keep me from leaving all that snug heat even for a second," I said as I used my hand on his ass to clutch him even closer to me. One or both of us was leaking so much pre-cum that our dicks slid against each other with ease and I could feel my body drawing up tight.

Another nod from Tate and a mumbled, "Yes."

"And when you finally come apart around me and you feel me shooting my cum inside you, you'll say my name, won't you?"

Whatever Tate said next wasn't even intelligible, but I had no trouble understanding him because his eyes had flipped open and he was nodding viciously.

"Say it now," I suddenly demanded, the need to hear my name falling from his lips undeniable.

"Hawke," he whispered harshly.

My heart seized up, but not in pleasure. I slowed my moves and released my hold on Tate's ass so I could press all of my weight down on him. As badly as I needed to come, I needed something more from him, but I was terrified of what it meant. A flash of emotion shot through me as I realized I would demand it of him despite what it would cost me. Because I needed all of him in that moment. But more than that, I needed to be all of me.

Tate's desire had eased enough that he was watching me in confusion. His hands were resting on the backs of my arms just above my elbows. I leaned down to kiss him and then cupped the sides of his face with my hands.

"Michael," I whispered against his mouth.

Tate didn't move or respond for the longest time. In fact, it felt like he was barely even breathing. But his eyes never left mine as he said, "Michael" in a barely-there voice.

"Again," I demanded.

"Michael," he said again, louder this time.

Pleasure flooded my entire body and I began thrusting my hips against his with ruthless precision.

"Again," I ground out as I braced my hands next to his head so I could bear my own weight as I rolled my lower body over his in heavy, weighted drags.

"Michael," he cried out, his voice growing more and more desperate. And after that, I didn't have to command him to say my name anymore. With every exhale, he called to me and I gave him what he needed, what we both needed. Tate went over seconds before I did and I felt his nails dig into my back where he was holding onto me as he screamed my name and his cum drenched us both. My own orgasm ripped through me without mercy and I dropped all of my weight onto Tate and gathered him into my arms as I rode out the endless waves of pleasure. The climax was so forceful that it bordered on painful and it was several long minutes before the brutally strong aftershocks eased enough that I stopped grinding my hips against Tate's. The roaring in my ears quieted enough to hear Tate still whispering my name.

I lifted my head enough to seal my lips over his in an unhurried kiss that was really just our lips pressed together for the few seconds between the deep breaths we were each sucking in to try to get our bodies back to some semblance of normal. I used my elbows to lift my weight up enough so I could run my fingers through Tate's slickened hair. The blissful expression on his face was one I would remember for the rest of my life, but nothing compared to the equal parts of pleasure and pain that tore through me when he said "Michael" one last time before closing his eyes.

Michael.

The name I'd never allowed anyone but my wife to call me.

CHAPTER 16

TATE

I waited a very long twenty minutes before I forced myself out of bed and padded over to the bathroom door. I felt childish with my ear up to the door trying to hear something... anything. I'd heard Hawke leave his bed, but hadn't opened my eyes until I'd heard the bathroom door close. It wasn't necessarily because I didn't want to confront Hawke...no, it was more like I needed time to build up the suit of armor I would need to face him.

Because I had no doubt that despite our moving encounter the night before, Hawke had nothing but regrets. He hadn't said that of course, and he hadn't done anything overtly obvious, but I'd felt it in every touch, every move after he'd eased himself off of me. The guilt in his eyes had been a living, breathing thing and I'd known it had nothing to do with what we'd done.

Michael.

I'd loved saying it. I'd loved seeing the pleasure flood his eyes every time I had. I'd loved knowing I had a piece of him that I knew in my gut not everyone did.

But I hated that it was that part of the night before that he would have changed if he could. And I hated that I was being measured against a dead woman who'd clearly deserved to be put on any pedestal her husband chose to put her on.

After the epic climax, I hadn't been able to move and I hadn't really wanted to despite the cooling cum all over my chest and abdomen. But the second Hawke had drawn me to my feet and sealed his mouth over mine, my body had started to come alive again. We'd ended up taking another shower together, but unlike the night before, Hawke's touch had been quick and efficient and while his movements had still turned me on, I'd felt all the warmth from my lingering orgasm fade and be replaced by a bitter cold that had been a thousand times worse than any I'd ever experienced before.

Because I was losing Hawke...again. Even though I'd never really had him.

After the shower, we'd dried ourselves off and I hadn't gotten a chance to taste Hawke again because he'd turned his back on me and crawled into his own bed, leaving me to the cool, empty sheets of mine. I'd managed to fall asleep at some point, but my brain had seemed to be even more hyper aware of Hawke than it had been before because I'd woken up every time he'd shifted in his bed. I'd given up trying to fall back asleep a couple of hours earlier and I'd spent the time trying to listen to the sound of Hawke's breathing to see if he'd found the peace of sleep.

Once he'd disappeared into the bathroom, I'd waited for the shower to come on. It hadn't. And then my disappointment had started to shift to concern.

Thus the standing in front of the door with my ear pressed up against it like a little kid. There was no sound of running water or a flushing toilet and I debated whether or not I shouldn't just seek the safety of my own bed. After all, did I really want to hear Hawke tell me last night was a mistake? Did I want to accept that the promise he'd made to me was one more in a long line of broken ones?

I didn't.

But I lifted my hand and knocked anyway. Because I couldn't keep guessing if Hawke's interest in me was based on needing to slake some physical need or if maybe there was something more there.

I care.

Hawke's whispered declaration sparked through me so when there was no answer, I knocked again and waited and then turned the knob.

He was standing in front of the vanity, his hands braced on the counter. He didn't seem surprised to see me and he didn't seem angry either. His eyes met mine in the reflection of the mirror and held me for a long time before he looked at his own reflection again.

I could see the remnants of shaving cream dripping off the parts of his face that weren't scarred, but it didn't look like he'd actually shaved. I moved farther into the bathroom and soaked in everything I could about him. He was wearing his athletic pants but no shirt. His right side was facing me and I could finally see that the burn scars went from his face and neck all the way down to his waist. In the reflection of the mirror I could see his tattoo on his other side and I sucked in a breath when I realized what I was seeing. What I'd thought were just strange words were actually words that were written in reverse so that they only made sense when viewed in a mirror.

I hadn't even realized I'd been staring until Hawke's arm shifted, blocking my view. But he was only reaching up to swipe away at some of the foam that had started to streak down his face as it began to break down.

"They're just for me," he murmured as his eyes once again met mine in the mirror.

I knew he was talking about the words that started on his chest just above his left nipple and went all the way down his side because he'd dropped his gaze to study them as he'd spoken.

"I'm sorry," I whispered, humiliation burning in my gut as I turned away. But then I felt his hand close around my wrist. Hawke didn't say anything as he pulled me closer to him. He didn't kiss me or hold me, he merely maneuvered me so that I was standing next to his right side.

"Revay used to write songs."

I swallowed hard in the hopes that I could find my own voice. "She was a singer?"

Hawke nodded. "She liked to sing, but her dream was to be a lyricist. She wanted to hear other people singing what she wrote."

"Was she successful?"

"She sold some songs, but mostly to local bands. To really pursue it, she would have had to move to some place like L.A."

"Why didn't she?" I asked, wishing like hell I could wrap my arms around Hawke because I could tell every word was costing him.

"She knew it would mean spending more time apart. I was Special Forces so I was deployed a lot on missions and sometimes I was only home for days at a time. I needed to be near wherever I was stationed so it wouldn't have been easy for me to fly to some place like L.A. or New York."

"She chose to be with you instead," I said in understanding.

Hawke nodded. "She gave up her dream so I could live mine." Hawke dropped his eyes to study the few puffs of foam that lingered in the sink. "I put in my papers just before my last mission. I was going to encourage her to pursue her dream and I'd be the one to follow her wherever she needed to go to make it happen."

"But she found out she was pregnant," I ventured.

Hawke lifted his eyes to meet mine in surprise.

"I overheard you and Ronan talking that day in the gym," I admitted.

Hawke studied me for a moment, but didn't comment on my revelation. "We'd been trying for a few years and had finally decided to go see a specialist when we got the news. We were floored," Hawke said with an uneven chuckle. "Revay had inherited the house in Wyoming from her parents after they died in a car accident so we decided to build a new life there."

"Is that where you guys were from?"

"Yeah. Revay grew up in that house. My uncle's property bordered her parents' ranch."

The more Hawke revealed, the more questions I had, but I held my tongue in the hopes that he would continue.

"We were living near the base I was stationed at in Texas. The night she was attacked was the night I got home from my last mission.

The guys in my team wanted to take me out for a celebratory drink so I was late getting home. In the hour that I was drinking shots and celebrating impending fatherhood, Revay was being raped. By the time I got home, the house was already on fire."

My gut clenched as the ugly reminder of the true nature of the connection I shared with Hawke raised its ugly head.

"I found her on the floor of our bedroom. She was naked and bleeding and the area rug she'd been lying on was on fire and had started to burn her. I was only able to get her as far as the front door before I was overcome with smoke."

My eyes shifted to the burn scars on Hawke's side. I couldn't stop myself from running my hand over the damaged skin. Hawke trembled beneath my seeking fingers, but he didn't move away from me or ask me to stop.

"Luckily the firefighters showed up right after that and got us both out. Ronan was working in the ER when we arrived. He saved Revay's life. She woke up long enough to tell me that it had been two men who'd assaulted her and that one of them had referred to the other as 'Pops' and then she told me she loved me. They had to intubate her right after that."

I stilled in my exploration of Hawk's scars and closed my eyes. So that was how he'd figured out that it was a father/son duo that had hurt his wife.

"I'm so sorry, Hawke," I whispered as I shook my head.

Hawke's touch on my chin as he lifted it was brief, but it was enough to see that he held no censure in his gaze. His eyes fell to the tattoo.

"The firemen were able to save part of the house. I found her notebook where she used to jot things down that she was working on in the kitchen, along with the ultrasound she'd had that day – the one that showed we were having a boy."

I let my hand rest on his side for another moment before I slowly worked my way around his back, trailing my fingers over the ripped muscles. When I reached his other side, my eyes fell on the reflection of the tattoo.

"Can I read it?" I asked.

Hawke watched me for a long moment in the mirror, his eyes dark with some unnamed emotion. And then he nodded.

I dropped my eyes to the tattoo and began reciting the words in my head when Hawke whispered, "Would you read it out loud?"

Emotion threatened to choke me, but I managed to swallow it down and began to read.

"I know I need to keep living
while I wait for you to come home
But I don't know how to tell my heart to stop hurting
since you're the reason it keeps beating on
My days are empty, my eyes full of tears
but the sound of your voice
and the promise of your smile
make it all disappear
You're the other half of my soul
the light that shows me the way
You're my yesterday and my tomorrow
The Angel that keeps me safe."

I could feel my own tears threatening to fall as I let my fingers dance over the beautiful words. I risked a glance up at Hawk and saw that he was barely holding it together.

"One fucking hour," he whispered in a guttural tone. Tears shimmered in his eyes and he angrily dashed them away. I lifted my hand to cup his cheek and forced my body between his and the counter. I drew him down until his head was resting against my neck.

"I'm so sorry," I managed to get out just before Hawke's arms went around me in a bone-crushing hold.

I felt warm moisture against my skin and knew what it meant. I kept my own emotions in check as I held on to Hawke as tight as I could. When he finally released his grip on me and leaned back, he quietly said, "Tate" as he shook his head dejectedly.

"You don't have to, Hawke," I interrupted. "Last night...tonight, whatever happens, you don't owe me any explanations. I'll take any piece of you I can get," I said. I searched out the shaving cream and put some in my hand. I pressed my lips against his in the briefest of kisses and whispered, "Just let me take care of you for a few minutes, okay?"

Hawke stared at me for the longest time and then nodded the tiniest bit. But as I began to spread the shaving cream over his face, I heard a small sigh leave his lips and there was the slightest release of tension in his big body.

And as I reached for his razor, I realized it was enough.

It would have to be.

CHAPTER 17

HAWKE

"*A*re you sure, Mr. Duncan?" Tate asked the frail old man who just kept shaking his head. Frustration coursed through me and I felt the urge to throw something. I took a step back on the small, rickety porch and braced my hands behind me on the porch railing so I wouldn't be tempted to do just that with one of the half dozen dying potted plants all around us.

"Ain't seen Buck or Denny for almost two years now," Mr. Duncan announced. "Rumor has it they died in that explosion."

Tate glanced over his shoulder at me and I did my best to school my reaction. We'd been interviewing people for several hours now and I knew the walk down memory lane wasn't good for Tate, especially considering how many people had looked at him with open distaste. I had no doubt that despite Tate's inherent goodness, he hadn't been able to escape the negative association forced upon him simply because he carried the Buckley name. Mr. Duncan, who it turned out had once been Tate's math teacher, had been the only one who hadn't spoken to Tate through the door. And so far he was the only one who'd had more than a few words to say about what may or may not have happened to Buck and Denny.

"Do you mean the explosion at the meth lab near the Weathersby farm?" Tate asked as he turned his attention back to the old man who was rocking back and forth in a decrepit rocking chair.

"Yup...they had the State Police down here for that one. Found a couple bodies too," Mr. Duncan said with a nod of his head as he reached for his glass of lemonade. "Course there wasn't much left to identify."

I ground my teeth together and turned around so that I was facing the street instead of the two men since I didn't want Mr. Duncan or Tate to see my building anger. In all the years I'd been searching for Buck and Denny, I'd never even considered the possibility that they were dead. My one goal had always been to see the two men dead and buried, but now that I faced the prospect that they already were, it felt hollow. I hadn't realized how much the prospect of hurting the two men, of making sure they suffered, had meant to me. Before it had just been a bonus, but now that I might not get it, I felt cheated.

Fuck, what kind of man did that make me?

Certainly not the kind of man who deserved to be with someone like Tate. Or Matty.

Jesus, I needed to get a fucking grip. I didn't want Tate or his kid. I wanted Revay. I wanted our son. Tate was just...a distraction. A warm, sweet, kind, gorgeous distraction.

It was my own voice that called me a liar this time around. I hadn't heard Revay's whisper in my ear in a while...not since I'd actually buried myself deep inside of Tate's body two nights ago. And worse, the only voice I now heard when I remembered the words scrawled across my body, my wife's final ode to what we'd had, was Tate's.

"You ready to go?"

I flinched when Tate's arm brushed mine as he leaned against the railing next to me. I hoped to God he hadn't noticed my reaction, but when he put several inches between us, I knew that he had. I glanced over my shoulder and saw that Mr. Duncan had gone inside at some point.

"Nothing?" I asked, since I'd ended up tuning out the end of their conversation.

Tate just shook his head.

Despite the intimacy we'd shared this morning in the motel's bathroom, we hadn't spoken much since then and I'd been incredibly careful not to touch Tate. Because he'd already seen me at my lowest. And touching him the way I wanted to just wasn't an option – because I couldn't give him more of what I'd only given to Revay. I would give him pleasure with my body and I'd take the same from him, but I couldn't give him what I knew he wanted...what I saw in his eyes every time he looked at me. What I'd felt in his embrace this morning as his skin had soaked up the few tears I hadn't been able to keep from falling.

"We could try talking to the sheriff about the explosion, but I'm not sure he'd tell us anything."

"Why not?" I asked as I followed Tate down the steps and towards my truck.

"He always looked the other way when it came to Buck and Denny. Pay was better, I guess."

"Buck paid him off?"

Tate nodded.

"How do you know?"

"It doesn't matter," Tate said as he reached for the truck's door handle. Despite my promise to myself not to touch him, I did just that and gently turned him to face me before he could open the door.

"It matters to me," I said as I backed Tate up until his back hit the door. He didn't struggle in any way and, in fact, he looked almost relieved.

"I asked him for help once."

"The sheriff?"

Tate nodded. "Buck made me run drugs for him when I was younger. I thought if I had the proof in my hands, the sheriff could arrest Buck."

"What happened?" I asked, though I pretty much knew the answer.

"He put me in his squad car along with the drugs, drove me back to my house and told Buck what I'd done. Buck handed him some cash, told him to keep the drugs as a bonus and then beat me so bad I blacked out right there in the driveway. I have no idea how long I was laying there for, but Denny dumped some water on me, pointed a gun at my head and told me he'd managed to talk Buck out of killing me. But if I ever opened my mouth again, Denny said he'd shoot me himself."

"Tate-"

"We should go, Hawke. There's one other person I want to talk to."

Tate's body had gone stiff as he'd spoken and as tempted as I was to try to coax some of the easiness back into it, I knew it wasn't the time or place so I nodded and stepped back. I walked around the truck and got in and tried not to feel disappointed that Tate refused to look at me. It was, after all, what I wanted...distance, time to think.

It only took a few minutes to get to our destination and I knew instantly who we were going to see when Tate told me to pull into the bank's parking lot. His piece of shit ex had worked in a bank and had been the one who'd told Buck where Tate was two years earlier.

"Your ex?" I growled.

"Reggie," Tate responded as he unbuckled his seat belt. "Although I suppose calling him my ex is generous. He was more of a fuck buddy and not a very good one at that."

Tate made a move to get out of the truck, but I grabbed him by the wrist to stop him.

"What does that mean?"

Tate sighed and then shrugged. "It's a small town, Hawke. Not a lot of options for a scrawny, scared kid with a homophobic father and brother."

"So you weren't in love with him?" I asked, hating the jealousy that was surging through me. Fortunately, Tate didn't seem to notice it.

"Love?" Tate said with a harsh chuckle. "I barely even liked him."

"Then why?" I pressed.

"Forget it," Tate murmured and tried to pull free of my hold.

"Why, Tate?"

He finally turned to face me, his expression an intriguing mix of defiance and shame.

"Because it was easy to pretend with him."

"Pretend?"

"Yeah, unlike you, I pretended all the time. I pretended he was my boyfriend and that I didn't feel cheap and used after he finished fucking me. I pretended I loved him and that we were going to build a life together. I pretended I didn't have to hide who I was and that for five God damn minutes, I was actually safe!"

Tate tried to tug free of my grip, but I pulled him closer and then sealed my mouth over his, not caring who might see us. I kissed him until he went soft beneath my lips and started kissing me back.

"You don't have to pretend anymore," I reminded him.

"Don't I?" Tate murmured, but before I could even try to figure out what he meant, he whispered, "Sorry," and tried to escape me again.

"Was there anyone else?" I asked. I had no idea why it was so important for me to suddenly know if there'd ever been someone special in Tate's life.

"No," Tate said as he dropped his gaze. "I went to a club once after Reggie moved away, but it wasn't what I thought it would be."

"What did you think it was going to be?"

"Do we have to talk about this?" Tate asked quietly.

"No," I finally said as I released him. The tension between us grew and I didn't try to stop Tate when he got out of the truck. He waited for me as I walked around it before heading into the small building.

Lulling had turned out to be a rural, almost desolate town with just a small town square. The population was just shy of a thousand people and my guess was that many of them either made their living running ranches on the surrounding farmland or made the hour long commute to San Antonio. The few businesses that remained were a throwback to another time and the bank was no exception. The décor as soon as we walked in screamed that the place hadn't seen an upgrade in several decades and there was only a singular teller standing behind the counter and one cubicle with a starchy older man punching numbers into an older model computer.

There was no doubt in my mind that the teller picking at something on the skin of his hand was Tate's ex and I had to curb the urge to walk up to the counter and drag the man through the little space that allowed him to interact with his customers. I sensed Tate tensing up next to me, but he didn't hesitate to make his way right up to Reggie.

"How may I help you today?" Reggie mumbled just before he lifted his dull eyes. They instantly widened at the sight of Tate.

"Chris," he whispered and then looked around the small space as if half expecting to see someone else. His eyes only stayed on me for a brief moment and I knew right away who he was expecting to see.

"Reggie," Tate acknowledged.

Reggie shifted back and forth uneasily on his feet. He was about the same height as Tate and I suspected his normal build would have been average to a little heavier set. But his gaunt frame, thin hair and clearly false teeth had me instantly realizing the man in front of us had betrayed Tate for one reason two years ago.

"What...what are you doing here?" Reggie asked as he crossed his arms and tucked his jittering hands under his armpits.

"We're looking for Buck."

"Buck?" Reggie whispered, his eyes once again darting around as if expecting Buck to magically appear. "I...I haven't seen him."

"Not even when you need your next fix?" I asked coldly.

Reggie's gaze shifted to me and then to the older man sitting in the cubicle. "I, um...I don't know what you're talking about."

"Reggie," Tate said crisply. "Buck and Denny, where are they?"

"I swear, Chris, I don't know."

"That's not his fucking name," I snarled as I brushed past Tate and snagged Reggie by his shirt collar and yanked him forward.

"Hawke," I heard Tate say calmly from behind me and then his hand was smoothing over my back. I stifled the half dozen names I wanted to call the piece of shit in front of me and released him. I stepped back just enough so Tate could make eye contact with the fucker, but that was it.

"Ch..." Reggie started to say to Tate and then bit off his words when his wide eyes darted to me. "I swear, I don't know where they are," he said and when I shifted my stance, he quickly continued. "No one's seen them since their lab exploded a while back. Most people think it was their bodies the cops found."

"But not you," Tate ventured.

Reggie shook his head. "I knew a couple guys who used to help Buck cook his stuff...I haven't seen them since it blew."

"Where would they have gone, Reggie?" Tate asked.

Reggie began to get more agitated as he kept checking the entrance for signs of anyone. His voice dropped to a low whisper when he said, "There's a rumor that Buck partnered with this dealer near the border. Laredo, I think." Reggie dropped his hands to the counter and leaned forward. "Chris," he began, too caught up in what he was saying to remember my warning about the name. "The guy's bad news. He's got a whole operation going on down there. Meth, heroin, coke."

"What's his name?" I asked.

Reggie looked at me and shook his head violently. I grabbed him again. "What the fuck is his name?"

"Davos," Reggie spit out. "Ricardo Davos."

Reggie tried to tug free of my hold, but I dragged him closer and said, "I'd like nothing more than to rip your nuts from your body and feed them to you, you little prick."

"Hawke," Tate said softly and I glanced up to see him shaking his head slightly. I looked over my shoulder to see the guy in the cubicle was watching us now, but surprisingly, he wasn't reaching for his phone or reacting in any kind of way.

I turned my attention back to Reggie and said, "Did you transfer the money two years ago?"

Reggie paled and then shot Tate a look before shaking head. "I... Buck told me not to. He wanted Chris to come back for it."

I shoved Reggie away from me and he stumbled, grabbing on to the counter to keep from falling. "Get it now!" I snapped.

"Um...Chris needs to fill out a withdrawal slip," Reggie began, but when I reached for him again, he stepped back and said, "Okay, okay" and began tapping on his keyboard. He kept shifting his eyes to Tate as he worked.

"I didn't have a choice," Reggie mumbled. "He said he'd kill me if I didn't tell him if you tried to get the money."

"And how the fuck did he know Chris had an account here?" I snarled, hating the way the name sounded coming from my lips, but not willing to share Tate's new name with Reggie.

Reggie's sallow skin flushed with color and I fought the urge to slam my fist into his face. He fumbled with the money he pulled from a drawer and started counting. It took several minutes for him to shove it in an envelope and slide it across the counter towards Tate.

"I'm sorry," Reggie whispered when Tate closed his hand over the envelope. But the second Reggie tried to touch Tate's hand, I grabbed his bony fingers and crushed them between my own. Reggie cried out in pain, but I stopped just short of actually breaking any bones.

"What are you sorry for, you little fuck? Selling him out for a lousy score two years ago or knowing you'd do it again in a heartbeat if you could?" I snapped. "Let's go," I said to Tate as I slammed Reggie's hand down on the counter and put my own on Tate's arm to steer him towards the door.

I was pleased when Tate didn't glance over his shoulder at Reggie, but as soon as we got outside, Tate froze and I realized why a second later when I saw a police officer walking slowly towards us. I guessed the man to be in his late fifties. His brown sheriff's uniform was tight across his heavyset frame and he was wearing a white cowboy hat. He was resting one hand on his holstered gun and the other hand was holding what looked like a check.

"Christopher Buckley," the Sheriff murmured as he came to a stop in front of us, his dark eyes looking Tate over quickly before settling on me. I didn't miss the way his fingers reflexively closed around his gun and I was innately pleased to know he instinctively knew I was a potential threat. Even with my gun stashed under the front seat of my truck, I could still take this man down in seconds. And I would have enjoyed doing it considering what he'd done to Tate years ago.

"What brings you back to town?" the sheriff asked, his eyes remaining on me.

"That an official business question?" I asked before Tate could answer.

The sheriff didn't respond, but I could see the tension in his jaw as he chewed whatever he had in his mouth. Chewing tobacco as far as I could tell from the smell.

"Chris, aren't you going to introduce me to your friend?" the guy asked smoothly as his eyes finally shifted to Tate who'd gone very quiet. We were standing close enough that I could feel a slight tremor in his body. I reached down to curl my fingers around his hand and gave him a gentle squeeze. He clamped down on my hand with a brutally tight hold and his palm was cold and clammy against mine.

"You can call me Hawke," I said coolly, not bothering to offer my hand. "Chris's boyfriend."

The sheriff actually took a step back, the repulsion in his eyes clear as day. "And you are?" I asked.

The man finally seemed to remember he'd been trying to intimidate us and he puffed out his chest. "Sheriff Graham Holden."

"Well, Sheriff Holden, to answer your question, Chris and I stopped by to get something he left behind when he got out of this piece of shit town of yours two years ago," I drawled.

The sheriff's jaw hardened and his gaze went back to Tate. "Seems I remember him leaving with something that wasn't his. His father was real sorry to see it and Chris go."

Tate tightened his hand on mine even more and I gently eased him forward past the sheriff. "Well, if you happen to see his father anytime soon, you tell him I'm going to stop by and see him real soon."

The sheriff's eyes widened for a moment and then held mine for several long seconds before he turned to enter the bank. I could tell Tate was barely holding it together so I quickly pulled him past the sheriff's patrol car and got him settled into my truck. The second I got behind the wheel, I reached for his hand and gently tugged him towards me until I could snag my other hand around the back of his neck.

"Tate, look at me," I said gently.

Tate was struggling to control his breathing and he shook his head. But a second later, he drew in a deep breath and opened his eyes. "I'm sorry," he whispered.

"For what?" I asked as I gently began massaging his skin with my fingers. The move seemed to help him relax somewhat.

"I wasn't prepared," he said. "I was for Reggie, but not him."

I knew he was talking about the sheriff. I leaned in and brushed my lips over his. "You did great," I said.

Tate shook his head. "I froze," he said. "I saw him and I was that scared sixteen-year-old kid again."

"You were fucking amazing," I said and then I dragged him to me and kissed him hard. Tate let out a rush of air as soon as I released his mouth, and then he was seeking me out for another kiss. I gave it to him and then gently pulled away from him. "Let's get going."

Tate leaned back in his seat and searched out his seat belt. "Laredo's only a few hours away. We can get there before it gets dark."

"No," I said. "We're heading back to the motel."

"It's still early-" Tate began to say.

"We're done," I said as I started up the truck. I looked at Tate and quietly repeated, "We're done." I put the truck in gear and forced myself not to look at Tate again when I said, "It's time for you to go home."

CHAPTER 18

TATE

*H*awke's declaration should have excited me. Even though it had only been a few days since I'd left Matty, I ached to see him again, to feel his little body in my arms. But it wasn't what Hawke had said that was bothering me so much.

It was what he hadn't said.

"You're going after them, aren't you?" I whispered as I pressed my hand to my stomach to stem the physical pain I was feeling.

When Hawke didn't answer me, I closed my eyes and tried to hold back the tears that threatened to fall. Everything inside of me had turned numb when Reggie had said Buck and Denny had teamed up with a drug lord and I'd feared this exact moment. Because Hawke would never stop hunting the men who'd stolen his entire life from him. But when it had been just Buck and Denny, he'd stood a chance of walking away.

"Hawke-"

The truck lurched to a stop in front of the motel and Hawke was out of the truck before I could finish my sentence. I followed him into the motel room and watched in silence as he gathered our few belongings. When he tried to walk past me and out of the room, I stepped into his path. "Please don't do this," I said quietly, trying like hell to keep my voice from breaking.

I held Hawke's gaze as he studied me for a long time. Hope sparked to life in my belly when he reached out to cup my face, his big, warm hand settling just behind my ear. I held my breath as I waited for him to kiss me, but instead of pressing his lips to mine, he dropped them to my forehead and lingered there for a moment before pulling back and saying, "We should get going."

And I knew in that moment that nothing I said or did would change his mind.

It was hours later when I finally became aware of my surroundings after I'd turned my gaze out the truck's window and kept it there. I had no idea what city we were in, or even what state, and I found that I didn't care. I hadn't spoken to Hawke and he hadn't said a word to me. I hadn't called Matty either and I couldn't even muster the energy to do that now.

Hawke had selected an exit from the Interstate that was well populated with hotels, restaurants and gas stations. He'd parked the truck in a parking lot of a drug store and when I forced myself to look at him, he said, "Why don't you drop off your film for one-hour processing and I'll get us checked in," he said as he motioned to the hotel next door. "We can eat while we're waiting for the pictures."

I managed a nod, but didn't trust myself to speak. With the line at the photo department, it took about ten minutes to drop off my film and I was assured it would be ready within the hour. Hawke was waiting for me outside the drug store. "That place okay?" he asked as he pointed to a diner on the opposite side of the drug store.

"Yeah," I managed to say.

We ate in silence, though I couldn't force more than a few bites past my lips and I ignored the dessert Hawke ordered for me. By the time we were on our way back to the drug store to get my photos, I truly feared I would lose what little I'd eaten right there in the parking lot. I was still in a daze as I waited for the clerk to get my pictures for me when Hawke murmured in my ear that he'd be right back. The clerk was already ringing me up when Hawke returned and I became instantly alert when he plopped something down on the counter and said, "This too please" to the clerk.

The sight of the bottle of lube had me lifting my eyes to seek out Hawke's and I saw the hunger in them. Despite my inner turmoil, my whole body drew up tight with anticipation. I barely noticed Hawke pay for both my pictures and the lube because all I was aware of was the moment Hawke reached down to link his fingers with mine. It felt so right that my heart surged with joy even as my brain fought to accept that what was going to happen between us would be just more pretending.

Because Hawke didn't really want me. My body, yes...me, no. And as hard as that was to accept, I knew it wouldn't change anything. Hawke was going to end up breaking my heart, and I was going to let him.

I let Hawke lead me to the truck. He didn't release me as we neared it and when we reached the passenger side door, he nudged me up against it until my back was pressed against the cool metal. "I need to know if you still want this," he said. The only place he was actually touching me was where our fingers were still joined, but his husky voice was like a sensual caress all over my body. I nodded.

"Tell me what you want," he ordered softly.

"You," I said simply.

Tremors of need surged through my body as Hawke tugged me forward, but he merely opened the door for me and waited until I got into the truck before closing it again. The drive to the hotel took less than a minute and when Hawke opened the door and motioned for me to enter before him, the very first thing I noticed was the bed.

The one bed.

The door closed behind me, cloaking the room in semi-darkness since only the inner white, gauzy curtains were drawn. I didn't even get a chance to turn around to face Hawke before he was reaching out and grabbing my arm. In one move, he turned me around and pressed me face first against the door. His whole body pressed up against mine and I shuddered when he pressed his cheek against mine, the burn scars teasing my skin. His hands covered mine and lifted them until they were above my head.

"You made me promise, do you remember?" Hawke whispered, his lips skimming the edge of my mouth.

I nodded. As much as I wished he was talking about the promise I'd just asked of him to not go after Buck and Denny in Laredo, I knew he was referring to the promise from the night before. The one where I'd asked him to fuck me again.

Hawke pressed his erection against my ass as his fingers played with mine where they were pinned to the door.

"Do you want me to keep it?"

I nodded again, my cheek scraping over the peephole in the door.

"Say my name," Hawke suddenly whispered desperately. "Please, Tate," he added as he nuzzled the back of my neck.

I turned my head so my forehead was pressed against the door and ignored the searing pain in my chest as I said, "Michael."

Hawke's whole body relaxed against mine and then his mouth was pressing kisses against my neck and cheek and when I turned my head back to the side for more, he sealed his mouth over mine. I moaned as he began slowly rolling his hips against my ass. His kiss was just as languid as the motion of his lower body, but it was over too soon.

"Leave your hands there," Hawke ordered firmly as he released my fingers and dropped his hands to my waist. I sucked in a breath when he moved them between the door and my groin and began playing with my erection through my jeans. But the torture didn't last nearly long enough because he was opening my pants a second later and shoving both them and my underwear down. His moves were rough and demanding as he dragged my shoes and socks off and yanked my pants away so I was completely naked from the waist down. A shiver of fear and excitement tore through me as I wondered if I was in for another rough ride. But instead of splitting me open, I felt Hawke's hands only smooth over my ass for a few seconds before he sought out my erection again and began stroking it. His free hand moved down to fondle my balls and I nearly swallowed my tongue when he kicked my legs farther apart. Because I had somehow missed him opening his own pants and by widening my stance, he'd given himself more room to work and his cock speared through my crease as he began teasing me with long strokes.

I began surging into his hand as my need grew and I could feel my pre-cum dripping down my dick and smoothing out Hawke's drags on my ultra-sensitive skin. "Please, Michael," I groaned as my lust began spiraling out of control.

"Please what, baby?" Hawke ground out against my ear before gently nipping on the lobe.

"Fuck me," I said.

"You want me in that tight little hole of yours again?"

"Yes," I nearly shouted and I risked dropping my hands so I could reach behind me to grab Hawke's ass. He stilled briefly at my touch, but then he began increasing his glides between my ass cheeks. The proof of his need moistened my heated skin.

Lips sought out mine in a brutal kiss as Hawke released my cock and closed his fingers over my hips. And then he was pulling away from me.

"Michael-" I cried in protest, but the remainder of my words died a quick death when I heard a tearing sound and was jerked backwards a little bit. What remained of my shirt hung in remnants from my arms as Hawke's lips sought out my collarbone and his hands dragged up and down my back. He pressed me hard against the door again and held me there with one hand in the middle of my back as his other hand pressed between the globes of my ass. He teased my hole with the rough pad of his finger and I shoved my ass back as much as I could to get more. Excitement flooded my system when I heard the telltale sounds of a plastic bag and then a second later, the snick of a cap. But no lube was brushed over my entrance, no slick cock slipped between my cheeks.

"Do you ever play with yourself here?" I heard Hawke ask as he pressed against me again and flicked his finger over my hole. Anticipation had me twisting my hips in the hopes he would give me more of what I needed. But when he pulled his finger away, I let out a harsh groan.

"Do you?"

I nodded, but I realized the admission caused me no humiliation, just more excitement. My cock was leaking like a faucet now and I sought relief by rubbing against the smooth surface of the door. But Hawke's next words stopped me cold.

"Show me."

Lust exploded in my belly as I understood what Hawke wanted and I immediately shook my head even as my brain cried out for me to do whatever he wanted.

"Work that pretty hole for me, Tate," Hawke urged and then he was pulling one of my hands from the door and covering my fingers with lube. My shirt was still hanging loosely from my arms, hampering my movements, so Hawke dragged it off of me. I should have protested Hawke's demand, but in truth, I was beyond turned on and I only hesitated for a second before reaching my fingers behind myself to seek out my hole. I could feel Hawke's eyes on me as I began massaging myself and a second later, his big hands split me open so he could see what I was doing.

"Fuck," Hawke, murmured as I began pressing the tip of one finger inside myself. The sting and burn drove my need to a whole new level and I ruthlessly shoved my finger in as far as I could, crying out in pleasure at the immediate burn that flared through my ass. I began thrusting in and out of my body and I risked turning my head to watch Hawke watching me. The raw lust and fascination in his gaze was heady and I used the moment to torment him the way he'd been tormenting me. I pulled my finger completely free of my body so he could glimpse my opening before it reflexively closed, then I pushed back in. I did it over and over until I felt my muscles starting to loosen and the burn beginning to fade. I started to add a second finger, but before I could, Hawke's thick digit was pressing into me, joining the finger I had jammed up my ass.

"Shit," I bit out as Hawke began to follow my motion as I fingered myself. The burn had returned the moment he'd slipped inside of me, but it wasn't enough. "More," I demanded as I pulled my finger free and braced my hands on the door. Another one of Hawke's fingers joined the first and I didn't hesitate to bump my hips back so I could fuck myself on them.

"You are so fucking beautiful," Hawke snarled just before his mouth closed over mine. He fucked my mouth as ruthlessly as he fucked my body and I could feel my orgasm starting to build. But then he took it all away in one swift move and I found myself being spun around and slammed back against the door. I saw what he needed from me as soon as our eyes connected, and the second his name slipped from my lips, he yanked me forward for a demanding, no holds barred kiss. And then he was dragging me down to the floor and covering my body with his.

CHAPTER 19

HAWKE

I'd promised myself to be gentle with Tate, but watching him finger fuck himself had done me in. My entire body was burning with need and my only hope was that I could keep my lust in check so that I wouldn't hurt him when I entered him. The reminder of what I'd done to him two nights ago actually sobered me in a way that words couldn't and as I settled my weight on top of Tate as I kissed him, I calmed my mind and focused on his needs rather than my own.

Because this time I would make it perfect for him.

Just in case it was the last time.

I hadn't been a hundred percent sure Tate would give himself to me after we'd left the drug store considering how distant he'd been from the time we'd left Lulling. From the moment I'd heard Reggie say Buck and Denny had aligned themselves with another drug dealer, I'd known Tate's role in helping me find his father and brother had come to an end. Because while I was sure I could handle myself in any situation that came up in Laredo or wherever my journey would ultimately lead me, I wasn't as certain I could protect Tate. And that had sealed it for me. I would keep my promise to Tate that he was going home to his son, and I would spend however many hours we had left trying to get as much of him as I could.

With that thought in mind, I eased off on the demanding kiss and just pressed gentle kisses against Tate's lips until his harsh breathing eased and he began to seek out more of my mouth. I let him take control of the kiss and reveled in the feel of his tongue sliding against mine. His arms came up to wrap around me, but the lack of contact between his skin and mine was a reminder that I was still wearing my shirt. I lifted just enough to pull it off, but Tate followed me up and wrapped his arm around my waist as he continued kissing me. I was on my knees between his spread legs and had a choice of trying to maintain the awkward angle or lowering Tate back to the floor. But as he pressed closer to me, I made up my mind and sat back on my heels, pulling Tate along with me so that he was straddling my lap. He took complete advantage of the new position and held my face as he kissed me with everything he had. His palms were pressed against my sides and I shivered as one hand stroked over my scarred flesh while the other hand settled on my left pectoral muscle...right over the spot where Revay's words were tattooed on my skin.

"You're so beautiful, Hawke," Tate whispered as he drew back from me a little bit. "So strong." His eyes held mine and he shook his head just a little bit. "I ache for you," he added and I could tell just by the open yearning in his gaze that he didn't mean just physically.

I waited for the expected shame to flood through me as I realized I knew exactly what he was feeling, but it wasn't there. I didn't know what to make of that and I didn't have time to consider it because Tate's hand drifted down to grip my cock and I groaned. I stole into Tate's mouth as he began stroking me and my promise to go slow disintegrated when he lowered his hand enough so that he could rub the pad of his finger over the sensitive skin behind my balls. I lowered Tate back to the floor and searched out the discarded bottle of lube at the same time that I kicked off my shoes and socks and shed my pants and underwear. By the time I managed to get some lube on my shaky fingers so I could slather it over my cock, Tate had lifted and separated his legs so that I had an unfettered view of his quivering hole. I scooted forward and added some more lube to the opening and then placed the head of my dick against it. Excitement flooded my entire system as I lifted my eyes to see Tate's hungry gaze on me.

He wanted this...me. No, he needed it. Just like I did.

I pressed forward slowly and dropped my eyes so I could watch Tate's body open to accept me. It wasn't until my leaking crown sank inside of him that Tate made a sound and when I looked up, I saw he had his eyes closed and his head thrown back.

"Tate-"

Tate shook his head before I could even continue and then his beautiful, bright, mismatched eyes opened and settled on me. "It feels so good, Michael," he breathed. "So good."

I nodded in understanding at the unfettered emotion in both his voice and gaze and I pressed forward a little more before pulling back and pushing in again. Tate gasped in pleasure and he released one of his legs long enough to reach his fingers down to cover my hand where it was pressed against the spot where his hip met his groin. I kept up the gentle rocking motion until I was completely seated inside of him and then I leaned forward to kiss him. I maneuvered my arms so that his legs were draped over them and the moment his hands were free, he grabbed the back of my head so I couldn't escape his kiss. Not that I wanted to...not even for a second.

Tate's body was gripping me so tight that I was sure I could come without even moving, but even if I'd wanted to stay like that forever, my body had other ideas. I pulled out of him and surged forward, capturing his moan as I did so. I repeated the move until I was sliding through his insanely tight heat with little resistance. Tate was still kissing me, but as his inner muscles began to tighten even more around me, he pulled his head back and looked down our bodies to where we were joined. His eyes were bright with excitement, his full, glistening lips open as he sucked in drags of air.

"Oh God," he cried out as I began thrusting into him harder. "Yes, right there!" he shouted and dropped his head and grabbed at my arms with his hands. It took me a moment to realize that a subtle shift of my hips was causing me to nail his prostate every time I surged into him. I slowed down dramatically and when Tate's eyes flew open, I jammed my hips forward. He shouted in pleasure. I did it over and over again until he was whimpering with need and his hands were closing over my ass in a desperate attempt to force me to give him what he needed. But instead of slamming into him again, I stopped all together.

"Michael, please," he said as the air seesawed in and out of him.

But I didn't move or speak. I just looked at him, trying to take in as much of him as I could in that moment. Because there'd only been one other person who'd looked so utterly perfect to me...who'd been all I'd ever needed or wanted.

Until now.

Until Tate.

I moved my arms, releasing Tate's legs, and he instantly wrapped them around my back. At some point he'd quieted beneath me, but none of the need had gone away. And I suspected he knew I was going through something more...something bigger than just finding my pleasure in his body or giving him his.

I dropped down to kiss him and reached for his arms. He understood right away what I wanted and dropped his hands from my shoulders where they'd been resting and linked his fingers with mine. I settled our joined hands on either side of his head, kissed him once more, and then began moving. But where I was frantic before, I was almost reluctant now. Because I didn't want it to be over.

I rolled my hips and flexed my ass as I powered into him and every time I pulled back, Tate clamped down on me with his inner muscles. The give and take continued as I surged into him over and over, painfully slow. My orgasm built with every thrust and drag, but it was both slow and strong and soon became almost unbearable. And Tate was my perfect counter because he matched everything I did, rolling his hips at the right exact time to suck me inside of him or to let me slide out. I had no doubt whatsoever that his orgasm was consuming him the same way mine was. As my balls began to draw up tight against my body and electricity fired up and down my spine, I began slamming into Tate harder. His body kept shifting along the carpet despite his legs being wrapped around me, so I released one of his hands and clamped it down on his shoulder. I felt his free hand snake between our bodies so he could jerk himself off and the feel of the backs of his fingers pressed against my groin only drove me higher.

"Harder," Tate ordered suddenly, his voice harsh in the quiet room. I pounded into him and kept angling my hips until I saw his mouth open wide on an empty scream. His free hand came up to wrap around my arm that was still pressed against his shoulder and he began calling my name every time I hit his gland. A few more strokes and he shouted in relief as his orgasm slammed into him. I managed to stave off my own release so I could watch him come and it was only when his fingers loosened on my arm just a little bit that I let go myself. I dropped my lips to Tate's neck and let out a muffled curse as my climax rocked through me. The brutal orgasm was so intense that my vision actually dimmed and I was sure my heart was going to pound right out of my chest. Tate moaned as my hot cum filled him and the feel of it bathing my own dick as I continued to saw in and out of him instantly triggered a powerful aftershock. The pleasure seemed endless and I couldn't have even begun to guess how long it went on for. It wasn't until I felt fingers threading through my hair that I even started to become aware of my surroundings.

Tate's warm body continued to cradle mine and he was pressing soft kisses against my temple as he held me to him. I didn't have enough strength to even lift my head to seek out his mouth, but I did manage to roll us enough so that Tate was lying on top of me. We'd managed to stay connected during the change in position and I groaned when Tate twisted his hips and then lifted just a little bit before sliding back down on me. I lifted my hands to close over his ass to help him bring us both gently down and opened my mouth when he sought entry.

"You okay?" Tate asked after several minutes passed and his body finally stilled on top of mine.

I nodded. "You?"

Tate smiled against my mouth. "That was..." He shook his head, unable to continue.

"I know," I said with a laugh. I had enough strength to get us both to a sitting position and the move finally forced my softening cock from his body. Tate wrapped his legs around me and pressed gentle kisses against my neck and collar bone, before finally resting his chin on my shoulder.

"I wish we could stay like this forever," he whispered.

Me too.

But I didn't say that. Because I couldn't.

Even if it was the truth.

CHAPTER 20

TATE

"Will you tell me about her?"

Hawke stiffened beneath me and his fingers stopped playing with mine. After our encounter on the floor, we'd showered together, gently washing each other's exhausted bodies. There'd been no more sexual activity, but that hadn't meant there'd been any less emotion. Afterwards, we'd dried each other off and crawled into bed. I'd automatically scooted over to the far side of the bed, closer to the wall, but within seconds of Hawke settling under the covers, he'd wrapped his arm around my waist and dragged me against him. I'd ended up resting my head on his chest and had started rubbing my fingers over his where they were pressed against his chest. He'd lifted our joined hands so we could watch our fingers play with each other, and that was when I'd focused on his wedding band.

I expected Hawke to say no and drop his hand, but instead, he began linking and unlinking our fingers. "What do you want to know?"

"What was she like?"

"Stubborn," Hawke finally said. "She never gave up on anything. But she was also really soft-hearted. That made it hard for her sometimes."

"How so?"

"It was like she took other people's pain into herself. She suffered along with them. She was also really outgoing and funny and she always latched on to people who she sensed needed just a little bit of extra attention. And she never stopped giving to other people...time, money, whatever it was they needed. But boy did she have a temper on her and if you threatened to hurt someone she loved..." Hawke said with a light chuckle.

I released Hawke's hand and turned over so I could face him. The hand that had been playing with mine immediately settled in my hair. I let my own fingers roam over his tattoo. "How did you know she was the one?"

Hawke shook his head slightly. "I'm not sure...it was just always there. I mean, when we were kids, we were best friends, but as we got older, I never had any interest in anyone else and neither did she."

"So you were never attracted to another woman?"

"I noticed them, but that was as far as it went. No one even came close to making me feel the way she did."

"What about men?" I asked cautiously.

"Do you mean was I attracted to them?"

I nodded.

Hawke was thoughtful for a moment. "I suppose I noticed if a guy was good looking or not, but no, I wasn't attracted to them."

"Does it bother you?"

"What?"

"Being with me?" I asked quietly, dropping my eyes. "I mean, you're not gay and it sounds like you aren't even bi."

I felt Hawke's fingers leave my head and lift my chin so that I was once again looking at him. "I'm not big on labels," he said. "People have been labeling me my whole life and it didn't mean shit." Hawke's finger traced over my lower lip. "You're beautiful, Tate...but that isn't what has me wanting more of you."

I felt my stomach drop out at Hawke's words.

"You're kind, even though all you've known is cruelty. You're strong despite all the times people have tried to break you. You gave up everything for that little boy from the second you saved him and you've been the father he needs and deserves despite not having had that yourself. I'm in awe of you, Tate Travers."

I swallowed hard around the knot of emotion in my throat and shook my head because I couldn't come up with even one single thing to say to that. I'd thought it had only been about physical attraction for Hawke, but to know he saw more than that...

Hawke's hand returned to my hair and we both fell silent for a while. But I couldn't miss out on the opportunity to know more about him so I said, "You said the house behind yours was your uncle's."

Hawke nodded. "It was mine too growing up."

"You lived with him?"

"Yeah, my mom and I moved in with him when I was eight. She died a few months later."

"What happened to her?"

"She had a brain tumor...inoperable."

I shook my head. "Hawke..."

"It's okay," Hawke murmured. "It was a long time ago."

"What about your father?"

"Never knew him. He worked on oil rigs and was killed in an explosion shortly after I was born. My mom and I moved from Louisiana to Wyoming when she found out she was sick."

I remembered Hawke's story about his first day of school. "It was bad, wasn't it?" I whispered. "Living with your uncle."

Hawke's fingers stilled in my hair. He finally nodded.

"Will you tell me?" I asked.

His eyes held mine for a moment and then shifted away. I could see the pain in them so I quickly said, "You don't-" but Hawke cut me off by placing a finger over my lips.

"After my mom died, he made sure to remind me on a daily basis that he didn't want me."

"He hurt you," I whispered.

Hawke nodded. "He drank a lot so after he smacked me around, I'd wait till he passed out and then I would crawl out of my window and walk through the woods to Revay's house. She always left her window unlocked and I'd get into bed with her...we were still kids back then so it wasn't more than her comforting me while I cried. After a while, I started going to her house every night. On the days where my uncle beat me so bad I could barely walk, she'd come to me." Hawke let out a pain filled laugh. "It was years before her parents found out. They were pissed and tried all sorts of things to stop her from sneaking out. But like I said, she was stubborn."

Hawke's next laugh was lighter and a small smile drifted across his mouth. "They finally gave up and set up a room for me and stuck a ladder outside the window so I wouldn't have to climb the big oak tree outside Revay's window. By the time I was fourteen, I was practically living with them full time."

"What happened to your uncle?"

"He got drunk one night and wrapped his car around a tree. I'd just turned eighteen so I didn't have to go into foster care or anything. Revay and I graduated a few weeks later and got married. We moved to Fort Benning in Georgia and she went to college to get a degree in music while I was going through basic training."

"What happened after you lost her?" I asked. "You'd left the army, right?"

"I re-enlisted about a year later. I...I couldn't sit around knowing the men who'd done that to her were walking around free. I left the army again about six years ago."

I nodded in understanding. I was about to ask another question when my phone rang. I sat up, but Hawke beat me to it and climbed out of bed. "I got it," he said and he grabbed my phone from my pants which were still laying in a discarded heap on the floor next to my torn shirt. I smiled at the memory and when Hawke came over to the bed to hand me the phone, there was a little smirk on his face that told me he was remembering the exact same thing as me. He leaned down to kiss me before handing me the phone.

I saw that the caller was Ronan and felt the automatic pang of fear go through me that I always did when he called. I'd talked to Matty earlier in the day and he'd been fine, but I couldn't get past my fear that one day I was going to get the call that things were no longer fine.

"Hi," I said after hitting the answer button. "Is Matty okay?"

"Hey. He's doing good, Tate."

Relief went through me and I glanced at Hawke who was in the process of moving his bag to the bed, probably so he could get his tablet out so I could video chat with Matty.

"Tate, I just wanted to give you a heads up about something before you talk to Matty."

The relief I'd felt a moment ago disappeared instantly. "You said he was okay," I whispered. Hawke appeared at my side with his tablet.

"Put it on speaker," he said quietly.

My hand was shaking so Hawke took the phone from me and did it himself. "Hey Ronan, you're on speaker, okay?"

"Hey," Ronan responded. "Tate, honestly, Matty's okay. It's just that his hair started falling out over the past couple of days and we talked him into shaving it off this morning. I wanted you to know before you saw him so it wouldn't be so much of a surprise."

I felt tears sting the backs of my eyes at the brutal reminder of what my little boy was going through. "Okay," I managed to say.

"Give me a minute and I'll start the video chat."

"Ronan, call my tablet, okay?" Hawke said.

"Yeah."

Ronan disconnected and Hawke put my phone away. "Hey," he said as he settled his hand on my back and put his head against mine. "He's okay. He's strong, Tate. Just like his dad."

I sucked in some air and nodded shakily. I blinked rapidly in an effort to clear the tears from my eyes. Hawke's tablet began ringing a minute later and he held it in front of me and hit the answer button.

Matty was sitting cross legged on his hospital bed. I managed to keep my composure at the sight of his bald head, but inside I felt like I was dying. "Hey, buddy," I said, my voice cracking. Hawke's hand at my back had a soothing effect.

"Daddy, look," Matty said as he pointed to his head.

"Wow, you look great," I said with a big smile. "How are you doing?"

"Good," Matty responded. "Guess what? Ronan says I look like Professor…" – Matty looked off-screen and whispered something, then nodded – "Xavier," he said proudly, struggling with pronouncing the name. "He's an X-Man, Daddy! He can read minds. Want me to read yours?"

I managed a nod. "Yeah, sure."

Matty closed his eyes for several seconds and scrunched his face up. Then his eyes popped open and he said, "You miss me lots!"

I managed to stifle my laugh and opened my mouth wide as if in shock. "That is exactly right! How did you do that?"

"Magic powers, Daddy. Is Hawke there? I want to read his mind too."

Hawke moved the tablet so Matty could see him. "I'm here, Matty."

Matty gave him a small wave. "Look!" he said as he pointed to his head again.

"You look just like the Professor," Hawke said. "But no way will you be able to read my mind."

"I bet I can," Matty insisted.

"Okay, you can try," Hawke said with a shake of his head, his doubt clear.

Matty once again got lost in thought, then opened his eyes and announced, "You miss me, too and you and Daddy are going to come see me soon."

My heart hurt as I watched the fleeting pain in Hawke's gaze as he looked at Matty. And I knew in that moment he was thinking about his own son. But he managed a smile and said, "Wow, you got it exactly right."

Matty nodded knowingly and Hawke shifted the tablet so Matty could see us both. "Daddy, guess what?"

"What?"

"Ronan and Seth knew how sad I was when they said I wasn't gonna have any hair for a while, so look."

The image teetered for a moment and when it came back into

focus, I slapped my hand over my mouth in disbelief. Because there on the bed next to my son sat Ronan and Seth, their heads completely bald.

"Hi!" Seth said with a wave.

"Isn't it cool, Daddy?" Matty said as he put one hand on Ronan's shaved head and the other on Seth's. The men looked so different, but I barely noticed that. All I noticed were their big smiles as they proudly showed off their new look.

"It's really cool," I managed to get out. Tears were flooding my eyes and I was helpless to hold them back. When Hawke used his arm to pull me against his chest, I gladly went. I knew my son and Ronan and Seth could see me, but I was too busy trying to hold it together.

"Daddy?"

"He's okay, Matty. He's just missing you," Hawke said quietly.

"Daddy," Matty called to me, his voice low and sweet.

"Yeah, buddy," I said as I pulled back from Hawke's chest and wiped at my eyes.

"Love you lots."

I let out a watery laugh. "Forever and ever," I finished.

"Hey, Matty's nurse is here to check his central line. We'll talk to you guys later, okay?" Ronan said.

I nodded. "Thanks, Ronan," I whispered as my eyes connected with the other man's. I hoped he heard what I couldn't put into words and when he nodded a moment later, I knew he had.

"Bye, Daddy!"

"Bye, Matty. I'll be home soon, okay. Love you."

"I love you too. Bye, Hawke."

"Bye, Matty," Hawke said quietly.

The screen went dark a second later and I instantly lost it and began crying. Hawke gathered me in his arms and lay down on the bed, taking me with him. I curled against his side and sobbed as he held me tight. It was several minutes before I quieted enough to say, "Thank you, Michael."

Hawke's arms tightened around me even more when I said his name.

"For what?" he asked.

"For everything," I said simply.

Hawke was silent for a moment and then he was rolling me onto my back as he hovered above me. His hand came up to cup my face. "I wish I could give you more, Tate. I wish I could be everything you needed."

And then he sealed his mouth over mine.

CHAPTER 21

HAWKE

"*H*ere."

I put down the towel I'd been using to dry my hair and took the picture Tate handed me.

After kissing Tate last night, I'd pulled him back into my arms and held him until we'd fallen asleep. I'd woken up with him in almost the same exact position and had lain there for nearly an hour before I'd forced myself to release him and get out of bed. For the first time since we'd left my house three days ago, I wasn't eager to start the day. Because by the end of it, Tate would be on his way home and I'd be alone again.

I looked at the picture and stilled when I saw the two men kneeling on the ground, rifles in hand as they held up the head of a dead deer with huge antlers. Both men were dressed in camouflage outfits, but it was their faces that I focused on. "Buck and Denny?" I asked.

Tate nodded. "I was just looking through the photos I had developed yesterday. They made me take this picture a couple of months before I left. I'd forgotten all about it."

I glanced up at Tate and shook my head in disbelief. He'd made it clear that he didn't want me going after Buck and Denny in Laredo, but he'd still given me the one thing I really needed to help me find them. "Thank you," I said.

Tate nodded and I could see that he wanted to say more, but he didn't. Instead, he turned and left the bathroom and I turned my attention back to the picture. Pain slashed through my belly as I took in the faces of the men who'd brutalized my wife and murdered her and my son. Buck looked nothing like what I'd imagined in my head. He was remarkably clean cut and good looking for his fifty odd years. He was a large man, but clearly took care of himself. But his eyes were cold and empty and my gaze fell to his big hands. Hands that had rained down on Tate's body over and over again. Hands that had held my wife down...

I shook myself loose from my thoughts and focused on Denny. He looked nothing like Tate as I would have expected. His grimy blond hair was long and stringy and his pockmarked skin was drawn tight over the sharp bones of his face. Like Reggie, the years of drug addiction had taken their toll on Denny and he almost looked as old as his father. And like his father, there was nothing in his dull eyes.

I put the picture down on the counter and lifted my eyes to look at myself in the mirror. My gaze fell to Revay's words and I let my finger trail over each sentence as I read them to myself. But it wasn't her voice I heard in my head. Not Tate's either. It was my own. And it wasn't Revay I was thinking of when I finally reached the last word.

～

"*Y*eah, thanks Daisy. Let me know what you find."

I hung up the phone and reached for my bag when I noticed Tate standing near the entrance to the bathroom. I hadn't heard him come out as I'd been speaking to Daisy about seeing what she could find on Ricardo Davos. But I could tell from Tate's worried look that he'd heard me talking to her.

"Does she work for you?"

"Who? Daisy?" I asked, focusing my attention on getting my bag repacked. My fingers hit on the picture of Revay and I realized it had gotten buried near the bottom of the bag.

Because I hadn't looked at it even once since the night I'd begged Tate to say my real name for the first time.

"Yeah."

"No, she works for Ronan."

"Do you work for him, too?"

I knew we were treading on dangerous ground so I said, "We should get on the road so you'll be able to drive over the pass tonight before it gets too dark."

The idea of watching Tate drive off caused a pain so sharp in my chest that I actually had to stop what I was doing so I could try to catch my breath. I heard Tate moving around behind me, but I didn't turn around as I grabbed my bag and left the room. I tossed my bag in the backseat of the truck and got it started. Tate appeared a moment later and climbed in beside me.

"You hungry?" I asked.

Tate didn't look at me. He just shook his head. I drove the truck across the street to a fast food place and ordered him a breakfast sandwich anyway, along with some coffee, but neither of us touched our food. Lunch was a repeat of breakfast, but when I told Tate he should try to eat something, he sent me a pained glance before turning his attention back out the window.

We were making good time until we hit rush hour traffic in Denver and then a major traffic jam on one of the mountain passes that added several hours to our trip. The sun had just started to set behind the mountains when we finally pulled in front of my garage. Tate was out of the car the second it rolled to a stop. I got out and went around the truck to watch him pull his bag from the backseat. He began rifling through it for a moment and then pulled the car keys for his rental out of one of the inner pockets. I'd parked his rental car next to the garage so I had no trouble seeing him as he went to the car, opened the trunk and tossed his bag in. My chest felt like it was going to explode as he walked around it to the driver's side and I realized he was actually going to leave without speaking to me. It took everything in me not to move forward and stop him. To demand he say something...anything that said these last three days had meant something to him...that they'd changed him the way they'd changed me.

But I couldn't ask that of him. Because even though being with Tate had changed me, it hadn't changed what I needed to do. It hadn't changed the fact that I couldn't let go of the one thing that I would need to in order to be with him the way I wanted.

Tate reached the door, but didn't open it. He just stood there staring at the handle like he didn't know what it was for. He finally looked up at me and even from where I stood, I could see the agony in his eyes. I moved a few steps forward without even thinking about it, but stopped myself when I was still several feet away.

Because if I touched him...

"She wouldn't have wanted this for you," Tate said so softly, I barely heard him.

But I *did* hear him. And I knew who *she* was. I couldn't help the flash of anger that went through me. "You have no idea what she would have wanted. You didn't know her."

Tate shook his head and dropped his eyes again. "Don't you get it, Hawke?"

I flinched at the use of my nickname...it sounded wrong coming from his lips after all the times he'd called me by my real name.

"Get what?" I asked.

"I know her because I am her." The strange statement made no sense to me, but I held my tongue as Tate turned to face me.

"I love you," he finally said and I felt my heart drop out of my chest. "I love you like she loved you. With everything I am. And that's how I know she wouldn't have wanted this life for you."

My mouth felt dry at the same time that heat flashed through my entire body. Tate loved me? I was so overcome that I almost didn't notice Tate shaking his head as he reached for the handle. I was on him in two strides and I slammed the door shut before he could open it all the way.

"No," I snapped angrily. "You don't get to say that to me and then just walk away!"

I pushed away from Tate and took several steps back as I tried to get control of my emotions. A maelstrom of them were going through me all at once. Joy, dread, confusion, fear.

Bone-wrenching fear.

Because I absolutely and completely believed Tate. And because it changed nothing. Except that I was going to end up hurting him again.

"It doesn't change anything, does it?" Tate asked quietly, eerily voicing my own thoughts.

"No," I finally managed to say.

"You could have something different, Hawke. With me...with Matty," Tate whispered desperately.

I felt like I was having a panic attack as the pain in my chest increased. Why the hell hadn't I just let Tate go after he'd made his admission?

"I can't just let her go, Tate," I said with a shake of my head. "What if every time I looked at you, all I saw was her? What if I only see the child I should have had when Matty's talking to me about something? He deserves better than that. You both do."

"We do," Tate agreed. "Goodbye, Hawke. Just...just stay safe, okay?" Tate said, his voice breaking as he turned back to the door.

I shook my head in disbelief at what was happening. And I knew in that moment that I wasn't ready.

I wasn't ready to tell him that I did love him. I wasn't ready to tell him how much I wished there was a place in my life for him and his son. But more than anything, I wasn't ready to let him go.

I closed the distance between us and used my body to press Tate's front against the car door. "Don't," I whispered in his ear as I wrapped my arm around his chest and dragged him back against me.

Tate was shaking in my hold as his hands came up to grab my forearm where I was holding him, but he didn't try to push me away.

"One more night, Tate," I begged, wrapping my other arm around his waist. He stiffened against me and I knew it was because I hadn't told him what he needed to hear. What I was asking was cruel, but I couldn't will myself to watch him walk away. I couldn't bear the idea of not feeling his body beneath mine one more time. I couldn't not taste him again.

The last time I'd begged for anything was the night I'd been in that ER watching Ronan work on my wife. And my desperation was just as clawing now as it had been then. "Please, Tate."

Tate let out a harsh sob and then he nodded and turned his head and searched out my lips. My whole body went weak with relief as Tate twisted in my arms until he was facing me and crushed our mouths together. And then his arms went around my neck and he buried his face against the crook of my shoulder. "I love you so much. So much, Michael."

I wanted so badly to say the words back.

But I couldn't.

I just fucking couldn't.

So I did my best to show him.

CHAPTER 22

TATE

*T*he only thing Hawke grabbed besides my hand after I'd whispered my admission for the second time was his bag from his truck. He released me long enough to unlock the front door and I barely managed to close the door behind me before he dragged me up the stairs. The second we were in his room, his mouth sought out mine and the last of my tears dried up as he made love to my mouth. As heartbroken as I was that he would never love me back, I needed Hawke more than I needed my pride. I'd pick up the pieces tomorrow. Tonight I would take enough of him to see me through the times in my life when I needed to pretend again.

I lifted my arms as Hawke tugged my shirt off and then I was reaching for his. Our mouths barely parted as we undressed one another and the second I was naked, Hawke maneuvered me to the bed and turned on the small lamp on the nightstand. But instead of laying me on my back, he urged me to lie down on my front and then he was hovering over me, his warm body blanketing mine. He kissed me for a long time before lifting up just enough so that he could kiss the back of my neck. As impatient as my body was for more, I loved every second of what he was doing to me. It was like he was worshiping me as he placed unhurried, gentle kisses all along my shoulders, collarbone and neck. And then his lips were trailing down my spine and I felt the goosebumps rise on my flesh as he grazed his nails over my back as he worked his way lower. I expected him to stop once he reached the globes of my ass, but he didn't. He just kept kissing me and didn't stop until he'd reached my feet. As turned on as I was, my body also felt boneless and I didn't protest when his hand closed over my hips and dragged me backwards until my ass was hanging off the bed, my feet flat on the floor.

Hawke split me open, but there was no lube pressed against my entrance, no finger seeking entry. Just cool air. I glanced over my shoulder at him and saw that he was staring at where he was holding me open. I looked at him questioningly and then held my breath when he licked his lips and suddenly dropped to his knees behind me.

There was no way he was going to...

But that was exactly what he did. I gasped when I felt his tongue tentatively flick over my hole. I'd never had anyone do this to me before and I had no idea what to expect. I'd never even been sure it was something I wanted because the idea of someone like Reggie rimming me had been a huge turn-off. And I definitely wouldn't have thought someone who was just starting to explore another side of his sexuality would do anything so intimate.

But after the first soft caress, another one followed, then another. And it wasn't just the tip of Hawke's tongue that was exploring me. His whole tongue, lips, teeth, they all worked together to put me in an agonizingly blissful haze of sensual pleasure. I felt fingers drifting over my cock and balls and then Hawke fisted my shaft as he continued to play with my hole. I gripped the bedding in between my fingers as the coil of need inside of me started to grow. And then I felt it...Hawke's tongue probing my hole more forcefully. Before I could even consider what was happening, I felt it push into me and I cried out at the sensation. Hands clamped down on my hips to hold me still, but that didn't stop me from trying to push back farther on the tongue that was thrusting in and out of me.

"Fuck, yes," I growled as Hawke's tongue licked my insides. "More," I ordered. But instead of continuing, Hawke pulled his tongue free and closed his lips over my hole and sucked gently. I began desperately rubbing my hips against the side of the bed in order to give my dick the friction it so badly needed, but Hawke took that away from me too by taking my leaking cock in his hand once again. He started dragging his thumb up and down the shaft as his mouth moved from my hole down to my balls and then licked along my cock before reversing direction.

"Michael, please," I whispered as the need inside of me became unbearable.

"Tell me what you want, baby," Hawke whispered against my skin, his soft breath stroking over my fluttering opening.

"I need to come," I begged shamelessly.

Hawke didn't answer me, but a second later his tongue was surging into me again and his hand began stroking me with hot, tight glides. And just like that I came. The buildup had been so slow and torturous, but the climax was the exact opposite because I was thrown over the edge with no warning at all. The orgasm was ruthless as it flashed through my body and seared every cell with pleasure. And through it all, Hawke kept fucking me with his tongue and fisting me with his hand. On the heels of the crushing ecstasy was the tingling that started in my core and spread out to all of my limbs.

I was struggling to catch my breath as the orgasm started to ease and I couldn't move when Hawke lay down on top of me, his front to my back and searched out my mouth. The second he kissed me, I knew exactly what the salty, bitter fluid was that transferred from his mouth to mine.

I was so sated that it was a struggle to kiss Hawke back, but I could tell he hadn't taken his own pleasure because his erection was nudging my ass. Hawke levered off of me and I felt his fingers massaging my hole. At the same time, I heard the distinctive sound of a cap being opened and I wasn't surprised when lube dripped onto my opening. It felt cold against my hot skin and I shivered as Hawke worked some inside of me. And then his slick cock was there and even in my exhausted state, I wanted it…him.

It took very little effort for Hawke's crown to push past my outer muscle since Hawke had done such a thorough job of relaxing it with his ministrations. He began fucking me with shallow thrusts that helped him work his way deeper into my body. My ass burned as it stretched to accommodate his thickness and once he bottomed out inside of me, he dropped down on my back and kissed my ear, my neck, my jaw.

"I need you so badly, Tate," he whispered.

"I'm yours, Michael. Always."

The kiss I got was desperate and needy and matched the frenetic pace Hawke set as he pounded into my body. I could feel my own cock responding as all the ridges of Hawke's cock massaged my inner walls. Hawke remained hunched over me and sought out my hands and linked our fingers together as he humped into me. His breath was hot against my neck and every grunt drove my own need to come higher and higher.

"Fuck," Hawke snarled as he began slamming into me urgently, signaling the end. He shifted his hips just the tiniest bit and hit my gland and I let out a hoarse shout. I couldn't move, couldn't think, couldn't do anything as Hawke controlled every aspect of my pleasure. I waited, I hoped and then I started begging Hawke to give me what I needed.

And then I was flying as I came again. Hawke shouted my name as he pummeled me with thrust after brutally deep thrust, and his weight held me to the bed as his release flooded my insides. My orgasm ratcheted even higher as I felt his dick slide through his juices before shoving into me hard one more time and holding there for several long seconds as more of his cum filled me. And then I heard it, barely a whisper.

"I love you, Tate."

And I wanted to cry.

Because I knew in my heart that it wasn't enough.

I wasn't enough.

CHAPTER 23

HAWKE

I hadn't meant to say the words. Not because I didn't mean them. Because I did. I'd known it the moment Tate had turned his back on me to get in that car.

To leave me.

No, I'd said them because as strong as my physical release had been, something deep inside of me had opened up at the same time and I'd felt whole again. But it had been fleeting – long enough for me to tell Tate the truth of what he meant to me, but not long enough to let go of the past or the promise I'd made.

Tate didn't respond to my declaration, but when I leaned in to kiss him, he kissed me back without hesitation. We stayed there like that until I knew my weight was too much for him and I carefully levered myself off of him and pulled free of his body. The sight of my release dripping from Tate's body set off something primal in me and I couldn't resist running my fingers through the sticky white fluid and spreading it into his skin. When I looked up, I saw that Tate was watching me over his shoulder with glassy eyes. I wrapped my hand around his arm and gently pulled him to his feet and he pushed into my arms and dragged me down for a kiss. I took his hand and led him to the bathroom.

The master bathroom was one of the only rooms that Revay's parents had gotten around to remodeling shortly before their deaths, so it sported a large walk in shower with a bench on one end. After I got the shower going, I changed the angle on the shower head to make sure the water would hit us the way I wanted it to and I led Tate to the bench and sat down. He didn't need any kind of urging to sit down on my lap and as we kissed, I searched out the soap and began washing him.

Both of us were hard by the time we were done cleaning each other. Tate took charge of our pleasure as he rubbed up against me, his erection brushing mine. At one point, he took us both in hand and began jerking us off at the same time, but without warning, he slipped from my lap and dropped to his knees between my legs. I watched in rapt fascination as he licked my length from base to tip and then teased my slit with the tip of his tongue. I wanted the sensual torture to both hurry up and slow down at the same time, but that was my last rational thought because Tate's mouth closed over my dick a second later. Blowjobs were something I'd gotten plenty of from Revay during our years together, but Tate's mouth felt entirely different. He seemed to know exactly how much pressure to exert, when to back off and when to barrel on so that I was always just riding the edge of my orgasm.

As Tate sucked me down to my base, I let out a hoarse shout and put my hands on his head to hold him still so I could fuck his mouth the way I wanted. I was close to coming when Tate released my cock and looked up at me.

"Scoot forward," he urged as his hands closed over my hips.

It took me a moment to realize why he wanted me to move. A niggle of uncertainty went through me as I understood what would happen next if I did as he asked. My relationship with Tate had progressed so quickly that I hadn't given much thought to having him touch me the same way I touched him. But one look at his patient eyes and I knew I wanted it. I wanted whatever he would give me. Because he wasn't doing it for him. He was doing it for me.

I shifted my hips forward until my ass was hanging off the bench.

The position put my upper body at an awkward angle, but that was all forgotten the second Tate put his finger in his mouth, got it nice and slick with spit, removed it, and then sucked my cock back into his mouth. I flinched when I felt his finger brushing over my hole, but I forced myself to remain still. Tate's mouth was still working me, but he'd eased up a little, probably so that I wouldn't be too distracted from what he was doing to my ass.

Tate's finger rubbed over my hole several times, the saliva making the motion smoother. At first I was struggling with the oddness of it all, but then I began to anticipate the little spark that shot through me every time the pad of his finger added just the slightest bit of pressure to my entrance. And when the finger disappeared, I actually started to protest until I saw Tate sucking his finger into his mouth to wet it again.

"Put your feet up on the bench," Tate urged. As soon as I did, I felt awkward and horribly exposed, but then Tate's finger was probing me again and he went back to work on my dick. And then Tate's long, thick finger pressed inside of me and I gasped at the sharp sting of pain that fired through my ass. Tate eased back a little, then pushed in again. He kept repeating the move over and over again, burying more of his finger inside of me each time. At some point the burning had eased and besides the odd feeling of being filled, a lovely sensation had started to build inside of me. Tate was still sucking me so between his mouth and his finger, I was trapped in a vortex of sensation.

Until he did something inside of me that rocketed through my entire body all at once. And I knew without having to ask that he'd hit my prostate. Tate did it again as he increased the suction on my dick and I soon found myself trying to impale my ass on his finger every time he slid it back into me. And if that wasn't enough, I looked down to where Tate's lips were wrapped around my cock and nearly came at the sight of him using his free hand to jack himself off. After that, I lost track of everything except the need to come.

"Tate!" I shouted as the pressure in my ass increased exponentially and I had no doubt Tate was now working two fingers in and out of my body. He rubbed over my gland a few more times as he hollowed out his cheeks and sucked hard and I was a goner. I shot load after load of cum in his mouth and even as hard as he worked to try and swallow it, some escaped his lips as he parted them when his own release hit him. As we both came down, Tate pulled his fingers from my body and I leaned down and yanked him up and sealed my mouth over his. The water had washed the cum on his mouth away, but I could still taste myself as I licked over his tongue and teeth. When I released his mouth, Tate wrapped his arms around me in a brutal hug and I just held him there like that.

Once my breathing had returned to normal, I took my time washing Tate and myself again and then dried him off and led him back to bed. He was asleep within minutes of me pulling him against my side, but I wasn't so lucky. I laid there for hours trying to process what I was feeling, but nothing made any sense to me and the lack of control was frustrating. And as the first filtered rays of sun seeped through the window, I gently rolled Tate onto his back and placed soft kisses on his mouth and face until he woke up. I made love to him again, slowly this time and I felt a rush of joy when he whispered that he loved me before falling asleep again. I got him cleaned up and stared at the clock next to the bed, willing it to slow down. But when Tate started to stir against me a couple of hours later, I closed my eyes and didn't open them again.

Not when he carefully eased himself from my hold.

Not when he got dressed.

Not when he leaned down to brush his lips over mine.

And not even when I heard the front door close and the sound of a muffled engine making its way down the driveway.

~

"I don't recall giving you permission to track my phone," I murmured as I heard the footsteps approaching from behind me. I was sitting on the dilapidated porch of my uncle's house staring at the overgrown yard, so my back was to Ronan as he came around the house and up the steps on the far end of the porch. The railing had long ago rotted and collapsed so I had an unfettered view of the woods and mountains beyond as I sat with my back against the wall of the house.

"And if it really bothered you, you would have turned the phone off or gotten a new one," Ronan said as he sat down next to me. I glanced at him and couldn't help the smile that flitted across my lips at the sight of the stubble covering his head. It had been nearly three weeks since Tate and I had video chatted with Matty after he'd gotten his head shaved and I suspected that Ronan had continued to shave his own head for some time afterwards because it was just now starting to grow back.

"What are you doing here?" I asked. A tremor of fear went through me as I quickly said, "Are Tate and Matty okay?"

"They're fine. Tate made it home with no problems and Matty's ANC count finally normalized a couple days ago. ANC stands for-"

"Absolute neutrophil count," I interrupted. "His white blood cell count had to get back to normal after the chemo killed all of them. That's why he had to stay in the Immunocompromised Services Unit at the hospital for so long after the chemo was finished. He was too susceptible to infections."

Ronan didn't respond so I glanced over at him. He was watching me with a mix of curiosity and pity and I turned back to focus on the horizon. There was no reason to explain that from the moment Matty had been admitted, I'd researched everything I could about his condition. Because Ronan would want to know why.

And I didn't have an answer for that.

Well, that wasn't quite true. I hadn't had an answer five weeks ago when I'd started researching the disease, but I had one now.

"He was released yesterday," Ronan said.

I nodded in understanding. Matty would only be out of the hospital for a week or so and then the whole process would start all over again. More chemo, more tests, more pain. My heart ached as I thought of all he and Tate would have to endure over the next six months. And a healthy outcome wasn't even a certainty.

"Why are you here, Ronan?" I asked tiredly.

"Why are you?"

When I glanced at him, he said, "I know you've been talking to Daisy. She found information that proves Ricardo Davos is in Laredo."

It shouldn't have surprised me that Ronan would know everything Daisy had told me. "Then you know that she didn't find any proof of Buck or Denny being part of Davos's crew," I said.

"Which is why I've spent the past three weeks monitoring your GPS so I would know when to send someone down there to back you up."

"What about whoever it is you have watching me?" I shot Ronan a glance and wasn't surprised to see not even an ounce of guilt. "Who is it?" I asked.

"Mav."

I nodded. Mav was a good guy to have your back. I hadn't been one hundred percent sure that I was being watched...it had been more of a feeling than anything else. But it hadn't surprised me that Ronan would take whatever steps necessary to make sure I was covered.

I'd planned to leave for Laredo the day after Tate had left, but I'd ended up putting off the trip until I'd gotten more information from Daisy. I'd gotten that information the very next day, but three weeks later and I still hadn't been able to bring myself to get in the truck and go.

And I had no idea why.

"Talk to me, Hawke," Ronan said quietly.

I sighed and shook my head. "I thought this place was so cool when my mom and I moved here," I mused as I scanned the property. "And then she was gone and I was left with him. I tried running away once – a few weeks after she died. I didn't even make it to the end of the driveway before he came after me. He locked me in a closet for three days."

I ran my hand along the back of my neck in agitation as I remembered that day. And then I remembered that I wasn't alone so I dropped it and forced my tense body to relax. "Then I met her and everything changed."

A dull pain settled in my chest as I remembered Revay's smile as she'd asked me if she could sit with me at the lunch table the same day we'd met for the first time. I turned to look at Ronan. "She was my best friend, Ronan. She was the only good thing in my life and I failed her."

"You didn't fail her, Hawke."

I blew out my breath as I realized I would never be able to make the man next to me understand.

"You think I should be able to just let her go," I finally said. "I should just move on."

"I didn't say that."

"If it were Seth, if you lost him, could you do it? Could you just let him go?"

Ronan shook his head. "No, never," he admitted. "But let me ask you this, Hawke. Did Tate ask you to let Revay go?"

I shot Ronan a glance. "What?"

"Did he ever ask you to choose?"

I thought back to my conversations with Tate and realized that he hadn't. All he'd ever done was ask about Revay...like he'd wanted to know more about her. I'd been the one who'd decided I needed to choose between them.

"What if I always see her when I look at him?" I asked. My voice shook as a terrible shame swept through me. "What if I'm with Tate and I start wishing it had been him instead of her?"

I blinked back the tears that threatened as I considered what it would be like if Tate were gone and I shook my head violently. "No," I whispered, realizing I'd answered my own question. Just like I couldn't choose Tate over Revay, I wouldn't have been able to choose her over him either. The sick what if game was messing with my head so I climbed to my feet and hurried down the steps and just began walking.

"Why did you hang on to this house, Hawke?"

"What?" I asked as I looked over my shoulder at Ronan who was following me.

"Your uncle's house," Ronan said as he motioned to the weathered structure behind me. I turned around to face the house that wasn't really a house anymore it. It was just some lumber held together by a few nails. I hadn't been inside the house even once since I'd left with Revay for Georgia, but I had no doubt it was just as much of a mess on the inside as it was on the outside.

I'd inherited the house after my uncle had died, but I hadn't ever given much thought as to what I should do with it. But I knew the answer to Ronan's question. I'd kept the house because despite all the bad memories it held for me, there was one really good one.

Revay.

Just like I'd crawled through her window so many times in the dead of night, she'd done the same thing. My eyes fell to the first floor window that had been my bedroom. I'd always been in so much pain after one of my uncle's beatings, both physically and emotionally, and she'd always been there, curled at my back, her slim arms holding me tight. She'd promised me we would always take care of each other and then she'd sung songs to me – songs she'd made up – until I'd fallen asleep.

"I don't want to ever forget," I admitted to Ronan, though I doubted he understood what I meant. It didn't matter because I did. It was the same reason I'd kept the house Revay had inherited from her parents...the one we were going to raise our family in. But I hadn't turned it into a home for myself. I'd left it as a shrine to her, to what we should have had together. I'd become stuck in time because it was the only way I could keep her close to me.

And I'd used my promise to her that I would find the men who'd hurt her as a way to get through each day. Because if I hadn't had that need for vengeance, I wouldn't have had a reason to go on.

But now I had a new reason.

"He'll never forgive me," I said softly. "The things I said about not really seeing him and Matty..."

"You'll never know unless you ask him," Ronan said as he came to stand next to me.

I shook my head even as a painful rush of hope swept through me. "I can't," I barely managed to say. "I have nothing to offer him. He doesn't even know what I've been doing for a living these past six years."

Ronan put his hand on my shoulder. "Let him make that choice, Hawke."

Denial reared its ugly head, but the aching need to know if I had a chance at finally having the life I wanted won out and I reached for my phone. My fingers were actually shaking as I tried to bring up the browser. "Um, I need to reserve a flight."

Ronan's hand closed over mine. "Seth and I chartered a jet," he said. "Matty wanted to bring Bullet with us."

I stilled as Ronan's words sank in and then my heart began pounding in my chest. "They're here?" I whispered in disbelief.

I brushed past Ronan even as he nodded, and began running. It took less than a minute to get through the woods that separated the two houses and when I rounded mine, I came to a thudding halt as I took in the sight before me. I only noticed Seth and Mav in my periphery because my eyes fell on Tate and Matty where they were bent over Bullet who was sitting in front of them, his big tail thumping on the dusty driveway. The German Shepherd saw me a second later and came running at me, but I kept my eyes on Tate and Matty as they both straightened. I locked eyes with Tate as he drew Matty back against him and dropped his hands on his shoulders.

I began striding forward, drawn in by the uncertainty in Tate's eyes.

Because that was the first thing I needed to change.

CHAPTER 24

TATE

I had to remind myself not to squeeze Matty's shoulders too hard as I watched Hawke stride towards us, his expression unreadable. I'd gone back and forth with myself on whether or not torturing myself with seeing Hawke again was a good idea, but in the end I couldn't deny my need to lay eyes on him again, even if it was just for a few minutes. But when Hawke didn't smile or even slow down as he neared us, a terrible fear went through me that I'd made a horrible mistake.

I shook my head as Hawke reached us and said, "Hawke, I'm sorry" but my words were abruptly cut off when Hawke's lips slammed down on mine. He swallowed my cry of surprise and stole into my mouth as his arms went around me. I recovered quickly and kissed him back, but my heart was pounding frantically in my chest as I struggled to process what was happening.

Hawke released my mouth and clasped my neck between his hands and pressed our foreheads together. "I love you so much, Tate," he whispered. He leaned in to kiss me again and then his arms wrapped around my shoulders in an almost painful hold. I felt tears threatening as I finally understood what was happening and I curled my arms around his back and just held on to him.

I didn't think it could get better until he whispered, "Stay with me," in my ear.

I was too overcome to speak so I just nodded frantically against him, hoping he'd hear my silent answer.

The past three weeks had been an endless struggle from the moment I'd left Hawke's bed. Matty's recovery couldn't have gone any better and I'd been beyond excited that he'd been cleared to leave the hospital for a week, but my joy had been tempered by the fact that my need for Hawke hadn't dwindled as each day had passed; it had grown and grown into an almost unbearable pain that made even the simplest of tasks a chore. The only time I'd really managed to focus was when the nurses had explained what I would need to do for Matty during the week he was home. Ronan had been by my side as the staff had explained how to change the bandage covering Matty's central line and the signs to watch for that would indicate any kind of infection. I'd also gotten a rundown of the antibiotics I would need to administer through the central line. I'd been terrified by the prospect of all the things that could go wrong, but one look at my son's happy face as he'd talked about seeing Bullet again and I'd pushed my fear aside.

And then Matty had started asking if we'd be able to visit Hawke.

I'd explained when I'd gotten back to Seattle that Hawke had had to stay behind so he could keep looking for the bad guys. That had mollified Matty for a few days, but then he'd started asking if we could call Hawke. Luckily, I'd been able to distract him long enough so that he eventually forgot about his request, but even the mention of Hawke's name would bring a rush of fierce longing and stark fear.

I'd confessed my fear for Hawke's safety when Ronan had picked me up at the airport and though I hadn't been one hundred percent clear what kind of professional relationship Ronan and Hawke had, my instincts had told me that Ronan wasn't the kind of man to sit idly by when one of his friends was in trouble. And I'd been right. That very day, Ronan had told me he was monitoring Hawke's location and had sent someone to watch Hawke's back when he went to Laredo.

Only he hadn't gone to Laredo.

I'd wanted to believe that it was a sign that maybe things could be different for him...for us. That maybe my words the night before I'd left had made a difference. But I'd been too afraid to hope.

Now it was all I felt as Hawke held me against him. I had no idea how long we clung to each other for, but when Hawke put some space between us, I finally remembered Matty and I looked down to see that he'd moved out of the way at some point when Hawke had been holding onto me. I had no idea what to even say to Matty since he'd never seen me act so intimately with another person. But the big grin on his face told me he had no problem with what he'd just witnessed and I guessed it was another thing I had Ronan and Seth to thank for since they were so openly affectionate around one another.

Before I could say anything, Hawke was lowering himself to Matty's level, but he didn't say anything. A part of me feared that he wasn't really seeing my son, but that disappeared when he pulled Matty gently into his arms. I noticed that he was careful not to put too much pressure against the place where the central line was located. Hawke whispered something into Matty's ear and then carefully lifted him into his arms. He held Matty with one arm and then drew me forward into another hug. A big sigh escaped his lips and his whole body seemed to relax as he held Matty and me close and I smiled because I knew no matter what, we'd figure the rest out.

Together.

~

"Is he asleep?" I asked when Hawke entered the bedroom. I was standing near the window that overlooked the open fields that surrounded the house, but it was so dark that I couldn't see a thing. There wasn't even a single light from a neighboring property.

"Yeah," Hawke said as he closed the door behind him. I couldn't explain why I was suddenly so nervous. Probably because Hawke and I hadn't had a chance to talk after he'd kissed me in the driveway. It had been close to dinner time when we'd arrived at Hawke's place and since he hadn't had enough food to feed everyone, we'd driven into town and eaten at a family style restaurant. Hawke had sat between me and Matty and while he'd held my hand beneath the table the entire time we hadn't been eating, he'd spent most of his time talking to Matty. Or listening, rather. Matty had talked almost nonstop about everything that had happened to him while he'd been in the hospital and had proudly showed off his little bald head and his central line. Then the discussion had turned to Matty's newest obsession with the X-Men superheroes that Ronan and Seth had introduced him to. And throughout it all, Hawke had done more than just listened. He'd asked Matty endless questions and heaped so much praise on my little boy for how brave he was, that I'd felt my love for Hawke go to a whole new level, something I wouldn't have even thought possible.

It had been late by the time we'd left and while Seth, Ronan and Mav had gone to the motel they'd booked, there'd been no question about where Matty and I would be staying. Matty hadn't even put up much of a fuss when he'd realized Bullet would be going with Seth and Ronan. Once we'd arrived back at Hawke's place, I'd given Matty a bath while Hawke had prepared the bedroom next to his for Matty. The pink walls had led me to suspect it was his wife's childhood room, but I hadn't been brave enough to ask Hawke. He'd opened a window to get the room aired out and I'd heard him feverishly vacuuming during the nearly hour Matty spent in the tub. There hadn't been even a speck of dust that I could see when I'd finally led Matty into the room. Hawke had joined us, Spiderman doll in hand, and had thanked Matty for gifting him with the doll to catch bad guys. He'd glossed over Matty's questions about whether he'd caught the bad guys and had sat on the bed to watch as I'd given Matty his meds and changed the dressing on his central line. He'd ended up asking several questions as I'd worked. And when Matty had insisted that Hawke was the one to read him his bedtime story, Hawke had readily agreed and I'd been dismissed.

"He told me I should get a dog," Hawke said as he came up to me and stood at my back. His arms went around me and his lips settled against the pulse point at my neck. "I told him I'd talk to you about it."

"It's your decision," I said with a laugh.

Hawke turned me in his arms. "It's our decision, Tate," he said firmly. "I want us to be a family."

I swallowed hard as my throat closed up. But I must have been quiet for too long because Hawke dropped his arms. "You don't want that, do you? This was just a visit-"

I grabbed Hawke and kissed him to shut him up. His fingers were biting into my upper arms where he was holding on to me when I released him and I whispered, "I want it. God, I want that so badly."

Hawke let out a rush of air and then he was wrapping his arms around me. "I missed you so much."

"Me too."

He pulled back enough so that he could look at me. "The stuff I said about not seeing you-"

I shook my head and placed my fingers over his lips. "I know you do," I said. "You never have to hide her from us, Hawke. You never have to hurt by yourself when you think of her or your little boy. You can share them with us as much or as little as you want."

Hawke nodded and I could see him blinking back tears. "I've been so afraid that I would start forgetting things about her so I tried to keep her with me. And then I met you and I thought I would have to let her go to be with you and I couldn't-"

Hawke's voice cracked as he shook his head. "I just couldn't do that to her, you know?"

I nodded. "I know, baby," I said as I pulled him against me and wrapped my arms around him. "She's a part of you and that makes her a part of us. I love you so much."

"I love you," Hawke whispered. He drew back and took my hand and led me to the bed. He kissed me, but kept it chaste and tugged me until I was sitting next to him on the mattress. He shifted so that he was facing me. "I need to tell you something...it's about what I do for a living."

"I already know," I interjected before he could continue. "Ronan told me."

Hawke stiffened and pulled his hands free of where he'd been

197

holding mine. He was clearly waiting for the recrimination he expected me to heap on him.

In truth, I'd struggled with what Ronan had shared with me the night before he'd told me he was flying to Wyoming to check on Hawke and that Matty and I could come with him if we wanted or we could stay at the house on Whidbey Island with Seth. The idea that Hawke had killed people, scores of them, was hard to swallow and a part of me had been horrified. But then Ronan had told me the story of how he and his fiancé had been beaten and brutally raped with a foreign object – an attack so vicious that his fiancé, Seth's older brother, had died from his injuries. And there'd been no justice for either of them when the military had refused to acknowledge the attack. Ronan had been upfront about Hawke's role in helping him seek vengeance. After that, he'd handed me a thick stack of papers and told me I needed to decide for myself.

I'd spent hours that night looking through the criminal records of all the men and even a few women who'd died at the hands of Ronan and the men who worked for his underground vigilante group, Hawke included. Among the descriptions of the horrendous crimes had been stories of failed justice and missed opportunities. And the victims…that had been the hardest part to read about. Some as young as Matty, some as innocent as Hawke's wife. By the time I'd finished, the sun had been rising and I'd gone to find Ronan before Matty had woken up and I'd told him that Matty and I would be joining him.

"It doesn't change anything," I said to Hawke as I sought out his hands again. "Ronan showed me everything and told me I had to decide for myself. We're here Hawke," I said as I squeezed his hands.

"You can't be okay with it," Hawke said in disbelief.

"Truth?"

Hawke nodded.

"If it's something you need to do, I'll figure out a way to deal with it. But if we're really going to do this – if we're really going to try and build a life together, I don't want to have to keep a secret like that from our son." At Hawke's indrawn breath I lowered my voice and said, "He'd be ours, Hawke. You would be his father."

My stomach clenched at the prospect that all of this might be over before it had really even had a chance to begin.

"Our son," Hawke said softly as if testing it. He nodded, a small smile gracing his strained features. "Ours," he repeated as he dropped his eyes. When he lifted them again, they were bright with emotion and he said, "I'll tell Ronan I'm out."

"Hawke-"

Hawke leaned forward and kissed me. "We're going to be a normal family, Tate. You, me and Matty." Hawke sifted his fingers into my hair and whispered, "He's going to get better and then we're going to have it all. Play dates, after school activities, PTA shit...all of it. Do you hear me?"

I laughed and nodded. "No more pretending."

"No more pretending," Hawke said softly and then he pulled me into his arms and kissed me.

The gentle kiss quickly turned heated and my body took over. I straddled Hawke's lap and took over the kiss as his palms skimmed down my back and settled on my ass. I'd already changed into my sweats so Hawke had no problem pushing his hands into my pants to grip my ass so he could grind our lower bodies together.

"I need you," I said as I leaned down to grab the hem of my shirt and yanked it off over my head so Hawke's hands wouldn't have to stop what they were doing.

But when I leaned down to kiss Hawke, he only gave me a quick kiss before he stopped everything he was doing and said, "Our last night together...in the shower," before stuttering to a stop. I watched in disbelief as color flooded his cheeks and I was innately glad he'd left the overhead lights on because I was sure I would have missed the show of embarrassment otherwise.

"Yeah," I urged as I cupped his face with my hands and forced him to keep looking at me. "Did you like it?" I asked, knowing exactly what part he was talking about. I'd taken a risk when I'd played with Hawke like that, but clearly it had paid off.

Hawke smiled and let out a little laugh. "You know I did, you little tease." Hawke began caressing my ass again. "I want more," he finally said. "I want all of you," he clarified.

I stilled because I hadn't expected that. I thought he'd want a repeat of what I'd done to him in the shower. The idea of being inside Hawke was both exciting and overwhelming.

"I...um, you should know I've never been with a guy like that before...Reggie wouldn't let me and the guy at the club was only interested-"

Hawke cut me off by putting his whole hand over my mouth and I didn't miss the anger that flashed across his face. "Sorry," I murmured against his hand as I realized bringing up my previous partners hadn't been the best way to go. I repeated the apology when Hawke removed his hand.

"I trust you, Tate. I really want this."

I swallowed around the knot in my throat and nodded. "Okay."

Hawke's smile did funny things to my heart and I kissed him hard. It took just minutes to get back to where we'd been, but it all went to hell when I reached down to pull his shirt off.

Because right after I realized that at some point Hawke had removed his wedding band and was now wearing it on a chain around his neck, I saw the new tattoo on his chest, right above Revay's.

The tattoo that was a perfect replica of the picture I'd taken so long ago of the two birds I'd hoped to one day follow to freedom.

CHAPTER 25

HAWKE

"Oh my God," Tate whispered just before he covered his mouth with his hand. His shocked eyes lifted to mine and he slowly lowered his hand. "How?" he asked, his voice cracking as tears flooded his eyes.

I'd stopped caressing Tate as soon as he'd seen the tattoo, but instead of answering him, I removed one of my hands from where I'd been holding him and reached into my nightstand drawer. I handed him the picture I'd taken from the trailer and he stared at it for a long time, letting his finger run over the pieces of tape I'd used to put the picture back together. The tattoo artist had gotten the image exactly right.

Tate lowered the picture and reached out to trail his finger over the ink on my skin.

"Why?" he asked.

I raised my fingers to wipe away his tears. "Because I needed something of you that I could keep with me. You may not have believed you were ever strong enough, Tate, but from the moment I met you, that's all I saw. You've taken on every storm in your path and come out the other side."

Tate shook his head in disbelief, but I was glad when he didn't argue with me. Of course, he seemed incapable of any kind of speech, so I wasn't sure if that wasn't part of the issue. His arms went around me and I held him for a long time – as long as he needed.

When he leaned back to once again look at the ink, his finger brushed over my wedding ring. It hadn't been as much of a struggle to take off as I'd thought it would be, but when I'd been faced with the prospect of hiding it away somewhere, I hadn't been able to do it.

"Does it bother you?" I asked.

Tate pressed his fingers over the ring and shook his head. "No," he choked out. "No, it doesn't bother me." He lowered himself back down and continued to play with the ring and the tattoo.

"Will you make love to me, Tate?" I said against his ear before brushing it with a kiss.

Tate nodded against me and then pulled himself back and wiped at his face. He climbed off the bed and held out his hand to me. He ran his hands up and down my sides, setting my skin on fire with his touch. "Does the door lock?" Tate asked.

"What?"

"The door? Does it lock?"

With Tate's caresses wreaking havoc with my mind and body, it took a moment to understand what he was asking and why. When I finally got it, I nodded and stepped away from him long enough to lock the door. But I hesitated before flipping the lock. "What if Matty needs us?"

Tate smiled. "He'll knock or he'll call out to us. Don't worry, we'll hear him. Parent hearing," he said with a chuckle as he tapped his ear.

I flipped the lock and returned to him. I leaned down and said against his lips, "I have a lot to learn."

"We'll figure it out together," Tate said and then he kissed me. It took only minutes to get back to the level of desire we'd been at before Tate had discovered the tattoo. Once we'd gotten each other undressed the rest of the way, Tate urged me to sit on the bed and then he said, "Scoot back a bit."

My nerves started to kick in as Tate fished the bottle of lube out of the drawer of the nightstand, but he merely dropped the bottle on the bed next to us and then crawled up my body and settled his weight on top of me as he kissed me. What followed was sensual torture unlike any I'd ever known. Because Tate touched me everywhere and with every part of himself. And when he was done with my front, he rolled me over and started on my back. Lips, teeth, tongue…he used every weapon in his arsenal to consume me and I was so hard by the time he reached my ass, I was sure I was going to explode the second he touched me there. By the time I felt my cheeks being opened, I didn't care how exposed I was. Not like that time in the shower.

I forced myself to wait for the feel of Tate's finger probing me, but it wasn't the rough pad of a fingertip that touched me. My whole body reverberated with shock when Tate's tongue licked over my entrance and I let out a harsh groan at how unexpectedly good it felt. His finger had been heaven, but his slick, wet tongue…it was indescribable. And he didn't just lick me. He nipped, he sucked, he kissed and then his tongue was pushing inside of me and I buried my face in the bedding to stifle my shout of pleasure. It could have been two minutes or twenty before I felt Tate's fingers touching my hole, but it was only to spread my hole open even farther so that he could sink more of his tongue into me.

"Too much," I ground out as I began humping the bed in the hopes I could make myself come.

Tate ignored my pleas and kept teasing me and then his finger was entering me. But instead of finger fucking me, he mixed it up so I was always on edge, not knowing how long it would be his tongue or his finger spearing inside of me. When it was his finger, he massaged my prostate, but the contact was too fleeting. Whimpers began erupting from my throat as my orgasm began to build, but the second I made a move to reach my hand between my body and the bed, Tate was pulling away from me and rolling me onto my back. I moaned when his tongue slipped inside my mouth and while the musky, forbidden flavor should have freaked me out, all it did was make me want more.

Tate used one of his hands to urge me to part my legs and as soon as I did, his cock brushed mine as he shifted his weight and then his finger was pushing inside of me again. I'd somehow missed him putting lube on it though, but feeling the cool liquid being spread around inside me both excited and frightened me. Because Tate's finger and tongue were one thing, his cock another.

"I can make you come like this," Tate suddenly said as he continued to finger fuck me. I loved that he was giving me an out, but I didn't need it.

"No," I said. "I want you inside of me when I come."

Tate nodded and leaned down to press a soft kiss over my lips before he sat up and reached for the lube. I forced myself to take even breaths as I watched him prepare his cock. His eyes connected with mine and then he reached for my legs and placed them on his shoulders. The position was strange to me, but as soon as Tate scooted forward and pressed his dick to my hole, I forgot all about it and held my breath.

"Push against me," Tate said softly and then he began to move. At first there was just a strong burning sensation as Tate's cock began to enter me, but it changed to full on pain the harder he pushed.

"Fuck," I muttered.

"Breathe, baby," Tate murmured as he stilled for a moment. I did as he told me and tried to force the rest of my body to relax. The pain got worse and the burn returned, but there was something else too. Something I couldn't put my finger on. Something inside of me that wanted more, even as my flaming entrance was screaming that it was enough. I focused my eyes on Tate and saw the fierce concentration in his features as he watched where we were joined and I knew in that moment that this was exactly what I wanted. The knowledge helped my body relax even more and I actually felt when my hole gave way and accepted Tate's thickness. Tate's eyes connected with mine as he gave me a few seconds to adjust and my heart swelled at the sight of the unfettered love I saw there.

After that, the pain became secondary to everything else and by the time Tate started giving me shallow thrusts, it was almost nonexistent. Heat had started to flood my limbs and I felt like electricity was firing through all my veins with every drag of Tate's cock. And when

Tate bottomed out inside of me, I whispered his name. He heard me and looked up and nodded in understanding.

Because it was fucking perfection.

Tate pulled out of me before slowly pushing back in and pleasure shot through me like a bullet. It happened every time he did it and he didn't even miss a beat in his rhythm as he lowered all his weight down on me and kissed me. I wrapped my legs around the backs of his thighs and reached down with my hands to cover his ass so I could feel the flexing muscles as he drove into me.

The pain had completely dissipated and my cock, which had gone soft at Tate's initial entry, swelled with need. Tate kept kissing me as he increased his pace and I grunted every time he buried himself inside of me as deep as he possibly could.

"Michael," he whispered against my lips. "Michael," he repeated, his voice filled with wonder. His lips skimmed over the raised skin on my cheek and jaw and then trailed down along my neck. They brushed briefly over the tattoo and then sought out my mouth again. I struggled to return Tate's kiss because the feeling of him driving into me with powerful lunges was nearly too much.

"I'm close," I managed to get out as I felt my balls draw up tight and electricity fired up my spine.

"Me too," Tate said as he sipped at my lips. "You feel so perfect, Michael. So tight," Tate breathed against my mouth. "I could stay inside of you forever."

I shuddered at his words, but couldn't manage to find my own voice. I dragged my hands up from his ass to his back and held on for dear life as my orgasm finally slammed into me and I shattered. Jet after jet of semen coated my abdomen as well as Tate's. I couldn't contain the harsh yell that left my lips, but Tate was there to swallow it down. And he came just seconds later. He was holding onto the bedding with one hand while the other slipped beneath my head to hold me still for his kiss. His muffled cries of relief mixed with mine as he slammed into me several times, driving my hips high. Heat flooded my insides which set off another, smaller orgasm deep inside of me. As Tate's thrusts finally slowed, I lifted my legs to wrap around his lower back so I could keep him inside of me for as long as possible.

"Love you," Tate said as he put one of his hands over my jackhammering heart.

I only managed to nod because I wasn't capable of speech.

Tate chuckled. "Does that mean we get to do that again?"

I managed a harsh laugh that sounded more like a groan and nodded again. Vigorously. I sucked in a deep breath and spit out, "We're definitely doing that again," before I dragged Tate down for another kiss.

CHAPTER 26

TATE

"I can't believe you did that," I joked after letting Matty out of the truck.

"Every kid needs a dog," Hawke murmured as he came around the front of the truck and brushed his lips over mine. He put his arm around me and we watched Matty carry the puppy across the driveway to a grassy area next to the house. "Besides, it was meant to be," Hawke said as he linked his fingers with mine and started leading me towards the house.

I was exhausted from the day's events and even though it was still light out, I knew there wouldn't be any issue with getting Matty to bed early because he was beyond tired. At least he had been until Hawke had stopped to speak to a neighbor of his who'd been parked near the grocery store we'd stopped at to grab some dinner from. The plan had been for Hawke to run in and grab a frozen pizza, but one look at the puppy the old rancher had been holding in his arms and Matty had begged to get out of the truck so he could play with it. I'd ended up going into the store to get the food and by the time I'd come back out, the rancher was gone and Matty was happily holding the small yellow puppy in his arms. Hawke had explained that it was the last of a surprise litter the rancher was trying to find homes for and the woman he'd been planning to give the puppy to had failed to show to pick it up.

Hawke had looked stricken when he'd remembered what he'd said about it being a decision we needed to make together, but I'd let him off with a smile and a shake of my head and had sent him back inside the store to pick up some puppy food while Matty had run through a list of superhero names and finally settled on another X-Men favorite, Storm, for the female puppy.

The day after Matty and I had arrived in Wyoming, we'd said our goodbyes to Ronan, Seth, Mav and Bullet. Ronan and Seth were headed home to Seattle for some alone time while Mav had plans to explore some of the mountain passes on his huge Harley Davidson motorcycle while he waited for his next assignment. I'd learned very little about the heavily tattooed man with the long black hair except that he fit the stereotypical biker to a T. Hawke had told me that he knew little about Mav's personal life, but I hadn't missed the respect he held for the man. The fact that he didn't appear to have a home to return to had bothered me greatly, but he'd declined our invitation to dinner the night Seth and Ronan had left. We'd spent much of that day exploring the town of Rocky Point and the surrounding area and at one point when we'd taken a short walk to check out Hawke's property, he'd taken my hand and veered us off the trail we'd been on. I hadn't had any clue what he'd wanted to show me and Matty, but it had become clear when we'd entered a clearing by a small lake and there had been a single headstone beneath the branches of a huge tree.

Hawke hadn't said much as we'd stood there, other than to explain that he and Revay had spent most of their summer vacations playing in the lake and laying on the sand dreaming of what their future would hold. Matty had been uncharacteristically solemn and I'd nearly lost it when he'd moved around me to stand on Hawke's other side so he could hold his hand too. Hawke and I had spent the rest of the night after Matty had gone to bed talking about our plans for the future and I'd been both worried and excited when he'd said he thought Seattle would be a good place for us to settle. I'd tried to tell him that we could make a life in Rocky Point after Matty's treatment was finished, but he'd refused, saying that we needed a fresh start...all of us. His only request had been that I be okay with him not selling the property since it was where Revay was buried. And when I'd asked about his pursuit of Buck and Denny, he'd simply told me it was over and I'd left it at that.

We'd made love again that night, but unlike the other times we'd been together, it was unhurried and we spent more time just exploring each other in a way that wasn't completely sexual. I'd discovered that for all his brawn and beauty, Hawke was supremely ticklish and Hawke had enjoyed finding every one of my erogenous zones and exploiting them. The next morning we'd ended up deciding on a spur of the moment trip to Yellowstone National Park which was just a couple of hours away. Matty had been in heaven as we'd explored the park both on foot and by car, but the highlight of the trip had been when we'd spotted a black bear and her two cubs crossing the road about a hundred yards from our car. We'd spent the night in a hotel and had spent the rest of today exploring before finally heading home.

Hence the exhaustion.

We'd just reached the porch when I heard Matty calling for me followed by a comment about him not being able to find the puppy.

"It's okay, I'll go," I said to Hawke as he started to follow me. "Can you put the pizza in while I check on him?"

Hawke nodded. "Can you grab my phone from the truck on your way back? I need to charge it."

"I told you not to show him those games on your phone," I said with a chuckle.

"Yeah, you did," Hawke acknowledged. "What can I say, the kid's got me wrapped around his finger. How was I supposed to know he'd play them till the phone died?" Hawke groused as he climbed the porch stairs. "Besides, I'm not the one who forgot my phone all together."

I shot him a dirty look and began walking towards the side of the house where I'd last seen Matty headed with the puppy. A twinge of concern went through me when I didn't see him anywhere and I began walking across the field towards a large, run down barn that Hawke had warned Matty not to play around.

"Matty!"

The lack of a response had me picking up my pace. "Matty, you answer me right now!" I shouted. I knew I was likely overreacting, but the thought that Matty could have climbed up into the hayloft and fallen through a broken floorboard flashed through my mind and I began running. I called his name again, but there was still no answer. And when I saw the barn door partially opened, I was gutted with fear and I shouted for Hawke.

But when I slid the door open wide enough so that I could fit through it, I was nowhere near prepared for the sight that greeted me.

Because there standing just behind my son in the middle of the barn pressing a gun against Matty's head, was Denny.

"Sorry, Daddy," Matty said, his voice uneven, and I knew he was just seconds away from crying.

At some point he'd found Storm because he was holding the quiet puppy in his arms. "It's okay, buddy. Just hold on to Storm and be real still and quiet while the grown-ups talk."

Despite my warning not to move, Matty nodded, but that was all he did. I lifted my eyes to Denny and shook my head. "Denny, please. He's just a kid. Just let him leave and you and I can talk."

"You shouldn't have taken him, Chrissy," Denny said, his hand shaking as he held the gun. "Pops, he was...you just shouldn't have taken him."

I glanced around the barn as subtly as I could, but didn't see Buck anywhere. But I knew without a shadow of a doubt that Denny wouldn't have had the forethought to do this on his own. Denny's eyes were wide and glassy and I suspected he was high or just coming down off of something. And that fact alone had sheer terror rolling through me. Because Denny was wholly unpredictable when he was in that condition.

"I had to, Denny. You know what Buck would have done to him. What he would have turned him into."

Denny pulled the gun away from Matty's head so he could wipe his brow with his arm. A sliver of relief went through me when he lowered the gun to his side instead of putting it back to Matty's head. But he still had his other hand clamped down on Matty's shoulder.

"Things didn't go well for me when he got home and found the kid gone," Denny said accusingly.

"I'm sorry, I didn't think about that when I took him."

Denny grew more agitated as he shook his head. "I told that stupid bitch to stay away."

I dropped my eyes to Matty as Denny seemed to get lost in himself and I gave my son what I hoped was a reassuring smile and a brief nod. Matty was clearly terrified, but he managed a small nod.

Denny was still ranting and I could tell he was getting more and more frustrated so I said, "Denny, talk to me. Who are you talking about?"

My brother looked at me as if he'd just now noticed my presence and I was surprised to see his face actually fall. "I really loved her, you know?"

"Who?"

"She was supposed to be the one. We were gonna be a family. You remember that, don't you Chrissy?" Denny said, his voice actually sounding dejected.

If the circumstances had been any different, I actually might have felt sorry for him.

"Daddy's name is Tate," Matty suddenly interjected, but instead of putting the gun back to Matty's head, Denny actually looked down at Matty strangely and then turned him and knelt down in front of him.

"He's not your daddy, Matthew," Denny said as he reached up with the hand that was holding the gun and tried to stroke Matty's face. Matty flinched and pulled his face away before Denny could make contact.

"Denny," I said desperately and I took several steps forward to get Denny's attention. The move worked and Denny jumped up and pointed his gun at me. "Talk to me, Denny," I ordered as I held out my hands.

"Fuck!" Denny bit out and he lowered the gun again. "This is all your fault! I could have convinced Buck not to…"

Denny started shaking his head and then he slammed his closed fist against his chest. It was a move I'd seen him do countless times when he was pissed and trying to get control of himself.

"Convinced Buck not to what?" I asked when Denny settled again.

"No loose ends, remember?"

I stilled at that and looked down at Matty. I shook my head in disbelief. "No," slipped from my lips as my father's motto rang in my ear.

"He was a three-year-old kid, Denny!" I nearly shouted.

"No loose ends," Denny repeated. "But I couldn't fucking do it. Not to my own kid."

I didn't correct Denny that he wasn't Matty's father because I knew it was the only thing of value I had. But his statement was telling and based on what he'd said earlier, he'd cared about Matty's mother.

"Who is she?" I asked.

Denny had quieted again and he solemnly said, "Jenna DuCane."

"Where is she, Denny?"

"Gone," was all Denny said.

"Gone where?"

"She came to the house that day looking for a fix. I'd told her never to come there."

"What happened to her?"

"She started yelling at me that if I didn't start helping her support the kid, she'd tell her dad who I was. She wanted cash and drugs. Then Buck came home and she started screaming that her dad was a cop."

I swallowed hard as I realized where Denny was headed. "She was only fourteen when she and I…she kept saying it was rape and her dad was going to put us all in jail. Buck hit her." Denny shook his head sadly. "I begged Buck to let me talk to her. I told him I could get her to come around. But he said she was a loose end. Him too," Denny said as he pointed to Matty.

"He put Jenna in his truck and told me to take the kid somewhere and get rid of him. But I couldn't."

Denny once again lowered himself to Matty's level. "He looks like me, huh?" he asked and then he reached for the baseball cap Matty was wearing and pushed it off his head. My brother's face went from strangely paternal to one of pure shock as he took in Matty's bald head. His eyes jumped to me. "He's sick?"

I nodded. "Leukemia."

Denny's horrified gaze settled on Matty again and this time when he lifted his hand – the one not holding the gun – to stroke Matty's face, Matty held still. I saw an opportunity that I hadn't expected. "Denny, just let him go. You can keep me...I'll tell Buck that Matty is staying with friends."

Denny glanced at me and then looked back at Matty longingly. He finally nodded his head and reached down for the baseball cap and settled it gently back on Matty's head.

"Matty," I said carefully. "Go take Storm and hide in the woods, okay? You stay there until you either see Hawke or police officers, do you hear me?"

"Yes, Daddy," Matty whispered.

Relief went through me as Matty stepped away from Denny and Denny let him go. I put my hand on Matty's shoulder as he slowly walked past me. "Run really fast, okay?"

Matty nodded. "Love you lots."

I managed a shaky nod and said, "Forever and ever."

I kept my eyes on him until he disappeared out the barn door and then I turned my focus on Denny.

"Tate," Denny murmured. "I didn't think you'd remember it."

"Remember what?" I asked.

"That name. You were so little when Pops changed it."

I stared at him in disbelief. "My real name actually is Tate?"

Denny nodded. "Pops always hated it so he used your middle name. He used to joke that Mom was high on something when she came up with that name."

"You remember our mother?"

"Yeah," Denny murmured. "She was real nice," he said thoughtfully. "Pops used to tell me that she hadn't wanted us anymore so she'd dumped us on him. But I never believed him."

Overwhelmed, I whispered, "Do you know where she is…is she still alive?"

"Don't know."

The lack of affect in Denny's tone was frightening, but my need for answers was too great so I barreled on and actually ended up stepping so close to Denny that I could have reached out to touch him.

"Denny, do you remember her name?"

"Layla," Denny said. "She used to play that song all the time."

"What about her last name? Was it Buckley?"

Denny shook his head. "Don't think so."

"So this is how you tie up loose ends?" I heard from behind me. I would have recognized who it was even if I hadn't turned around. And the second I did, I regretted it because as my father stepped into the dark barn, I saw him pulling my son behind him, the puppy still clutched in his arms. Tears were streaking down Matty's face.

"I couldn't run fast enough, Daddy," Matty cried.

I began striding towards Buck and Matty, not caring what the man did to me, but like Denny, he pulled out a gun and pointed it at Matty and I stopped in my tracks.

"Hello, Son," Buck sniped as he kept walking forward, forcing me back towards Denny.

"It's okay, Matty. You did real good," I said gently as Matty began to cry in earnest.

"Pops-" Denny began.

"Shut the fuck up," Buck snapped and then he turned his attention on me as he walked around me until he was facing the doorway, presumably so he could see anyone coming. Even though it had been only minutes since I'd entered the barn looking for Matty, it had felt like hours. But I had no doubt that Hawke would be coming to check on us any minute now and I just needed to keep Buck and Denny talking until then.

But even before I finished the thought, I heard a gunshot ring through the air. A few seconds later, there was another one.

"You hear that?" Buck said with a smile. "That's called a double-tap."

Terror rolled through me as I realized the shots had come from the house.

"Now those Mexicans, they know something about how not to leave loose ends," Buck said with a chuckle.

I felt tears stinging the backs of my eyes, but I forced myself not to think about Hawke.

"I'll do anything you want," I said to Buck. "Just let Matty go. He's not a part of this."

Buck laughed. "You think this is about you, you little faggot?"

My eyes fell to Matty and I shook my head. "He's just a kid, Pops." I hated referring to him in any way as my father, but I knew better than to piss him off by calling him Buck, a name I as his son wasn't permitted to use since he considered it a display of disrespect.

"You want to know the ironic part?" Buck said, ignoring my plea. "I was all prepared to let you keep this little shit" – Buck jerked Matty back and forth several times – "Until you and your fudge packer boyfriend showed up in Lulling asking questions."

"Who told you?" I asked, hoping to stall Buck long enough until I could figure out what to do. "The sheriff?"

"That lazy SOB always did like an easy payday. All he had to do was run your plates," Buck responded and I realized he meant the license plates on Hawke's truck which would have led to Hawke's address. Buck's eyes shifted to Denny. "Finish it," he suddenly said and then motioned to me with his gun.

Denny was standing next to me, but his gun was hanging loosely by his side. "Pops, maybe we should just let 'em go. The kid's sick-"

"The kid wouldn't be here if you'd just done what I told you to do two years ago."

"He's my son…" Denny said desperately and I almost felt a sliver of pity for him.

"He's not yours," I said to Denny as I flashed him a glance.

215

"What?" Denny asked.

"He's not yours, Denny," I said again, though I kept my eyes on Buck. "I'm thinking Pops here wanted you to tie up *his* loose end, not yours."

"No," Denny whispered and I looked at him to see that his eyes were on Buck whose snide smile had disappeared. "You promised me," Denny murmured. "You promised me you weren't with Jenna like that."

"Shut up and do as I say, boy!" Buck snarled.

"I told you I loved her! You promised me I wouldn't have to share her!"

Denny's rage was palpable and I saw Matty close his eyes as even he sensed the rising tension between the two men. Thankfully, Buck's gun wasn't aimed at Matty's head, though the hand holding the weapon was on Matty's shoulder.

"And I told you what would happen if she told her father about you."

"Not me!" Denny screamed. "You! She loved me! She never would have told him about us, but you! Did you fucking rape her you sick fuck?"

"Enough!" Buck roared and Denny actually fell silent, though I could feel his fury wafting off of him as he stood next to me. Buck's rage filled eyes shifted to me and then he aimed his gun at me.

Panic went through me as I realized I had nothing left to delay the inevitable and I looked down at Matty and whispered, "Close your eyes, buddy." I was glad when Matty did as I said and when the gunshot rang out a second later, I tried to call up an image of him and Hawke from earlier in the day to mind.

A weight hit me hard and knocked me to the ground and it took me a second to realize it hadn't been a bullet tearing through my flesh that had been the cause. I heard a terrible gasping sound and I scrambled to my knees as my fear for Matty overruled everything else. But it wasn't Matty who'd been shot either.

It was Denny who was lying next to me, a bloom of bright red blood staining the front of his shirt. Shock tore through me as I realized my brother had pushed me out of the way, putting himself in the path of the bullet that had been meant for me.

"Denny?!" I shouted and then my instincts took over and I pressed my hands down on his chest. I looked up at Buck in disbelief and saw that he actually seemed to be in a state of shock himself. Matty still had his eyes squeezed shut.

"Denny, hold on, okay?" I said desperately as blood seeped through my fingers. Denny's shocked eyes held mine as he struggled to breathe.

"I'm sorry," he choked out.

I shook my head. "It's okay, just hang on."

"Should have protected you," Denny managed to say, though his last words faded out as his pupils grew larger and then he lowered his head to the floor and his body jerked several times before finally stilling beneath my hands.

I pulled my bloody hands from Denny's chest and stared at them for several long seconds before wiping them on my pants. "Why?" I asked, though I wasn't expecting an answer. When I turned my attention to Buck, I saw that his gun was once again pointed at me.

"Put it down."

The sound of Hawke's voice behind me went through me like a wave and I actually let out a sob when I heard it. I wanted so badly to look over my shoulder at him, but I didn't dare move because the second Hawke spoke, Buck's gun went from me to Matty.

"Daddy?" Matty whispered, his eyes still closed.

"I'm here, buddy," I managed to get out as I kept my eyes trained on my son. The puppy who'd been quiet throughout the entire ordeal began to lick Matty's chin. "Just keep holding onto Storm, okay? It's going to be over soon."

Matty nodded.

"Drop your weapon," Buck snapped. "I've already killed one son. Don't think for a second I won't kill another," he warned.

"Hawke," I pleaded.

"It's okay, Tate," was all Hawke said and I could hear his footsteps getting closer and I sensed he was only inches from me. But I didn't give a shit about me.

"Remember your promise," I whispered. "No matter what happens to me," I said, hoping like hell he would remember his promise to always put Matty first.

"I remember," Hawke said.

"Put the fucking gun down," Buck said, his voice ice cold. I couldn't see Hawke, but I heard the sound of metal on wood and I knew he'd put the gun down on the floor.

"Kick it away."

A part of me wanted to die when I heard the gun slide across the wooden floor.

"Matty," Hawke said calmly. "I need you to do something for me, okay?"

Matty nodded, his eyes still closed.

"I need you to try to read my mind like Professor Xavier does. But because it's so noisy in here, you need to concentrate real hard and not move at all. Not even a muscle, okay?"

Matty nodded again and then he briefly opened his eyes to look at Hawke and then me. "It's okay, Matty. Go ahead and read Hawke's mind," I urged.

Matty closed his eyes again and I watched as he scrunched up his face, his brow furrowed.

"Very touching, Chrissy," Buck drawled and I held my breath as an ugly smile split his lips and he raised his gun. But it wasn't pointed at me. It was pointed at Hawke.

"His name is Tate," Hawke whispered and then everything happened so fast, I barely understood what I was seeing. I saw a flash of silver in my peripheral vision and a split second later, Buck was screaming in pain as a knife pierced the wrist of the hand he was holding the gun with. The gun discharged, but the force of the knife had caused his arm to swing wide and instead of the bullet flying over my shoulder towards Hawke, it slammed into the floor several feet to Buck's right. At nearly the same time, Hawke launched his body over me, hitting Buck hard and knocking him to the ground. Matty went down with them, but as I scrambled towards him, I saw that neither man had landed on him. I dragged him into my arms and lifted my eyes just in time to see Hawke yank the knife from Buck's wrist and jam it into his neck. Buck let out a terrible gurgling noise as blood sprayed everywhere and I had to turn away from the gruesome sight.

Even as my father struggled with his last breaths, I turned all of my attention on Matty and began checking him for injures.

"Matty, does it hurt anywhere?" I asked.

Matty was crying and it took several seconds before he finally shook his head. "Can I open my eyes, Daddy?" he asked as the puppy squirmed in his arms.

I glanced over at Hawke who'd climbed to his feet. My father's body was still twitching and there was blood everywhere so I said, "No buddy, not yet," and pulled Matty against me as I stood. I carried him out of the barn and then dropped to my knees in the grass and put him down in front of me.

"Okay, buddy, you can open them."

Matty slowly opened his eyes and then looked around briefly before he burst into tears and launched himself into my arms.

"It's okay, Matty. It's over," I whispered as I held him against me. The puppy was stuck between us, but all she did was lick at Matty's face so I left her where she was. "You were so brave," I said as I patted Matty's back once his sobs slowed.

"They were bad men," Matty announced as he pulled back from me.

"They were," I said. "But they can't hurt you ever again, okay?"

Matty nodded and then looked over my shoulder. I followed his gaze to see Hawke walking towards us. His shirt was covered in blood, but I knew it wasn't his. I was stunned to see Mav walking behind him. And I knew instantly where the knife that had hit Buck in the wrist had come from.

Hawke dropped to his knees beside me. His face was drawn tight with emotion as he dragged Matty into his arms and buried his face in his shoulder.

"I read your mind," Matty announced when Hawke released him.

"Oh yeah?" Hawke said, his voice thick and uneven. He shifted his gaze to me and I nearly lost it when his hand went around my neck and he just held me like that. I didn't need words to know what he was thinking. I pressed up against his side as I focused on my son.

Our son.

"You were thinking about saving me and Daddy."

Hawke lifted his other hand to stroke Matty's cheek. "That's exactly right," he said.

"And you know what else?" Matty announced as he wiped at his tear stained face.

"What else?"

"You were thinking that Daddy and I should stay with you forever."

I felt my own throat tighten as Hawke and I exchanged another look. Hawke nodded slowly and then he was pulling Matty into his arms. His free arm dragged me closer and he held us both as he said, "Forever and ever."

EPILOGUE

HAWKE

*O**ne month later*
I took my eyes off the sight in front of me only when Ronan tapped my shoulder with the bottle of beer. "Thanks," I said as I took it from him. He settled down onto the concrete step next to me and took a sip of his beer.

"So when were you planning on telling me you're out?" Ronan asked.

We were sitting on the steps that led from the patio to the office at Seth and Ronan's Whidbey Island house and while the back of the house sported an amazing view of the water and surrounding mountains, I had eyes only for what was happening on the expansive grass in front of us. But it wasn't just Tate and Matty I was focused on as they played soccer with Seth and the two dogs. Of course, the puppy, Storm, wasn't really interested in the ball because all she did was chase after Bullet as Bullet tried to steal the ball from the players. No, it was the fourth participant in the game I had my attention on. His name was Magnus DuCane and he'd turned out to be nothing like I'd expected.

From the second I'd walked into my house a month earlier, I'd known something was off, but before I'd been able to even call out to

221

Tate in warning, two men had jumped me. My fear for Matty and Tate had consumed me as I'd fought the men, but they hadn't been just any lackeys and I'd only managed to snap the neck of one of them when the other had managed to put his gun to my head. I'd had a moment where my life had flashed before my eyes as I'd waited for the bullet to pierce my brain and it had turned out to be a really great moment. Because it had been filled with memories of Revay and Tate and Matty and there hadn't been even one regret or doubt. But I'd felt nothing as the first gunshot rang out and by the time I'd opened my eyes, Mav was already standing over the guy who'd been about to shoot me and he'd put a second bullet in his head.

There'd been no time for explanations as to how Mav had known what was happening, but I'd found out later that Daisy had been tracking the men in Ricardo Davos's circle and one of them had used a credit card to buy gas in a town just twenty miles from Rocky Point. Ronan had tried to call both me and Tate to warn us, but since my phone's battery had died just after we'd left Yellowstone and Tate had forgotten his, we'd been sitting ducks. Although Mav had already left town, he'd managed to make it out to my house in time. Ronan had called the police as well, but they hadn't arrived until well after the whole thing had ended.

Mav and I'd had only precious seconds to come up with a plan as we'd hurried from the house to the barn where we'd heard a gunshot and my heart had been in my throat the entire time as I'd run the short distance. My relief at seeing both Tate and Matty unharmed had been almost crippling, but I'd been able to keep my wits about me as I'd waited for Mav to get into position. He'd managed to climb up the rusted out machine that had once been used to move hay bales from the ground into the hayloft and as I'd done my part to make sure Matty didn't move so Mav wouldn't inadvertently hit him with the knife, Mav had taken aim. The second I'd seen the knife hit Buck, I'd done my best to take him down without hurting Matty and then I'd plunged the knife into his thick neck before he'd even had a chance to try and take another shot at me. And it wasn't just Revay's image that had flashed through my mind as I'd taken his life; Tate's and Matty's had been there too.

After the police had arrived and questioned us, Tate and I had taken Matty to the hospital to be checked out and then we'd gone to a motel to spend the night. Tate and I hadn't spoken much as I'd held him in my arms and he'd held Matty in his as Matty had slept. We hadn't needed to say anything. Because we'd both been aware of how close we'd come to losing each other and our son.

The next day I'd learned more about what had driven Buck to seek us out and when I'd had Daisy investigate Jenna DuCane, I'd been led to her father, Magnus, a Texas Ranger. Tate had been scared to reach out to Matty's maternal grandfather, but he'd known it needed to be done. His biggest fear had been that the man would try to seek custody of his grandson. We'd been back in Seattle at that point and Matty had been undergoing his second round of chemo, so I'd flown down to Texas to talk to Magnus so I could try to feel him out. What I'd found was a devastated, broken man who'd been searching for his then seventeen-year-old daughter and three-year-old grandson for two years. He hadn't known about Buck and Denny and it was me who'd ended up having to tell him his daughter was likely dead based on Buck's comments to Tate in the barn.

At only forty years old, Magnus DuCane was still a young man, but I could tell that his daughter's disappearance had aged him signifi-cantly and I'd understood the raw pain he'd been enduring both in the two years he'd been searching for her and the day I'd told him she wasn't coming home. The only thing that had caused the tiniest spark of hope to flare in the man's eyes was when he'd learned his grandson was alive. I'd spoken with Tate that night on the phone and had explained what Magnus had been going through and it had been his idea to bring the man home with me so he could see Matty for himself.

Three weeks later and Magnus was still here.

We'd taken our time explaining who Magnus was to Matty and although he'd understood that the man was his grandfather, he hadn't asked too many questions about his mother. But we knew there would be a day when he would and Magnus would be the only one who could tell him who she'd been. Tate had been welcoming to Magnus, but his fear that Magnus would try to take Matty away from us hadn't eased until Magnus had pulled us both aside one day when Matty had been asleep in his hospital bed and thanked us for giving him a chance to know his grandson again. He'd gone on to thank Tate for saving Matty's life and he'd told him that he could think of no two better parents to raise Matty. His only ask was that he could still be included in Matty's life. After that, Magnus had been enfolded into our little family and I had no doubt that the man stood no chance against Matty's persistent request asking him to stay.

Matty's second round of chemo had progressed much like the first, though he'd been more worn out this time around and had spent a lot of time sleeping or just lying in bed. There'd been some rough days too as Matty had struggled with the inevitable pain that came along with his treatments, but between all of us, we'd managed to build a good support system for him. His recovery from the events of that terrible day in the barn had been slow and he'd been plagued with nightmares. A child psychologist was helping him work through the trauma and expected that Matty would eventually completely recover. There'd been some concern that Ricardo Davos would send someone after us to get rid of any potential links to his organization, but between Daisy monitoring the man and Ronan bringing in several of his guys to give all of us round the clock protection, I knew Matty and Tate were safe. And Matty had found himself his own personal body-guard in Mav who spent nearly every day at the hospital stationed outside of Matty's room. The only time he gave up his post was when he was forced to get some sleep.

Tate and I hadn't started the process of looking for a house in Seattle yet since we spent so much time at the hospital. We'd ended up taking up residence at the same hotel Ronan and Seth had gotten Tate set up in for the first round of Matty's chemo. I also hadn't started looking for a job since Matty's treatment was scheduled to last another four months. I had managed to talk Tate into taking a photography course so that he'd be able to spend some time outside the hospital and after much reluctance, he'd finally consented to try it and had ultimately been excited to have something back in his life that had always brought him so much pleasure. In hopes of encouraging Tate to one day pursue his passion as a career, I'd also surprised him with an expensive camera that his instructor had recommended.

I'd been fortunate enough to have plenty of money saved up for both Matty's treatment and for Tate and I to live off of, but I knew I had the man next to me to thank for that because he'd paid considerably better than the army ever had. But my loyalty to Ronan had also made it difficult to admit that my professional relationship with him was over. Since I hadn't taken any cases in the two months since I'd met Tate, I suspected Ronan already knew what my plan was. His question confirmed it.

"I owe you so much-" I began to say, but Ronan cut me off.

"No you don't," he said simply. "We saved each other, Hawke. You know it. I know it. Let's just leave it at that."

"Are you going to keep the group going?"

Ronan nodded. "It does too much good not to." His eyes were on Seth when he said, "But I'm not going to be picking up a gun again anytime soon," he said.

"What will you do?" I asked.

"I'm looking into going back into medicine," he admitted. He nodded at Matty. "I can still save kids like him. I'll just use a scalpel to do it."

I smiled at that.

"What about you?" Ronan asked.

"I'm thinking about doing something in security," I said. "There's a security firm out here that has a really good reputation."

"Barretti Security Group," Ronan said. "I've heard good things about them. They'd be lucky to have you," Ronan said.

"What about the group? Who's going to run it?"

"Not sure. Mav seems interested in being second in command, but he doesn't want to be lead. I've got another guy in mind, but he's not exactly a team player."

"Who?"

Ronan glanced at me. "Memphis."

I chuckled and shook my head. "Good luck with that," was all I said before I took a sip of my beer. I'd only worked with Memphis Wheland on one occasion and while he was the ultimate killer, his interpersonal skills were considerably lacking.

"Yeah," Ronan agreed. "When are you going to tell Tate about his mom?"

"Tonight," I said. "Thanks for keeping an eye on Matty for us."

"Are you kidding?" Ronan said. "Seth can't get enough of that kid."

"Just Seth?" I asked knowingly.

Ronan smiled – it was something I still couldn't get used to. "No, not just Seth," Ronan murmured.

I turned my focus on Tate who'd fallen to the ground in mock exhaustion and had been promptly piled on by a dog, a puppy and a very happy five-year-old. I knew what I had to tell Tate tonight would be yet another heavy thing for him to process, but I also suspected he'd eventually see the joy in it too. But until then, I would take pleasure in seeing the man who'd changed my entire life enjoy every moment he could with our ever expanding family.

&

"*B*aby, I need to talk to you about something," I murmured between the kisses Tate was stealing as we walked to our hotel room.

"Okay," Tate said against my lips, but instead of giving me some space, he crowded me against our door as I fumbled with the key card to get it open. I gave up and wrapped my arms around his waist as he stole into my mouth and teased me with his tongue. I growled when he refused to give me what I wanted and I quickly spun him until his back was up against the door. I took over the kiss and by the time I was done taking what I wanted, Tate was rubbing up against me, his hands gripping my ass as he tried to pull me closer to him so he could grind our erections together.

I managed to finally get the key card in the door when Tate started

226

fumbling with the buttons on my shirt, and the second we were inside, I ripped my shirt off and then went to work on his. Tate was rubbing my erection relentlessly with his hand and I knew I wasn't going to last. Since the bedroom was too far away, I dragged Tate to the counter that separated the kitchen from the living area in the small suite and shoved him back against it. I managed to get his pants undone and off of him, but when Tate's fingers pushed past my waistband at my back and began smoothing over my ass, I was a goner and I ruthlessly turned Tate around and shoved him face down over the counter. I placed my hand on Tate's neck to hold him in place as I freed my cock from my pants with the other hand and searched out my wallet for the packet of lube I kept there.

"You like it like this, don't you baby?" I growled as I slid my cock between his cheeks.

"Yes," Tate said breathlessly as he pushed his ass against me. "Fuck me really hard, Michael."

The sound of my name always did it for me and since Tate only used it when we were alone, it never failed to elicit a primal response in me. I kept my hand on Tate's neck to hold him still as I tore the packet of lube open with my teeth and slathered the contents on my dick. I didn't bother lowering my pants because I knew Tate liked it when I fucked him while I was still partially or fully dressed and he was completely naked. I placed some lube on Tate's hole, but I didn't prepare him because I knew it was something else he liked. There were days when we both needed slow, sweet, pleasurable lovemaking that lasted hours, and then there were other days like this where we needed each other too much to go slow.

After wiping my hand on my pants, I lifted it to join the other one around Tate's neck and while I didn't apply anything more than subtle pressure, I could practically feel Tate's excitement ripple off of him as I took complete control. My cock was so hard that I had no trouble searching out his hole and as I began to push into his tight body, he moaned and whispered my name. I didn't give him much time to adjust to my shaft and from the way he was begging me to go faster, I knew he was fine with that. Once I was inside of him, I leaned over his back so I could feel his skin against mine and then I began thrusting in long, heavy drags. I fucked him ruthlessly after that and the only time I removed my hand from his neck was when I finally reached down to start jacking him off. I could have made him come without the using my hand, but my own lust had spiraled out of control as soon as Tate's tight heat had gripped me and I knew I wouldn't last.

"Fuck! God, yes, right there!" Tate screamed as I began hitting his prostate. It took just seconds for him to come after that and as soon as his orgasm started to slow, I put both my hands on his shoulders and held him in place as I pounded into him. Less than half a dozen strokes later, I was filling him as my climax tore through me. I dropped my lips to the back of his neck as I cried out his name. When his body had taken everything from me that it could, Tate searched out my lips and I kissed him deeply.

"I love you," I whispered.

"Me too," he managed to say as his body went limp beneath mine.

After getting us both cleaned up in the shower, we climbed into bed and as soon as Tate snuggled up against me, I said, "I need to talk to you about something."

"Okay."

I loved that he didn't tense up against me. It was a testament to how much he trusted me.

"Daisy found your mom."

At that, Tate did tense up and then he turned his head to look at my face before he pulled free of my arms and sat up so he could face me. "She did? How?"

"She did a search on missing kids named Tate and Dennis and found that a woman named Layla had reported them missing almost twenty years ago. She claimed that her ex-boyfriend kidnapped them. She and Buck were never married and she'd left him shortly after you were born."

"Is...is she still alive?" Tate asked shakily.

"She is. Her name is Layla Hemmings. She lives in Omaha. She's married with two kids. Both girls. One is thirteen, the other is ten."

Tate sat in silence as he tried to take it all in.

"She has red hair, Tate."

His eyes lifted. "The woman from my dream," he whispered. "It was real?"

I nodded. I sat up and brushed my fingers over his upper arms. "I called her."

"You did?" he asked.

"I did," I said, worried that he'd be angry with me. "I wanted to find out what kind of person she was."

Tate nodded. "You wanted to know if she still wanted me."

"Yeah," I admitted. "I wanted to protect you-"

Tate cut me off with a kiss. "Thank you," he whispered. He leaned against me and I laid back down, taking him with me. "Does she want to see me?"

"Yes, she does. She was really upset and crying a lot. I told her I'd talk to you first, but that I couldn't promise anything."

"Did you tell her you were my boyfriend?"

I tightened my hold on Tate as I guessed his line of thinking. His father and brother had ridiculed him because of his sexuality, so it wasn't a reach to suspect his mother would do the same thing.

"I did. She was fine with it, Tate. She asked me all sorts of questions about myself. I didn't tell her about you and Matty, but I told her a little bit about me. She kind of lost it when I told her how much I loved you."

Tate didn't respond, but I felt his fingers stroking over the tattoo on my chest. His tattoo.

"There's no rush, Tate. You can call her whenever you're ready. And if you're never ready, that's okay too."

Another round of silence and then Tate lifted up on his elbow and kissed me. "I'm ready," he whispered. I nodded and reached for my phone. I pulled up the number from my call list, but didn't hit the dial button. Instead, I handed it to him.

"I love you, Tate."

A broad smile spread across Tate's mouth and he leaned in to kiss me again. "I love you, Michael. Forever and ever."

He glanced down at the phone, took a deep breath and then hit dial. When I shifted so I could see his reactions better, he put his hand on my chest and said, "Stay with me?"

I ran my fingers through his hair and whispered, "Forever and ever."

And when I heard a woman's voice on the phone answer, I drew Tate against me just as Tate said, "Um, hi, this is Tate."

I dropped a kiss to his head when I heard crying on other end of the phone and I held him tight when his own tears started to fall.

The End

Scroll to the next page for a Sneak Peek of Mav's story

SNEAK PEEK

FORSAKEN (THE PROTECTORS, BOOK 4)
(M/M)

PROLOGUE

MAV

I didn't see him at first because unlike so many of the other times he'd been walking down the busy hallway towards the hospital room I was guarding, his head was hung and he didn't speak to any of the various nurses and other staff who greeted him. In fact, he was so distracted that he nearly slammed into me as he turned to enter the door. I managed to grab him by the upper arms just before he walked into me and I didn't miss his startled gasp right before he lifted his eyes to meet mine.

The young man was nothing like the men I usually went for. First of all, because he was just way too young. He was in his early twenties at best. Second, I liked them a little on the beefier side. This man was so lean and slight, I would have had to worry about breaking him if I put all of my weight down on his back while I was fucking him from behind. And third, and most importantly, he was skittish. Exceedingly so. I didn't mind a little shyness here and there, but I wasn't into fucking guys who were terrified of me. And with the way his whole body seized up when I'd first grabbed his arms, I knew that was exactly what he was.

"Sorry," he whispered, though it was hard to hear him over the din of the people coming and going through the hallway.

"No problem," I responded, though I had yet to let him go. With it being summer, he was wearing a short-sleeved shirt so my fingers were in contact with his bare skin and that was wreaking havoc on my senses. Not to mention his big, luminous dark brown eyes and his slightly parted lips that looked so full that I couldn't help but wonder if he'd just been kissing someone or if they were just naturally that plump and supple looking.

I'd first noticed him a couple of weeks earlier when the young boy I was keeping an eye on, Matty Travers, had been readmitted to the Immunocompromised Services Unit of the children's hospital. I'd only met the little boy about six weeks earlier when my boss, Ronan Grisham, had asked me to keep an eye on one of my colleagues, Hawke, in case he decided to single-handedly pursue the men who'd murdered his wife. Under normal circumstances, Hawke wasn't the kind of guy who needed backup, but when Ronan had learned that the murderers had taken up with a Mexican drug lord, all bets were off and he'd ordered me to stick to Hawke like glue.

Weeks had passed, but Hawke hadn't gone looking for the men as expected and when the man he'd lost his heart to, Tate Travers, and his five-year-old son had shown up to visit him at his ranch in Wyoming, I'd been there to witness the reunion and I'd known then that Hawke had chosen a future with them rather than seeking vengeance for the rape and murder of his wife and unborn child ten years earlier. I'd ended up sticking around town for a couple days so I could explore the mountain ranges surrounding Rocky Point, but on the day I'd finally gotten on my Harley to head to my next assignment, Ronan had frantically called me and told me to get back to Hawke's house because the men he'd given up on hunting had found him instead.

I'd made it back to Hawke's ranch just in time to save him from the bullet one of the drug lord's lackeys had been about to put in his brain, and then he and I had managed to get Tate and Matty to safety. For someone so young, little Matty had been beyond brave as a gun had been held to his head and I'd felt a kinship with him from the start. So when Ronan had asked me if I'd stay in Seattle for a while to keep an eye on the family, in case the drug lord made a play for them, I'd readily agreed.

And that was when I'd seen the young man.

He arrived every day like clockwork to spend time with Matty and I'd learned from Hawke who had given me the okay to let the guy past me, that he was someone who had just started volunteering in the pediatric oncology unit. I hadn't missed how beautiful he was with his dark skin tone that hinted at Hispanic heritage and pretty, expressive eyes, but I'd dismissed my intense attraction to him because of the way he'd looked at me that very first day when he'd told me his name as he'd sought entry into Matty's room.

Eli.

I'd let the name roll off my tongue as I'd automatically flirted with him, but when he'd looked at me like I was going to jump him, I'd let him pass without further comment and I'd done my best to ignore him all the other days that he'd stopped by. But it had been an almost impossible task because there was always this inevitable moment when Eli stepped past me, that his eyes would lift to look at me for the briefest of moments and I wouldn't see fear in them...I'd see something different. Something that had my stomach knotting up with anticipation and my fingers itching to reach up and stroke over the smoothness of his cheek.

But now as I held on to him, he wasn't only looking terrified, he was practically shaking in my grip, so I quickly released him.

I knew I wasn't the safest looking guy in terms of appearance, especially considering the tattoos that covered my arms, torso and back, my large build, long hair and the leather motorcycle pants I wore, but it wasn't like I'd overtly come on to the guy or anything that would cause him to be so fearful of me.

I expected Eli to quickly move away from me and rush into the room, but other than taking a step back, he didn't do anything else. His eyes held mine as he tried to get control of his breathing and then he shook his head slightly. "I'm sorry," he said again, a little louder this time, but still very low and quiet.

I had no doubt the second apology had nothing to do with running into me and I desperately wanted to ask him what he was sorry for. But then I saw it.

Longing.

My breath caught in my throat as I realized what the look meant, but before I could question Eli or even respond, he stepped past me and into the room. I heard both Matty and Tate happily greet him and there was no fear or tentativeness as Eli greeted them in return. The idea that Eli might actually be attracted to me was an unexpected distraction and it took everything in my power to keep from looking through the glass walls into Matty's room to see him and Eli interacting. My job was to focus on my surroundings and keep the little boy inside that room safe.

It was only about a half an hour later that Eli left the room and I willed myself not to look at him as he passed, but I failed miserably when I sensed his gaze on me. Our eyes met briefly and I felt my cock harden uncomfortably in my pants. Eli was the one to tear his gaze away first, but I kept my eyes on his slim back as he hurried down the hall towards another room and it wasn't until he disappeared inside of it that I finally managed to snap out of whatever spell I'd fallen under. Irritation flooded my system and I cursed both my own traitorous body, as well as the young man who'd fucked with my head for those few seconds with just one look.

My shift outside Matty's door lasted only another hour and when Hawke arrived to relieve me, I said my goodbyes to Matty and Tate and hurried towards the parking garage so I could get my Harley between my legs and use the massive bike to work off some of the tension that was still lingering in my system. It took just a few minutes to get to the garage and I automatically bypassed the elevator for the stairs that would lead to the lowest floor of the garage where I'd left my bike. But the second I opened the door, I went on high alert when I heard someone yelling, "Stay the fuck away from him, do you hear me?"

The sound of flesh striking flesh had me moving and when I heard someone let out a small cry, I leaned over the stair railing and yelled, "Hey! What's going on down there?"

There was another distressed cry and then a door was opening and closing. I knew the assailant would be long gone by the time I reached the bottom landing, but I took the stairs as fast as I could anyway so I could make sure whoever had been struck was okay.

I saw the young man immediately before I even reached the last step. He was sitting on the concrete floor, his back to the wall and his arms over his head. I could hear him crying softly.

"Hey, you okay?" I asked as I knelt on the floor in front of him. He flinched when I carefully tried to pull his arms away from his face. "You're safe now," I murmured as he finally relaxed his muscles enough to drop his arms. And when I put my fingers under his chin to lift his face, I held my breath as I realized who it was under the bruise that was already forming along one cheek, the blood trickling from the split lip and the tears streaking down his face.

Eli.

ABOUT THE AUTHOR

Dear Reader,

I hope you enjoyed Hawke and Tate's story. They will be back in Mav's story.

For those of you who have read *Logan's Need* which is the last book in my Escort series and the book that introduces characters from my Barretti Security series, you may be wondering if Mav's Eli is the same Eli from Logan and Dom's story. The answer is yes. And this won't be the first time you will be meeting some of the other boys mentioned in the Barretti Security series epilogue at the end of *Freeing Zane*. In fact, all of the older boys I mentioned in that epilogue will be getting their own stories either as part of the Protectors series or as another book in my Finding series. So be sure to keep checking in with me for more information on that!

As an independent author, I am always grateful for feedback so if you have the time and desire, please leave a review, good or bad, so I can continue to find out what my readers like and don't like. You can also send me feedback via email at sloane@sloanekennedy.com

Join my Facebook Fan Group: Sloane's Secret Sinners

Connect with me:

www.sloanekennedy.com

sloane@sloanekennedy.com

ALSO BY SLOANE KENNEDY

(Note: Not all titles will be available on all retail sites)

The Escort Series
Gabriel's Rule (M/F)

Shane's Fall (M/F)

Logan's Need (M/M)

Barretti Security Series
Loving Vin (M/F)

Redeeming Rafe (M/M)

Saving Ren (M/M/M)

Freeing Zane (M/M)

Finding Series
Finding Home (M/M/M)

Finding Trust (M/M)

Finding Peace (M/M)

Finding Forgiveness (M/M)

Finding Hope (M/M/M)

The Protectors
Absolution (M/M/M)

Salvation (M/M)

Retribution (M/M)

Forsaken (M/M)

Vengeance (M/M/M)

A Protectors Family Christmas

Atonement (M/M)

Revelation (M/M)

Redemption (M/M)

Non-Series

Letting Go (M/F)

Made in the USA
Lexington, KY
04 February 2018